Star Song
and Other Stories

Star Song
and Other Stories

Timothy Zahn

Five Star • Waterville, Maine

3/03 24.95

Five Star First Edition Science Fiction and Fantasy Series.

Published in 2002 in conjunction with Tekno-Books and Ed Gorman.

Set in 11 pt. Plantin.

Printed in the United States on permanent paper.

Library of Congress Cataloging-in-Publication Data

Zahn, Timothy.
    Star song and other stories / Timothy Zahn.
        p. cm.—(Five Star first edition science fiction and fantasy series)
    ISBN 0-7862-4696-0 (hc : alk. paper)
    1. Science fiction, American. I. Title. II. Series.
PS3576.A33 S7 2002
    813'.54—dc21   2002029725

For Dr. Stanley Schmidt:
Who, 24 years ago, rescued me from the slush pile.
Thanks, Stan.

Table of Contents

Introduction

I've always liked short stories. I've especially always liked short story collections.

That's not just because you're holding a collection of mine in your hands right now, deciding whether or not to dive into it. It's also not just because I started my career with short stories, though that is in fact what I did. For me, short fiction was a great way for a novice writer to learn the craft of putting narrative and character and plot together, rather like climbing a series of foothills before tackling the awesome and slightly terrifying mountain of a full-fledged novel. I published seven stories before even beginning my first novel (and wrote a lot more that were never published), and had published twenty-two of them before that novel finally saw print.

No, my love of short fiction is a lot older than that. It goes back to the days of my youth, back when I first began my exploration of the universe of science fiction. My pattern then was to pick a new author off the local library's SF shelves and try a book by him or her. If I liked it, I would read the shelves dry, and then (if I had any spare money that month) hunt up whatever newer works might be available at the bookstore.

But unless there was a novel by Author X that looked particularly intriguing, I always preferred to start with a short-story collection if one was available.

Why? Very simply, because a collection gave me a better idea of the author's range than a single novel ever could. It let me see variations in style and character, plus a wider sampling of the kind of ideas he or she liked to play with. The full extent of the author's sense of humor was often better represented, too. Whereas humor might be almost totally absent in a particularly grim novel (or overly lavished in a deliberately silly one), a collection would again give the kind of balance to let me know if this was someone I wanted as my guide into worlds of wonder over the next few weeks or months.

Which brings us back to this particular collection. In putting it together, I've tried to give a fair sampling of the sort of stories I've been writing over the years. There's everything from serious to humorous; from very short vignette to novella length; from my somewhat older efforts ("Point Man," 1987) to more modern ones ("Star Song," 1997).

A quick rundown of the particular stories, in case you're interested:

"Point Man" was the third of a series of interconnected stories (modeled after Larry Niven's Known Universe series) that somehow never got any farther than these three. I have that problem sometimes with series: I get distracted by something else, and never quite get back. Maybe someday . . .

"Hitmen — See Murderers" was one of those ideas that let me edge a little ways into philosophy, as well as getting to figure out ways that something that looked so useful and good could generate such bad results. I was probably at least partially influenced by Arabian Nights–type stories, and seeing how a malevolent genie could mess up a perfectly good set of wishes. (Tip for beginning writers: read everything. It all gets used eventually.)

"The Broccoli Factor." Don't even ask. Too much time spent around small children, I guess.

"The Art of War" was commissioned (sort of) by Kris Rusch, who was editing *Fantasy & Science Fiction* at the time. She had been intrigued by my *Star Wars* character Grand Admiral Thrawn and his way of connecting art and war, and thought there was something else I could do with that pairing. This may not have been exactly what she had in mind, but it's what came out.

"The Play's the Thing" was inspired by my first trip to New York City since childhood, and my first-ever Broadway play. Until I can write, produce, or star in one myself, I guess this story will have to suffice.

And finally, "Star Song" was one of the handful of stories I've written where I was able to draw on my love of music. It was also one of those maddening times where I quickly had all of the story except for one crucial piece. In this case, a comment from my son was the key to that piece, after which everything fell into place. I made the mistake of giving him 5% of the payment in thanks. Never do that with a teenager. He now figures any residual money that comes in from the story is partially his, and as a paralegal student he knows how to argue from precedent. I'm just glad I didn't offer him 10%.

So there you have it: background, history, and, hopefully, a little appetite whetting. All that's left now is the stories themselves.

Enjoy!

Point Man

Everyone, my mother used to tell me, had a special talent. Every human being, in one way or another, stood head and shoulders above all those around him. It was, she'd firmly believed, part of what made us human; one of the few things that stood us apart from the lower animals and even from the sophisticated alien hive minds that plied the galaxy.

She never told me just what she thought my talent was while I was growing up, of course. At the time I figured that she simply didn't want to prejudice me. Looking back from the perspective of five decades, it has gradually become apparent that she hadn't told me what my talent was because she was never able to *find* any. But she was too kind to tell me outright that I was so uniformly average . . . and so I left home and spent thirty solid years looking for something in which I could excel.

Eventually, I found it. I found that I had a genuine and unique knack for being at the wrong place at the wrong time.

I remember vividly the day that conclusion suddenly came to me; remember almost as well the solid month afterwards that I fought it. But eventually I had to give in and accept it as truth. There were just too many instances scattered throughout my life to blame on coincidence and accident. There was the time I walked into my college room just as my roommate was frying his cortex with an illegal and badly overset brain-stretch stimulator. I was eventually ex-

13

onerated of all blame, but the trauma and stigma were just as bad as if I'd been thrown out of school, and eventually led to the same result. I joined the Services and had worked my way up to a very promising position in starship engineering when I was transferred to the *Burma* . . . three months before the ship's first officer attempted a mutiny and damn near made it. Again, the wrong place at the wrong time, and this time the stigma of association effectively ended my Services career. I eventually went into the merchant fleet, kicking around various ships until my special damn talent landed me in another innocent mess and I was forced to move on.

So given my history, I shouldn't have been surprised to be on the *Volga*'s bridge when it broke out of hyperspace on that particularly nasty evening.

I shouldn't even have been *on* the bridge, for starters. That fact alone should have tipped me off that my perverse talent was about to do me dirty again. Second Officer Mara Kittredge was at the command console, Tarl Fromm and Ing Waskin were backing her up at helm and scanners, and there was absolutely no reason why anyone else should have been needed, least of all the ship's third officer. But I was feeling restless. We were about to come out of hyperspace over Messenia, and I wanted to make sure this whole silly stop was handled as quickly as possible, so I was there. I should have known better.

"Thirty seconds," Waskin was saying as I arrived. He glanced up at me, then quickly turned back to his scanners. Probably, I figured, so that I wouldn't see that faintly gloating smile he undoubtedly had on his skinny face.

Kittredge looked up, too, but her smile had nothing but her normal cool friendliness in it. She was friendly because she felt professionals should always be polite to their infe-

14

riors; cool, because she knew all about my career and clearly had no intention of being too close to me when the lightning struck again. "Travis," she nodded. "You're a little early for your shift, aren't you?"

"A shave, maybe," I said, drifting to her side and steadying myself on her chair back. She wasn't much more than half my age, but then, that was true of nearly everyone aboard except Captain Garrett. Bright kids, all of them. Only a few with Kittredge's same hard-edged ambition, but all of them on the up side of their careers nonetheless. It made me feel old. "Was that thirty seconds to breakout?"

"Yes," she said, voice going distant as the bulk of her attention shifted from me to the bank of displays before her. I followed her example and turned to watch the screens and readouts. And continued my silent grousing.

We weren't supposed to be at Messenia. We weren't, in fact, supposed to be anywhere closer than a day's hyperdrive of the stupid damn mudball on this particular trip. We were on or a bit ahead of schedule for a change, we had all the cargo a medium-sized freighter like the *Volga* could reasonably carry, and all we had to do was deliver it to make the kind of medium-sized profit that keeps pleasant smiles on the faces of freighter contractors. It should have been a nice, simple trip, the kind where the crew's lives alternate between predictable chores and pleasant boredom.

Enter Waskin. Exit simplicity.

He had, Waskin informed us, an acquaintance who was supposed to be out here with the Messenia survey mission. We'd all heard the rumors that there were supposed to be outcroppings of firebrand opaline scattered across Messenia's surface — opaline whose current market value Waskin just happened to have on hand. It was pretty obvious that if someone came along who could offer off-world

15

transport for some of the stone — especially if middlemen and certain tax and duty formalities happened to get lost in the shuffle — then that someone stood to add a tidy sum to his trip's profits. The next part was obvious: Waskin figured that that someone might as well be the crew of the *Volga*.

It was the sort of argument that had earned Waskin the half-dozen shady nicknames he possessed. Unfortunately, it was also the sort of argument he was extremely adroit at pushing, and in the end Captain Garrett decided it was worth the gamble of a couple of days to stop by and just assess the situation.

I hadn't agreed. In fact, I'd fought hard to change the captain's mind. For starters, the opaline wasn't even a confirmed fact yet; and even if it *was* there, it was less than certain what the Messenia survey mission would think of us dropping in out of nowhere and trying to walk away with a handful of it. Survey missions like Messenia's were always military oriented, and if they suspected we were even *thinking of* bending any customs regulations, we could look forward to some very unpleasant questions.

And I, of course, would wind up with yet another job blown out from under me.

But freighter contractors weren't the only ones to whom the word "profit" brought pleasant smiles . . . and third officers, I'd long ago learned, existed solely to take the owl bridge shift. Half the ship's thirty-member crew had already made their private calculations as to how much of a bonus a few chunks of opaline would bring, and my arguments were quickly dismissed as just one more example of Travis's famous inability to make winning gambles, a side talent that had made me the most sought-after poker player on the ship.

Waskin always won at poker, too. And got far too much

satisfaction out of beating me.

Abruptly, the lights flickered. Quickly, guiltily, I brought my attention back to the displays, but it was all right — the breakout had come off textbook-clean.

"We're here," Fromm reported from the helm. "Ready to set orbit."

"Put us at about two hundred for now," Kittredge told him. "Waskin, you want to try and contact this friend of yours and find out about this opaline?"

"Yes, ma'am," he nodded, swiveling around to the comm board.

"Was there anything else?" Kittredge asked, looking up at me.

I shook my head. "I just wanted to make sure we knew one way or another about the rocks before anyone got too comfortable here."

She smiled lopsidedly. "I doubt you have to wor—"

"Holy Mother!"

I snapped my head around to look at Waskin, nearly losing my hold in the process. He was staring at the main display. As I shifted my eyes that direction, I felt a similar expletive welling up like verbal fire in my throat.

We'd come within view of the mission's base camp . . . or rather, within view of the blackened crater where the base camp was supposed to be.

"Oh, my God," Kittredge gasped as the scanners panned over the whole nauseating mess. "What *happened?*"

"No idea," I said grimly, "but we'd better find out." My long-ago years in the Services came flooding back, the old pages of emergency procedures flipping up in front of my mind's eye. "Waskin, get back on the scanners. Do a quick full-pattern run-through for anything out of the ordinary, then go back to infrared for a grid survivor search."

"Yes, sir." There was no cockiness now; he was good and thoroughly scared. With an effort, he got his face jammed into the display hood, his hand visibly trembling as he fumbled with the selector knob. "Yes, sir. Okay. IR . . . those fires have been out a minimum of . . . eighteen hours, the computer says. Could be more." His thin face — what I could see of it, anyway — was a rather pasty white, and I hoped hard that he wouldn't pass out. Time could be crucial, and I didn't want to have to man the scanners myself until we could get another expert up here. "Shortwave . . . nothing in particular. No broadcasts on any frequency. Neutrino . . . there's a residual decay spectrum, but it's the wrong one for their type of power plant. Tachyon . . . uh-oh."

"What?" Kittredge snapped.

Waskin visibly swallowed. "It reads . . . it reads an awful lot like the pattern you get from full-spectrum explosives."

Fromm caught it before the rest of us did. "Explo*sives*, plural?" he asked. "How many are we talking about?"

"Lots," Waskin said. "At least thirty separate blasts. Maybe more."

Fromm swore under his breath. "Damn. They must have had a stockpile that blew."

"No," I said, and even to me my voice sounded harsh. "You don't store full-specs that close to each other. Someone came in and bombed the hell out of them. Deliberately."

There was a long moment of silence. "The opaline," Kittredge said at last. "Someone wanted the opaline."

For lousy pieces of rock . . . ? I forced my brain to unfreeze from that thought. Messenia had been militarily oriented. . . . "Waskin, cancel the grid search for a second and get back on the comm board," I told him. "Broadcast our

18

ship ID on the emergency beacon frequency and then listen."

Kittredge looked up at me. "Travis, no one could have survived a bombing like that —"

"No one *there*, no," I cut her off. "But there would have been at least a few men out beyond the horizon from the base — that's standard procedure."

"Yeah, but the radiation would have got 'em," Waskin muttered.

"Just do it," I snapped.

"I'd better get the captain up here," Kittredge said, reaching for the intercom.

"Better get a boat ready to fly, too," I told her. My eyes returned to the main display, where the base was starting to drift behind us. "With the doc and a couple others with strong stomachs aboard. If there are any survivors, they'll need help fast."

She nodded, and that was that. If I hadn't been there, they'd have done a quick, futile grid search and then gone running hotfoot to report the attack to some authority or other without trying the emergency beacon trick. We'd have missed entirely the fact that there was indeed a survivor of the attack.

And we sure as hell would have missed getting mixed up in mankind's first interstellar war.

His name was Lieutenant Colonel Halveston, and he was dying.

He knew that, of course. The Services were good at making sure their people had any and all information that might have an influence on their performance or survival. Halveston knew how much radiation he'd taken, knew that at this stage there was nothing anyone could do for him . . .

but countering that was a strong will to hold out long enough to let someone know what had happened. The Services were good at developing that, too.

We didn't get to talk to him on the trip up from Messenia, partly because the doc needed Halveston's full attention for the bioloop stabilization techniques to work and partly because long chatty conversations on an open radio didn't seem like a smart idea. It was nerve-racking as hell . . . and so when the captain, Kittredge, and I were finally able to gather around Halveston's sickbay bed, we weren't exactly in the greatest of emotional shapes.

Not that it mattered that much. Halveston's report would have been a full-spec bombshell no matter what our condition.

"It was the Drymnu," he whispered through cracked lips. "The Drymnu did this."

I looked up from Halveston to see Captain Garrett's mouth drop open slightly. That, from the captain, was the equivalent of falling over backwards with shock . . . which was about what *I* felt like doing. "The . . . Drymnu?" he asked carefully. "*The* Drymnu? The hive race?"

Halveston winced in a sudden spasm of pain. "You know any other aliens by that name?" he said. I got the impression he would have snarled it if he'd had the strength to do so.

"No, of course not," the captain said. "It's just that —" He paused, visibly searching for a diplomatic way of putting this. "I've just never heard of a hivey attacking anyone before."

A little more of Halveston's strength seemed to drain out of him. "You have now," he whispered.

The Captain looked up at Kittredge and me, back down at Halveston. "Could it have been a group of human pirates, say, pretending they were a Drymnu ship?"

Halveston closed his eyes and shook his head weakly. "Outposts get a direct cable feed from the main base's scanners. If you'd ever seen a Drymnu ship, you'd know no one could fake something like that."

"Travis?" the captain murmured.

I nodded reluctantly. "He's right, sir. If he actually saw the ship, it couldn't have been anyone else."

"But it doesn't make any sense," Kittredge put in. "Why would any Drymnu ship attack a human outpost?"

It was a damn good question. All the aliens we'd ever run into out here were hive races, and hive races didn't make war. Period. They weren't constitutionally oriented that way, for starters; aggression in hivies nearly always focused on studying and understanding the universe, and as far as I knew the Drymnu were no exception. It was why hivies nearly always discovered the Burke stardrive and made it into space, while fragmented races like humanity nearly always blew themselves to bits before they could do likewise.

"I don't know why," Halveston sighed. "I don't have any idea. But whatever the reason, he sure as hell did it on purpose. He came in real close, discussing refueling possibilities, and when he was too close for us to have any chance at all, he just opened up and bombed the hell out of the base."

The speech took too much out of him. His eyes rolled up, and he seemed to go a little more limp beneath his safety webbing. I looked up, caught the captain's eye.

"We'd better get out of here," I said in a low voice. "It looks like he's long gone, but I don't think we want to be here if he comes back."

"And we need to report this right away, too," Kittredge added.

"No!"

I would've jumped if there'd been any gravity to do it with. "Take it easy, colonel," the captain soothed him. "There's no one else alive down there — trust us, we made a complete infrared grid search while you were being brought up. We've got to warn the Services —"

"No," Halveston repeated, much weaker this time. "You've got to go after him. *Now,* before he gets too far away."

"But we don't even know what direction he's gone in," Kittredge told him.

"My pack . . . has the records of our . . . three nav satellites." Clearly, Halveston was fading fast. "He didn't think . . . take them out. Got the . . . para-Cerenkov rainbow . . . when he left."

And with the rainbow recorded from three directions we did indeed have the direction the ship had taken — at least until he came out of hyperspace and changed vectors. But it would normally be several days at the least before he did that. "All the more reason for us to go sound the alarm," I told Halveston.

"No time," Halveston gasped. "He'll get away, regroup with other Drymnu ships . . . never identify him then. And the whole mind will know . . . how easily he got us."

And suddenly, for a handful of seconds, the pain cleared almost entirely from his face and a spark of life flared in his eyes. "Captain Garrett . . . as a command-rank officer of the Combined Services . . . I hereby commandeer the *Volga* . . . and order you to give chase . . . to the Drymnu ship . . . that destroyed Messenia. And to destroy it. Carry out your . . . orders . . . captain."

And as his eyes again rolled up, the warbling of the *life-failure* alert broke into our stunned silence. Automatically, we floated back to give the med people room to work. We were still there, still silent, when the doc finally shut off the med sensors and covered Halveston's face.

"Well?" the captain asked, glaring at the intercom and then at Kittredge and me in turn. "*Now* what do we do?"

The intercom rasped as First Officer Wong, who had replaced Kittredge on the bridge, cleared his throat delicately. "I presume there's no way to expunge that . . . suggestion . . . from the log?"

"That your idea or one of Waskin's?" the captain snorted. Perhaps he was remembering it was Waskin's fault we were here in the first place. "Of course there's no way. And it wasn't a suggestion, it was an order — a legal one, our resident military expert tells me." He turned his glare full force onto me.

I refused to shrivel. He'd asked me a question, and it wasn't *my* fault if he hadn't liked the answer.

"But this is crazy," Wong persisted. "We're *a freighter,* for God's sake. How in hell did he expect us to take on a warship with eighteen thousand Drymnu aboard?"

"It wasn't a warship," I put in. "Couldn't have been. The Drymnu don't have any warships."

"You could have fooled *me,*" Kittredge growled. "I hope you're not suggesting he just *happened* to have a cargo of full-spectrum bombs aboard and somehow lost his grip on them."

"I said he didn't have any warships," I shot back. "I *didn't* say the attack wasn't deliberate."

"The difference escapes me —"

"Let's keep the discussion civil, shall we?" the captain interrupted. "I think it's a given that we're all on edge here. All right, Travis, you want to offer an explanation as to why a race ostensibly as peaceful as the Drymnu would launch

23

an unprovoked attack on a human installation?"

"I don't *know* why he did it," I told him. "But keep in mind that the Drymnu isn't really 'peaceful' — I wouldn't call him that, anyway. He isn't warlike, but he's competitive enough, to the point of having deliberately wiped out at least one class of predators on his home world. All the hivies are that way. It's just that in space there's so much room and territory that there's no reason for one of them to fight any of the others."

"But we're different?" the captain asked.

I spread out my hands. "We're a fragmented race, which means we're warlike, and we've gotten into space, which means we're flagrant violations of accepted hivey theory. Maybe the Drymnu has decided that the combination makes us too dangerous to exist and is beginning a campaign to wipe us out."

"Starting with Messenia?" Wong interjected from the bridge. "Why? To show that his war machine can blow up a couple hundred Services men, developers, and scientists? Big deal."

"Maybe it wasn't the entire Drymnu mind behind it," I pointed out. "Each ship is essentially autonomous until it gets within thirty thousand klicks or so of another Drymnu ship or planet."

"Could this one part of the mind have gone insane?" Kittredge suggested hesitantly. "Become homicidal, somehow?"

"God, what a thought," Wong muttered. "A raving maniac with eighteen thousand bodies running around the galaxy in his own starship."

I shrugged. "I don't know if it's possible or not. It's probably more likely that Messenia was an experiment on his part."

"A *what?*" Kittredge growled.

"An experiment. To see if we could handle a sneak attack, with Messenia chosen because it was small and out of the way. You know — club a sleeping tiger or two first to get the technique down before you tackle one that's awake."

Wong and Kittredge started to speak at once; the captain cut them off with a wave of his hand. "Enough, everyone. As I see it, we have three possibilities here: that the entire Drymnu mind has declared war on humanity; that this one ship-sized segment of the Drymnu mind has declared war on humanity; or that some portion of the Drymnu mind is playing war with humanity to see how we react. Does that about cover it, Travis?"

My mouth felt dry. There was a glint I didn't at all care for in the captain's eyes. "Well . . . I can't see any other alternatives at the moment, no."

He nodded, the glint brighter than ever. "Thank you. Any of the rest of you? No? Then it seems to me that we've got no choice — ethically as well as legally. Halveston said it himself: if that ship gets back to one of the Drymnu worlds and reports how easy it was to club this sleeping tiger to death, we may very well find ourselves embroiled in an all-out war. Wong, pull the raider's direction from those tapes and get us in pursuit."

There was a moment of stunned silence. None of the others, I gathered, had noticed that glint. "Captain —" Wong began, and then hesitated.

Kittredge showed less restraint. "Captain," she said, "the last time I checked, the *Volga* was *not* a warship. Doesn't it strike you as just the *slightest* bit dangerous for us to take on that ship? Our chief duty at this point is to report the attack."

"And if Messenia was merely a single thrust of a more comprehensive and synchronized attack?" the captain said quietly. "What then?"

She opened her mouth, closed it again. "Then there may not be any human bases left anywhere near here to report to," she said at last, very softly. "Oh, God."

The captain nodded and started unstrapping himself from his chair. "Bear in mind, too, that even if we're able to guess where he'll come out of hyperspace, we'll have a minimum of several days to prepare for the encounter. Travis, as the nearest thing to a military expert we've got, you're in charge of getting us ready for combat."

I swallowed. "Yes, sir."

The wrong place, the wrong time.

Twenty minutes later we were in hyperspace, in hot pursuit of the Drymnu ship, and I was in my cabin, wondering just what in hell I was going to do.

A Drymnu hive ship. Eighteen thousand — call them individuals, bodies, whatever — there were still eighteen thousand of them, each part of a common mind. The concept was bad enough; the immediate military consequences were even worse.

No problems with command or garbled orders. Instant communication between laser operators and those at the scanners. Possibly no need for scanners at all at close range — observers watching from opposite ends of the ship would give the mind a binocular vision that would both make scanners unnecessary and, incidentally, render useless many of the Services' ECM jammers. The ship itself would be a hundred times larger than the *Volga*, with almost certainly the extra structural strength a craft that big would have to have. More antimeteor lasers. More speed.

In other words, warship or not, if we went head-to-head against the Drymnu, we were going to get our tubes peeled.

What in the hell were we going to *do?*

The smartest decision would be to quit right now, try to talk the captain out of it, and if that didn't work, simply to refuse to obey his order. *Mutiny.* The memory of the *Burma* incident made me wince. But this wasn't the Services, and it was nothing like the same situation. *Mutiny.* In this case, it was far and away the best chance of getting all of us out of this alive. And *that,* it seemed to me, was where my loyalty ought to lie. I respected the captain a great deal, but he had no idea what he was getting all of us into. These people weren't trained — weren't volunteers for dangerous duty like Services people were — and sending the *Volga* out to be point man in this war was mass suicide. Maybe Captain Garrett felt legally bound to carry out Colonel Halveston's dying order, but I didn't feel myself nearly so tied.

In fact, it occurred to me that by refusing the captain's orders, I might actually be doing him a favor. Halveston's order had been directed at him; but if he was prevented from carrying it out, he would be off the legal hook. Any official wrath would then turn onto me, of course, but I was prepared to accept that. Unlike Captain Garrett, I was used to having my career dumped out with the sawdust. Surely enough of the others would back me in this, especially once I explained how it would be for the captain's good, and we could just head to the nearest Services base . . .

Assuming there *were* still Services bases to head for. Assuming the Messenia attack had been a one-shot deal. Assuming the Drymnu had not, in fact, launched an all-out war.

And if those assumptions were wrong, running from the Drymnu now wouldn't gain us anything but a little time.

Maybe not even that.

Which was where the crux of my dilemma lay. Saving the *Volga* now for worse treatment later on wouldn't be doing anyone a favor.

I was chasing the logic around the track for the fifth time when my door buzzed. "Come in," I called, the words releasing the lock.

I'd expected it to be the captain. It was, instead, Kittredge. "Busy?" she asked, stepping inside with the peculiar gait that rotational pseudogravity always gives people in ships the *Volga*'s size.

A younger man might have expected it to be a social call. I knew Kittredge better than that. "Not really," I said as the door slid closed behind her. "Just plotting out the victory parade route for after we've whipped the Drymnu's sauce. Why?"

The attempt at humor didn't even register on her face. "Travis, we've got some serious trouble here."

"I've noticed. What do you suggest we do about it?"

"Call the whole thing off," she growled. "We can't take on any Drymnu hive ship — it's completely out of the question."

If it had been Wong who'd tossed my own ideas back at me like this, we would have been off to lay out our ultimatum before the captain in thirty seconds. But Kittredge was so intense and by-the-book . . . Perversely, my brain shifted into devil's advocate mode. "You're suggesting Captain Garrett disobey a duly given and recorded order?"

She snorted. "No one in the Services would even think of holding us to that. What, they'd rather we go in and get blown up for nothing than come back with valuable information?"

Maybe it was a remnant of my Services pride come back

to haunt me, or maybe it was just Kittredge and the fact that I was the one in charge of planning this operation. Whatever it was, something like a psychic burr began to work its way under a corner of my mind. "You assume the outcome would be a forgone conclusion."

"You bet I do — and don't give me that look. You were a minor petty officer aboard a third-rate starship. I hardly expect they overloaded you with battle tactics, especially against an enemy we weren't ever supposed to have to fight."

The burr dug itself in a little deeper. "You might be surprised," I told her stiffly. "The *Burma*'s engineering section was designed to operate independently in case of massive destruction to the rest of the ship. We were taught quite a lot about warfare."

"Against hivies?" she asked pointedly.

"Not exactly, no," I admitted. "But just because the hivies weren't supposed to be warlike doesn't mean no one ever considered what it might mean to fight one of them. I remember one lecture in particular that listed three exploitable weaknesses a hive ship would have against a human ship in battle."

"Oh? I don't suppose you remember what they were?"

I felt my face getting hotter. "You mean is the old man losing his memory at wholesale rates?"

"Well?" she replied coolly. "Are you?"

"I wouldn't bet on it if I were you," I snapped. "You'll see what shape my memory and mind are in when I give the captain my preliminary plan in a couple of days."

"Uh-*huh*." A faint look of scorn twitched at her lip. "I'm sure it'll be Crécy all over again. You'll forgive me if I still try and talk the captain out of it."

"That's up to you," I said as she turned around and

walked, stiff-backed, to the door. It opened for her, and she left.

With an odd feeling in my stomach, I realized that I had just set a pleasant little bonfire in the center of my line of retreat. If I didn't come up with a workable battle plan now, I would humiliate myself in front of Kittredge — and probably everyone else aboard ship, too. In my mind's eye I could see Kittredge's I-knew-you-couldn't-do-it contempt, the captain's maddeningly understanding look, Waskin's outright amusement . . .

Alone in my cabin, the images still made me cringe. More undeserved shame . . . and for once, I suddenly decided I would rather die than go through all of that again. I *would* draw up a battle plan — and it was going to be the best damned plan Waskin or Kittredge had ever seen.

I would start with a concerted effort to dredge up those three vaguely remembered hivey weaknesses from their dusty hiding places in my memory. And maybe with a trip through the ship's references to find out just what the hell this Crécy was that Kittredge had referred to.

We started making preparations immediately, of course. Unfortunately, there weren't a lot of preparations that could be made.

The *Volga*, as was pointed out to me with monotonous regularity, was not a warship. We had no shielding beyond the standard solar radiation and micrometeor stuff, our sole weapon was a pair of laser cannons designed to blow away more dangerous meteors — those up to a whopping half-meter across — and our drive and mechanical structure had never been designed for anything even resembling a tight maneuver. We were a waddling, quacking duck that could be blown into mesons half a second after the Drymnu decided we were dangerous to it.

The trick, therefore, was going to be to make the *Volga* seem as harmless as possible . . . and then to figure out how we could stop being harmless when we wanted to. That much was basic military strategy, the stuff I'd learned my second week in basic. Fortunately, there was one very trivial way to accomplish that.

Unfortunately, it was the *only* way I could think of to accomplish it.

Across the room, the door slid open and Waskin walked in, a wary expression on his face. "I hope like hell, sir," he said, "that this isn't what I think it is."

"It is," I nodded, keying the door closed. "I'm tapping you for part of my assault team."

"Oh, sh—" He swallowed the rest of the expletive with an effort. "Sir, I'd like to respectfully withdraw, on grounds —"

"Stuff it, Waskin," I told him shortly. "We haven't got time for it. How much has the ship's grapevine given you about what I've got planned?"

"Enough. You're having a meteor laser taken out and installed aboard one of the landing boats. If you ask me, your David/Goliath complex is getting a little out of hand."

I ignored the sarcasm. Everyone else, even Kittredge, had started treating me with new respect, but it had been too much to hope for that Waskin would join that particular club. "I take it you don't think it would be a good idea to send a boat out after the Drymnu ship. Why not?"

He looked hard at me, decided it was a serious question. "Because he'll blow us apart before we get anywhere near our own firing range, that's why. Or have I missed something?"

"You've missed two things. First of all, remember that this isn't a warship we're going up against. The Drymnu isn't likely to have fine-aim lasers or high-maneuverable missiles aboard."

"Why not?"

"Why should he?"

"Because he knows we'll eventually be sending warships and fighter carriers after him."

"Ah." I held up a finger. "Warships, yes. But not necessarily carriers."

Waskin frowned. "You mean he might not know we've got them?"

I shook my head. "I'm guessing that the concept of fighters won't even occur to him."

"Why wouldn't it? You could put a handful of Drymnu bodies aboard something the size of a fighter, and as long as they didn't get too far from the mother ship, they'd still be connected to the hive mind."

And at that moment Waskin sealed his fate. Everyone else that I'd had this talk with had needed to be reminded that hivies couldn't function at all in groups of less than a few thousand . . . and *then* had needed to be reminded that the thirty-thousand-klick range meant that small scouts or fighters could, indeed, have limited use for them. "You're right," I nodded to Waskin. "Absolutely right. So why won't the Drymnu expect us to use small fighters?"

He made a face. "You're enjoying this, aren't you? This is your revenge for all the poker games you've lost, right?"

God knew there wasn't a lot about this situation that was even remotely enjoyable . . . but in a perverse way I *did* rather like being ahead of Waskin for a change. The fact that my years in the Services gave me a slight advantage was totally irrelevant. "Never mind me," I told him shortly.

"You just concentrate on *you*. Why won't he expect fighters?"

He snorted, then shook his head. "I don't know. Maybe a single ship-sized mind can't handle that many disparate viewpoints. No, that doesn't make sense."

"It's actually pretty close," I had to admit. "It's loosely tied into the reason for that thirty-thousand-klick range. That number suggest anything?"

"It's the distance light travels in a tenth of a second," he said promptly. "I'm not *that* ignorant, you know."

He was right; that part of the hivies' limitation was pretty common knowledge. "Okay, then, that leads us immediately to the fact that the common telepathic link behaves the same way light does, with all the same limitations. So what do you get when you have, say, a dozen high-speed fighters swarming out from the mother ship vectoring in on your target?"

"What do you — ? Oh. Oh, sure. High relative speeds mean you'll be getting into relativistic effects."

"Including time dilation," I nodded. "A pretty minor effect, admittedly. But if a section of mind can't handle even a tenth of a second time lag, it seems reasonable that even a small difference in the temporal *rate* would foul it up even worse."

He nodded slowly and gave me a long, speculative look. "Makes sense. Doesn't mean it's true."

"It is," I told him. "Or it's at least official theory. We've observed Sirrachat and Karmahsh ships occasionally using small advance scouts when feeling their way through a particularly dense ring system or asteroid belt. The scouts behave exactly as expected: they stay practically within hugging range of the mother ship and keep their speeds strictly matched with it."

"Uh-huh. I take it this is supposed to make me feel better about going up against Goliath? Because if it is, it isn't working." He held up some fingers and began ticking them off. "One: if we can think like hivies, it's just possible he's been able to think like humans and will be all ready for us to come blazing in on him. Two: even if he *isn't* ready for us right at the start, a hive mind learns pretty damn quickly. How many passes is it going to take us to hit a vital spot and put his ship out of commission — twenty? Fifty? And three: even if by some miracle he doesn't catch on to the basics of space warfare through all of that, what makes you think we're going to be able to take advantage of it? None of *us* are soldiers, either."

"What do you think *I* am?" I asked.

"A former Services engine room officer who got everything he knows about tactics by pure osmosis," he shot back.

I forced down my irritation with an effort. The fact that he was right didn't make it any easier. "Okay," I growled. "But by osmosis or otherwise, I've still got it. And as far as *that* goes, you and Fromm have both had more than *your* share of experience using the meteor laser. Haven't you."

I had the satisfaction of seeing him flinch. He and Fromm had had a private duel of LaserWar going on down in the game room for the past six months, and I knew for a fact that they both occasionally brought the competition into duty hours, using the *Volga*'s lasers for live practice. Strictly against regulations, naturally. "A little, maybe," he muttered. "But mostly that's just a game."

"So? Hivies don't get even *that* much practice — they don't play LaserWar or any other games. Which brings me to our second advantage over them; a hive mind may learn fast, but all eighteen thousand bodies on that ship are going

34

to start exactly even. It's not as though there's going to be anyone there who has even a smattering of practical experience with tactics, for instance, or anyone who excels at hitting small, fast-moving targets. We do, and I intend to use that advantage to the fullest."

"By making Fromm and me your chief gunners?" Waskin snorted.

"By making Fromm my chief gunner," I corrected. "You I'm making my second-in-command."

His eyes bulged. "You're — *what?* Oh, now wait a minute, sir —"

"Sorry, Waskin, the job's yours." I glanced at my watch. "All right. We'll be having a meeting to set up practice sessions in the lounge in exactly one hour. Be there."

For a moment I thought he was going to argue with me. But he just took a deep breath and nodded. "Yes, sir. Under protest, though."

"I wouldn't have expected it any other way."

He left, and I took a deep breath of my own. There was nothing like a willing team, I reflected, letting my eyes defocus with tiredness. None of the six I'd chosen had any real enthusiasm for what they saw as a stupid decision on the captain's part, but at least only Waskin was even verbally hostile about it.

That would probably change, of course, at the meeting an hour away, when I told them about the rest of my plan. It wasn't something I was especially looking forward to.

But in the meantime . . . Stretching hard, I cracked the tension out of my back and settled more comfortably into my seat. *One: hivies won't be able to think in terms of small-group efficiency. Two: a given hivey mind-segment won't have the same range of abilities and talents that a human force will have. Three: . . .*

No good. Whatever that third hivey weakness was, it was still managing to elude me. But that was okay; I still had a couple of days until breakout, and surely that would be enough time for my subconscious to dig it out of wherever it was I'd tucked it away.

They didn't like the plan. Didn't like it at all.

And I couldn't really blame them. The landing boat assault was bad enough, relying as strongly as it did on Hive Mind Weaknesses One and Two — weaknesses they had only my unsupported word for. But the full plan was even worse, and none of them were particularly reticent about voicing their displeasure.

It could have come to mass mutiny right there, I suppose, with the crew going to the captain en masse and demanding either a decent plan of action or else that he scrap this whole thing. And I suppose that there was a part of me that hoped they would do so. It had been rather pleasant, for a change, to be treated with a little respect aboard the ship — to be Tactician Travis, the man who was guiding the *Volga* into battle, instead of just plain Third Officer Travis, who always lost at poker. But none of that could quite erase the knowledge that I could very well be on the brink of getting some of us killed, me included. I'd already burned my own spaceport behind me, but if the captain decided to quit now, I for one wasn't going to argue too strenuously with him.

But he didn't. Perhaps he felt he'd also come too far to back down; perhaps he really believed that he was obligated to Colonel Halveston's dying order. But whatever the reason, he came out in solid support of both me and my plan, and in the end everyone fell grudgingly into line behind him. Perhaps, with so much uncertainty still remaining as to whether we'd even catch the Drymnu ship, no one wanted to stick his or her neck too far out.

A fair portion of that uncertainty, though, was illusory. True, we had only the Drymnu's departure vector to guide us, and it was true that he could theoretically break out and change his direction anywhere along a path a hundred light-years long. But in actuality, his choices were far more limited: by physics, which governed how long a ship could generate heat in hyperspace before it had to break out and dump it; and by common sense, which said that in case of breakout problems you wanted your ship reasonably close to raw materials and energy, which meant somewhere inside a solar system.

There was, it turned out, exactly one system along the Drymnu's vector that fit both those constraints.

So even while my team complained and muttered to one another about the chances this would all be a waste of time, I made sure they worked their butts off. Somewhere in that system, I was pretty sure, we would find the Drymnu.

Four days later, we broke out into our target system, a totally unremarkable conglomeration of nondescript planets, minor chunks of rock, a dull red sun . . . and one Drymnu ship.

He wasn't visible to the naked eye, of course, but by solar system standards we arrived practically on his landing ramp. He was barely three million klicks away, radiating so much infrared that Waskin had a lock on him two minutes after breakout. Captain Garrett gave the order, and we turned and drove hell for leather straight for him.

The *Volga* was capable of making nearly two gravs of acceleration, but even at that, the Drymnu was a good seven hours away. There was, therefore, no question of sneaking up on him, especially since half that time we would be decelerating with our main drive blasting directly toward him. There was little chance he would escape into hyperspace — not with the amount of heat he clearly had yet to get rid of — but I'd expected that he would at least make us chase him through normal, gain himself some extra time to study us.

We were less than half an hour away from him when we all were finally forced to the conclusion that he really *did* intend to simply stand there and hold his ground.

"Damn," Waskin muttered under his breath at the scanners. "He knows we're here — he *has* to have seen us by now. He's waiting for us, like a — a giant spider in his web —"

"That'll do, Waskin," the captain told him, his own voice icy calm. "There's no need to create wild pictures; I think we're all adequately nervous. Just remember that chances are at least as good that he's waiting because he figures we're a warship and that running would be a waste of time."

"Running doesn't sound like a waste of time to *me*," Kittredge said tensely.

The captain turned a brief stare on her, then looked at me. "Well, Travis, looks like this is it. Any last-minute changes you want to make in the plan?"

I shook my head. *One: hivies don't form small groups. Two: all members of a hive mind have the same experience level. Three: . . . Three, where the hell are you, damn it?* "No, sir," I told him with a quiet sigh. Half an hour to battle. No way around it; we were just going to have to make do without Hive Mind Weakness Number Three, whatever it was. "I'd better get the team into the boat."

He nodded and motioned someone else to take Waskin's place at the scanners. "We'll signal just before we drop you," he told me. "And we'll let you know if there's any change in the situation out there. Good luck."

"Thank you, sir."

Waskin beside me, I headed out the bridge door and did a fast float down the cramped corridor toward the landing boat bay. "So this is it, isn't it?" Waskin murmured. "Your big chance to be a hero."

"I'm not doing this for the heroics of it," I growled back.

"No? Come on, Travis, I'm not *that* stupid. You and the captain dreamed up this whole landing boat assault just so that he can pretend he's obeying Halveston's damned order while still keeping the *Volga* itself from getting blasted to dust."

"The captain has nothing to do with it," I snapped. "It's — it just happens to make the most sense this way."

"Aha," he nodded, an entirely too knowing look on his face. "So you're trying to con the captain along with the rest of us, are you? I should have guessed that. He wouldn't have been able to send us out to get fried on his behalf. Not with a straight face, anyway."

I gritted my teeth. Somehow, I'd thought I'd covered my intentions better than that. "You're hallucinating," I snarled. "There's not a scrap of truth to it — and you'd sure as hell better not go blabbing nonsense like that to the rest of the team."

"Don't get so mad — it's working, isn't it? The *Volga*'s going to come out okay, and you're going to get to go out in a blaze of glory. Along with six more of us lucky souls."

I gritted my teeth some more and ignored him, and we covered another half corridor in silence. "There wasn't really any Services list of hive mind weaknesses, was there?" he said as we maneuvered through a tight hatchway. "You made all that up to justify this plan."

I exhaled in defeat. "No, it was — it is — an actual list," I told him. "It's just that — look, it was a long time ago. The two I gave you are real enough. And there's one more — an important one, I'm pretty sure — but I can't for the life of me remember what it was."

"Uh-huh. Sure."

Or in other words, he didn't believe me. "Waskin —"

"Oh, it's all right," he interrupted. "If it helps any, I actually happen to agree with the basic idea. I just wouldn't have picked myself to be one of the sacrificial goats."

"I'm hoping we'll come out of it a bit better than that," I told him.

"Uh-huh. Sure."

We finished the rest of the trip to the bay in silence, to find that the captain had already had the other five members of the team assemble there.

I tried giving them a short pep talk, but I wasn't particularly good at it and they weren't much in the mood to be pepped up, anyway. So instead we spent a few minutes checking one last time on our equipment and making as sure as we could that our specially equipped suits and weapons were going to function as desired.

Afterward, we all sat in the boat, breathed recycled air, and sweated hard.

And I tried one last time to think. *One: hivies don't form small groups. Two: all members of a hive mind have the same experience level. Three: . . .*

Still no use.

I don't know how long we sat there. The plan was for the captain to take the *Volga* as close in as he could before the Drymnu's inevitable attack became too much for the ship to handle, but as the minutes dragged on and nothing happened, a set of frightening possibilities began to flicker through my already overheated mind. The *Volga*'s bridge blown so quickly that they'd had no time even to cry out . . . the rest of us flying blind toward a collision or to sail forever through normal space . . .

"The Drymnu's opened fire," the captain's voice crackled abruptly in our headsets. "Antimeteor lasers; some minor sensor damage. Get ready —"

With a stomach-jolting lurch, we were dumped out through the bay doors . . . and got our first real look at a Drymnu hive ship.

The thing was *huge.* Incredibly so. It was still several klicks away, yet it still took up a massive chunk of the sky ahead of us. Dark-hulled, oddly shaped, convoluted, threatening — it was all of those, too, but the only word that registered in that first heart-stopping second was *huge.* I'd seen the biggest of the Services' carriers up close, and I was stunned. God only knows how the others in the boat felt.

And then the first laser flicked out toward us, and the time for that kind of thought was thankfully over.

The shot was a clean miss. We'd been dropped along one of the Drymnu's flanks, as planned, and it was quickly clear that lasers designed for shooting oncoming meteors weren't at their best trying to fire sideways. But the Drymnu was a hive mind, and hive minds learned fast. The second and third shots missed, too, but the fourth bubbled the reflective paint on our nose. "Let's get moving," I snapped.

Kelly, our pilot, didn't need any coaxing. The words weren't even out of my mouth when she had us jammed against our restraints in a tight spiraling turn that sent us back toward the stern. Not *too* close; the drive that could actually move this floating mountain would fry us in nanoseconds if it occurred to the Drymnu to turn it on. But Kelly knew her job, and when we finally pulled into a more or less inertial path again, we were no more than two-thirds of the way back toward the stern and maybe three hundred meters from the textured hull.

This close to a true warship, we would be dead in seconds. But the Drymnu wasn't a warship . . . and as we flew on unvaporized, I finally knew for a fact that my gamble had paid off. We were inside the alien's defenses, and he couldn't touch us.

Now if we could only turn that advantage into something concrete.

"Fromm, get the laser going," I ordered. "The rest of you, let's find some targets for him to hit. Sensors, intakes, surface radiator equipment — anything that looks weak."

My headset crackled suddenly. "*Volga* to Travis," the captain's voice said. "Neutrino emission's suddenly gone up — I think he's running up his drive."

"Acknowledged," I said. "You out of his laser range yet?"

"We will be soon. So far he seems to be ignoring us."

A small favor to be grateful for. Whatever happened to us, at least this part of my plan had worked. "Okay. We're starting our first strafing run —"

Abruptly, my headset exploded with static. I grabbed for the volume control, vaguely aware of the others scrambling with similar haste around me. "What happened?" Kelly's voice came faintly, muffled by two helmets and the thin atmosphere in the boat.

"It's occurred to him that jamming our radios is a good idea," I shouted, my voice echoing painfully inside my helmet.

"Took him long enough," Waskin put in. "What was that about the drive? He trying to get away?"

"Probably." But no matter how powerful the Drymnu's drive, with all that mass to move, he wouldn't be outrunning us for a while, anyway. "We've still got time to do plenty of damage. Get cracking."

We tried. We flew all the way around that damn ship, skimming its surface, blasting away at anything that looked remotely interesting . . . and in the process we discovered something I'd somehow managed not to anticipate.

None of us had the faintest idea what Drymnu sensors, intakes, or surface radiator equipment looked like.

Totally unexpected. Form follows function, or so I'd always believed. But there was clearly more room for variation than I'd ever realized.

Which meant that even as we vaporized bits of metal and plastic all over that ship, we had no idea whatsoever how much genuine damage we were doing. Or even if we were doing any damage at all.

And slowly the Drymnu began to move.

I put off the decision as long as possible, and so it wound up being Waskin who eventually forced the issue. "Gonna have to go all the way, aren't we?" he called out. "The full plan. It's either that or give up and go home."

I gritted my teeth hard enough to hurt. It was my plan, and even while I'd been selling it to the others I'd been hoping like hell we wouldn't have to use it. But there was literally no other choice available to us now. If we tried to escape to the *Volga* now, it would be a choice of heading aft and being fried by the drive or going forward and giving the lasers a clean shot at us. There was no way to go now but in. "All right," I sighed, then repeated it loudly for everyone to hear. "Kelly, find us something that looks like a hatchway and bring us down. Anyone here had experience working on rotating hulls?"

Even through two helmets I could hear Waskin's sigh. "I have," he said.

"Good. You and I will head out as soon as we're down."

The hatches, fortunately, *were* recognizable as such. Kelly had anchored us to the hull beside one of them, and Waskin and I were outside working it open, when the Drymnu seemed to suddenly realize just what we were doing. Abruptly, vents we hadn't spotted began spewing gases all over the area. For a bad minute I thought there might be acid or something equally dangerous being blown out the discharge tubes, but it registered only as obvious waste gases, apparently used in hopes of confusing us or breaking our boots' pseudoglue grip. Once again, it seemed, we'd caught the Drymnu by surprise; but Waskin and I still didn't waste any time forcing the hatch open.

"Looks cramped," he grunted, touching his helmet to mine to bypass the still-jammed radio.

It was, too, though with Drymnu bodies half the size of ours, I wouldn't have expected anything else. "I think there's enough room for one of us to be inside and still have room to work," I told him, not bothering to point out we didn't have much choice in the matter. "I'll go. You and Fromm close the outer hatch once I'm in."

It took a little squeezing, but I made it. There didn't seem to be any inside controls, which was as expected; what I hadn't expected was that even as the hatch closed behind me and I unlimbered my modified cutting torch, my suit's exterior air sensors suddenly came alive.

And with the radio jammed, I was cut off from the others. I waited, heart thumping, wondering what the Drymnu had out there waiting for me. . . . As the pressures equalized, I threw all my weight upwards against the inner hatch. For a second it resisted. Then, with a *pop!* it swung open and, getting a grip on the lip, I pulled myself out into the corridor —

To be faced by a river of meter-high figures surging directly toward me.

There was no time for thought on any rational level, and indeed I later had no recollection at all of having aimed and fired my torch. But abruptly the hallway was ablaze with light and flame . . . and where the blue-white fire met the dark river there was death.

I heard no screams. Possibly my suit insulated me from that sound; more likely the telepathic bodies of a hive mind had never had reason to develop any vocal apparatus. But whatever else was alien about the Drymnu, its multiple bodies were still based on carbon and oxygen, and such molecules were not built to survive the kind of heat I was focusing on them. Where the flame touched, the bodies flared and dropped and died.

It was all over in seconds, at least that first wave of the attack. A dozen of the bodies lay before and around me, still smoldering and smoking, while the others beat an orderly retreat. I looked down at the carnage just once, then turned my eyes quickly and firmly away. I was just glad I couldn't smell them.

I was still standing there, watching and waiting for the next attack, when a tap on my helmet made me start violently. "Easy, easy, it's me," a faint and frantic voice came as I spun around and nearly incinerated Waskin. "Powers is behind me in the airlock. Are there any buttons in here we have to push to cycle it?"

"No, it seems to be set on automatic," I told him. "You have everyone coming in?"

"All but Kelly. I thought we ought to leave someone with the boat."

"Good." Experimentally, I turned my radio up a bit. No good; the jamming was just as strong inside the ship as it had been outside. "Well, at least he probably won't have any better hand weapons than we do. And he ought to be even worse at hand-to-hand than he is at space warfare."

"Unfortunately, he's got all those eighteen thousand bodies to spend learning the techniques," Waskin pointed out sourly.

"Not that many — we only have to kill maybe fourteen or fifteen thousand to destroy the hive mind."

"That's not an awful lot of help," he said.

Actually, though, it was, especially considering that the more bodies we disposed of the less of the mind would actually be present. *Weakness Number Three: destroying segments of the mind eventually destroys the whole?* No, that wasn't quite it. But it was getting closer. . . .

The Drymnu was able to get in two more assaults before the last four of our landing party made it through the airlock. Neither attack was particularly imaginative, and both were ultimately failures, but already the mind was showing far more grasp of elementary tactics than I cared for. The second attack was actually layered, with a torch-armed backup team hiding under cover while the main suicide squad drew us out into the corridor, and it was only the fact that we had heavily fire- and heat-proofed our suits beforehand that let us escape without burns.

But for the moment we clearly still held the advantage, and by the time all six of us were ready to begin moving down the corridor the Drymnu had pulled back out of sight.

"I don't suppose he's given up already," Fromm called as we headed cautiously out.

"More likely cooking up something nasty somewhere," Waskin shouted back.

"Let's kill the idle chatter," I called. My ears buzzed from the volume I had to use to be heard, and it occurred to me that if we kept this up we would all have severe self-inflicted deafness long before the Drymnu got us. "Keep communication helmet-to-helmet as much as possible," I told them.

Fromm leaned over and touched his helmet to mine. "Are we heading anywhere specific, or just supposed to cause as much damage as we can?"

"The latter, unless we find a particular target worth going for," I told him. "If we analyze the Drymnu's defenses, say, and figure out that he's defending some place specific, we'll go for that. Pass the word, okay?"

Good targets or not, though, we were equipped to do a lot of incidental damage, and we did our damnedest to live up to our potential. The rooms were already deserted as we got to them, but they were full of flammable carpeting and furnishings, and we soon had a dozen fires spewing flames and smoke in our wake. Within ten minutes the corridor was hazy with smoke — and, more significantly, with *moving* smoke — which meant that whatever bulkheading and rupture-control system the Drymnu was employing, it was clear that the burning section wasn't being well sealed off from the remainder of the ship. That should have meant big trouble for the alien, which in turn should have meant he would be soon throwing everything he had in an effort to stop us.

But it didn't happen. We moved farther and farther into the ship, setting fires and torching everything that looked torchable, and still the Drymnu held back. For a while I wondered if he was simply waiting for us to run out of fuel; for a shorter while I wondered if he had indeed given up. But the radio jamming continued, and he didn't seem to care that we were using up our fuel destroying his home, and so for lack of a better plan we just kept going.

We got up a couple of ramps, switched corridors twice, and were at a large, interior corridor when we finally found out what he had in mind.

It was just the fortune of the draw that Powers was point man as we reached that spot . . . just the fortune of the draw that he was the one to die. He glanced around the corner into the main corridor, started to step through — and was abruptly hurled a dozen meters sideways by a violent blast of highly compressed air. Waskin, behind him, leaned into the corridor to spray torch fire in that direction, and apparently succeeded in neutralizing the weapon. But it cost us precious seconds, and by the time we were able to move in and see what was happening to Powers, it was too late. The dark tide of bodies withdrew readily from before our flames, and we saw that Powers, still inside his reinforced suit, had nevertheless been beaten to death.

"With tools, looked like," Fromm said. Even through the muffling of the helmets his voice was clearly shaking. "They clubbed him to death with ordinary tools."

"So much for him not understanding the techniques of warfare," Waskin bit out. "He's figured out all he really needs to know: that he's got the numbers on his side. And how to use them."

He was right. Inevitable, really; the only mystery was why it had taken the Drymnu this long to realize that. "We'd better keep moving," I shouted as we pressed our helmets together in a ring.

"Why bother?" Brimmer snarled, his voice dripping with anger and fear. "Waskin's right — he knows what he's doing, all right. He's suckered us into coming too far inside the ship and now he's ready to begin the slaughter."

"Yeah, well, maybe," Fromm growled, "but he's going to have one hell of a fight before he gets us."

"So?" Brimmer shot back. "What difference does it make to *him* how many of his bodies he loses? He's got *eighteen thousand* of them to throw at us."

"So we kill as many as we can," I put in, struggling to regain control. "Every bit helps slow him down."

"Oh, *hell!*" Brimmer said suddenly. "Look — here they come!"

I swung around . . . and froze.

The entire width of the hallway was a mass of dark bodies charging down on us — dark bodies, with hands that glinted with metal tools.

This was it . . . and down deep I knew Brimmer was right. For all my purported tactical knowledge, I'd been taken in by the oldest ploy in human military history: draw the enemy deep inside your lines and then smother him. I glanced around; sure enough, the bodies filled the corridor in the other direction, too.

And for the last time in my life I had wound up in the wrong place at the wrong time. Except that this time I wouldn't be the only one who paid the price.

We had already shifted into a back-to-back formation, and three lines of torch fire were licking out toward each half of the imploding waves. Leaning my head back a few degrees, I touched the helmet behind me. "Looks like this is it," I said, trying hard to keep my voice calm. "Let's try to at least take as much of the Drymnu down with us as we can — we owe Messenia that much. Go for head shots — pass it down to the others."

The words were barely out of my mouth when I was deafened by another of the air blasts that had gotten Powers. Automatically, I braced myself; but this time they'd added something new. Along with the burst of air threatening to sweep us off our feet came a cloud of metal shrapnel.

It hit Waskin squarely in the chest.

I didn't hear any gasp of pain, but as he fell to his knees I clearly heard him utter something blasphemous. I gave the approaching wave one last sweep with my torch and then dropped down beside him. "Where does it hurt?" I shouted, pressing our helmets together.

"Mostly everywhere," he bit out. "Damn. I think they got my air system."

As well as the rest of the suit. I gritted my teeth and broke out my emergency patch kit, running a hand over his reinforced air hose to try and find the break. Suit integrity per se shouldn't be a big problem — we'd modified the standard suit design to isolate the helmet from everything else with just this sort of thing in mind. But an air system leak in an unknown atmosphere might easily prove fatal, and I had no intention of losing Waskin to suffocation or poisoning while he could still fight. I found the leak, gripped the piece of metal still sticking out of it —

"Oh, hell, Travis," he gasped. "Hell. What am I using for brains?"

"What?" I called. "What is it?"

"The Drymnu, damn it. Forget the head shots — we got to stop killing them."

Hysteria so quickly? "Waskin —"

"Damn it, Travis, don't you see? It's a hive mind — a *hive mind*. All experiences are shared commonly. *All* experiences — *including pain!*"

It was like a tactical full-spec bomb had gone off in the back of my brain. *Hive Mind Weakness Number Three: injure a part and you injure the whole.* "That's it!" I snapped, standing up and slamming my helmet against the one behind me. "Fire to injure, everyone, not to kill. Go for the arms and legs — try and take the bodies out of the fight without killing them. Pass the word — we're going to see if we can overload the Drymnu with pain."

For a wonder, they understood, and by the time Waskin and I were back in the game ourselves it was already becoming clear that we indeed had a chance. It was far easier to injure the bodies than to kill them — far easier and far quicker — and as the incapacitated bodies fell to the deck, their agonized thrashing hindered the advance of those behind them. The air-blast cannon continued its attacks for a while, but while all of us got painfully pincushioned by the flying shrapnel, Waskin's remained the only seriously life-threatening injury. We kept firing, and the bodies kept charging, and I gritted my teeth waiting for the Drymnu to switch tactics on us.

But he didn't. I'd been right, all along: for all his sophistication and alien intelligence, the Drymnu had no concept of warfare beyond the brute-force numbers game he'd latched onto. Even now, when it was clearly failing, he could come up with no alternative to it, and with each passing minute I could feel the attack becoming more sluggish or more erratic in turn as the Drymnu began to lose his ability to focus on us. Eventually, it reached the point where I knew there would be no more surprises. The Drymnu, agonized probably beyond anything he had ever felt before, and with more pain coming in faster than it could be dealt with, had literally become unable to think straight.

Approximately five minutes later, the attacking waves finally began to retreat back down the corridor; and even as we began to give chase, the radio jamming abruptly ceased and the Drymnu surrendered.

The full story — or at least the official story — didn't surface from the dust for nearly two months, but it came out pretty nearly as we on the *Volga* had already expected it to. The Drymnu — either the total thing or some large fraction of it — had apparently decided that having a fragmented race out among the stars was both an abomination of nature and highly dangerous besides, and had taken it upon himself to see whether humanity could indeed be destroyed. Point man — or point whatever — in a war that was apparently already over. The Drymnu, defeated by a lowly unarmed freighter, had clearly learned his lesson.

And I was left to meditate once more on the frustrations of my talent.

Sure, we won. Better than that, the *Volga* was actually famous, at least among official circles. To be sure, our medals were given to us at a private ceremony and we were warned gently against panicking the general public with stories about what had happened, but it was still fame of a sort. And we *did* save humanity from having to fight a war of survival. At least this time.

And yet. . . .

If I hadn't been standing there next to Waskin — hadn't decided to take the time to repair his air tube — we would very likely all have been killed . . . and I would have been spared the humiliation of having to sit around the *Volga* and listen to Waskin tell everyone over and over again how it had been *his* last-minute inspiration that had saved the day.

The wrong place at the wrong time.

Hitmen — See Murderers

It had been a long, slow, frustrating day, full of cranky machines, crankier creditors, and not nearly enough customers. In other words, a depressingly typical day. But even as Radley Grussing slogged up the last flight of stairs to his apartment he found himself whistling a little tune to himself. From the moment he'd passed the first landing — had looked down the first-floor hallway and seen the yellow plastic bag leaning up against each door — he'd known there was hope. Hope for his struggling little print shop; hope for his life, his future, and — with any luck at all — for his chances with Alison. Hope in double-ream lots, wrapped up in a fat yellow bag and delivered to his door.

The new phone books were out.

"Let your fingers do the walking through the Yellow Pages." He sang the old Bell Telephone jingle to himself as he scooped up the bag propped up against his own door and worked the key into the lock. Or, rather, that was what he *tried* to sing. After four flights of stairs, it came out more like, "Let your . . . fingers do the . . . walking through . . . the Yellow . . . Pages."

From off to the side came the sound of a door closing, and with a flush of embarrassment Radley realized that whoever it was had probably overheard his little song. "Shoot," he muttered to himself, his face feeling warm. Though maybe the heat was just from the exertion of climbing four flights of stairs. Alison had been bugging him lately about getting more exercise; maybe she was right.

He got the door open, and for a moment stood on the threshold carefully surveying his apartment. TV and VCR sitting on their woodgrain stand right where they were supposed to be. Check. The doors to kitchen and bedroom standing half-open at exactly the angles he'd put them before he'd left for work that morning. Check.

Through his panting Radley heaved a cautious sigh of relief. The existence of the TV showed no burglars had come and gone; the carefully positioned doors showed no one had come and was still there.

At least, no one *probably* was still there. . . .

As quietly as he could, he stepped into the apartment and closed the door, turning the doorknob lock but leaving the three deadbolts open in case he had to make a quick run for it. On a table beside the door stood an empty pewter vase. He picked it up by its slender neck, left the yellow plastic bag on the floor by the table and tiptoed to the bedroom door. Steeling himself, panting as quietly as was humanly possible, he nudged the door open and peered in. No one. Still on tiptoe, he repeated the check with the kitchen, with the same result.

He gave another sigh of relief. Alison thought he was a little on the paranoid side, and wasn't particularly hesitant about saying so. But he read the papers and he watched the news, and he knew that the quiet evil of the city was nothing to be ignored or scoffed at.

But once more, he'd braved the evil — braved it, and won, and had made it back to his own room and safety. Heading back to the door, he locked the deadbolts, returned the vase to its place on the table, and retrieved the yellow bag.

It was only as he was walking to the kitchen with it, his mind now freed from the preoccupations of survival in a hostile world, that his brain finally registered what his fingers had been trying to tell him all along.

The yellow bag was not, in fact, made of plastic.

"Huh," he said aloud, raising it up in front of his eyes for a closer look. It *looked* like plastic, certainly, like the same plastic they'd been delivering phone books in for he couldn't remember how many years. But the feel of the thing was totally wrong for plastic.

In fact, it was totally wrong for *any*thing.

"Well, that's funny," he said, continuing on into the kitchen. Laying the bag on the table, he pulled up one of the four more-or-less-matching chairs and sat down.

For a minute he just looked at the thing, rubbing his fingers slowly across its surface and digging back into his memory for how these bags had felt in the past. He couldn't remember, exactly; but it was for sure they hadn't felt like *this*. This wasn't like any plastic he'd ever felt before. Or like any cloth, or like any paper.

"It's something new, then," he told himself. "Maybe one of those new plastics they're making out of corn oil or something."

The words weren't much comfort. In his mind's eye, he saw the thriller that had been on cable last week, the one where the spy had been blown to bits by a shopping bag made out of plastic explosive. . . .

He gritted his teeth. "That's stupid," he said firmly. "Who in the world would go to that kind of trouble to kill *me?* Period; end of discussion," he added to forestall an argument. Alison had more or less accepted his habit of talking to himself, especially when he hadn't seen her for a couple of days. But even she drew the line at arguing aloud with himself. "End of discussion," he repeated. "So. Let's quit this nonsense and check out the ad."

He took a deep breath, exhaled it explosively like a shotputter about to go into his little loop-de-spin. Taking another deep breath, he reached into the bag and, carefully, pulled the phone book out.

Nothing happened.

"There — you see?" he chided himself, pushing the bag across the table and pulling the directory in front of him. "Alison's right; there's paranoia, and then there's para-*noi*-a. Gotta stop watching those late cable shows. Now, let's see here . . ."

He checked his white-pages listings first, both his apartment's and the print shop's. Both were correct. "Great," he muttered. "And now" — he hummed himself a little trumpet flourish as he turned to the Yellow Pages — "the pièce de résistance. Let your fingers do the walking through the Yellow Pages, dum dum de dum . . ." He reached the L's, turned past to the P's . . .

And there it was. Blazing out at him, in full three-color glory, the display ad for Grussing A-One-Excellent Printing And Copying.

"Now *that*," he told himself proudly, "is an *ad*. You just wait, Radley old boy — an ad like that'll get you more business than you know what to do with. You'll see — there's nowhere to go but *up* from now on."

He leafed through the pages, studying all the other print-shop ads and trying hard not to notice that six of his competitors had three-color displays fully as impressive as his own. That didn't matter. His ad — and the business it was going to bring in — would lift him up out of the hungry pack, bring him to the notice of important people with important printing needs. "You'll see," he told himself confidently. The *Printers* heading gave way to *Printers — Business Forms*, and then to *Printing Equipment* and *Printing Supplies*.

"Huh; Steven's has moved," he noted with some surprise. He hadn't bought anything from Steven's for over a year — probably about time he checked out their prices again. Idly, he turned another page —

And stopped. Right after the short listing of *Prosthetic Devices* was a heading he'd never seen before.

Prostitutes.

"Well, I'll be D-double-darned," he muttered in amazement. "I didn't know they could advertise."

He let his eyes drift down the listings, turned the page. There were a *lot* of names there — almost as many, he thought, as the attorney listings at the other end of the Yellow Pages, except that unlike the lawyers, the prostitutes had no display ads. "Wonder when the phone company decided to let this go in." He shook his head. "Hoo, boy — the egg's gonna hit the fan for sure when the Baptists see *this.*"

He scanned down the listing. Names — both women's and a few men's — addresses, phone numbers — it was all there. Everything anyone so inclined would need to get themselves some late-night companionship.

He frowned. Addresses. Not just post office boxes. Real street addresses.

Home addresses.

"Wait just a minute, here," he muttered. "Just a D-double-darned minute." Nevada, he'd heard once, had legal prostitution; but *here* — "This is nuts," he decided. The cops could just go right there and arrest them. Couldn't they? I mean, even those escort and massage places usually just have phone numbers. Don't they?"

With the phone book sitting right in front of him, there was an obvious way to answer that question. Sticking a corner of the yellow bag in to mark his place, he turned backwards toward the E's. *Excavating Contractors, Elevators* — oops; too far —

He froze, finger and thumb suddenly stiff where they gripped a corner of the page. A couple of headings down from *Elevators* was another list of names, shorter than the prostitutes listing but likewise distinguished by the absence of display ads. And the heading here . . .

Embezzlers.

His lips, he suddenly noticed, were dry. He licked them, without noticeable effect. "This," he said, his words sounding eerie in his ears, "is nuts. Embezzlers don't advertise. I mean, come *on* now."

He willed the listing to vanish, to change to something more reasonable, like *Embalmers*. But that heading was there, too . . . and the *Embezzlers* heading didn't go away.

He took a deep breath and, resolutely, turned the page. "I've been working too hard," he informed himself loudly. "Way too hard. Now. Let's see, where was I going . . . right — escort services."

He found the heading and its page after page of garish and seductive display ads. Sure enough, none of them listed any addresses. Just for completeness, he flipped back to the M's, checking out the massage places. Some had addresses; others — the ones advertising out-calls only — had just phone numbers.

"Makes sense," he decided. "Otherwise the cops and self-appointed guardians of public morals could just sit there and scare all their business away. So what gives with *this*?" He started to turn back to the prostitute listing, his fingers losing their grip on the slippery pages and dropping the book open at the end of the M's —

And again he froze. There was another listing of names and addresses there, just in front of *Museums*. Shorter than either the prostitute or embezzler lists; but the heading more than made up for it.

Murderers.

He squeezed his eyes shut, shook his head. "This is crazy," he breathed. "I mean, *really crazy.*" Carefully, he opened his eyes again. The *Murderers* listing was still there. Almost unwillingly, he reached out a finger and rubbed it across the ink. It didn't rub off, like cheap ink would, or fade away, like a hallucination ought to.

It was real.

He was still staring at the book, the sea of yellow dazzling his eyes, when the knock came at his front door.

He fairly jumped out of the chair, jamming his thigh against the underside of the table as he did so. "It's the FBI," he gasped under his breath. It was their book — their book of the city's criminals. It had been delivered here by mistake, and they were here to get it back.

Or else it was the *mob's* book —

"Radley?" A familiar voice came through the steel-cored wood panel. "You home?"

He felt a little surge of relief, knees going a little shaky. "There's paranoia," he chided himself, "and then there's para-*noi*-a." He raised his voice. "Coming, Alison," he called.

"Hi," she said with a smile as he opened the door, her face just visible over the large white bag in her arms. "Got the table all set?"

"Oh — right," he said, taking the bag from her. The warm scent of fried chicken rose from it; belatedly, he remembered he was supposed to have made a salad, too. "Uh — no, not yet. Hey, look, come in here — you've got to *see* this."

He led her to the kitchen, dropping the bag on the

counter beside the sink and sitting her down in front of the phone book. The yellow bag still marked the page with the *Prostitutes* heading; turning there, he pointed. "Do you see what I see?" he asked, his mouth going dry. If she *didn't* see anything, it had suddenly occurred to him, it would mean his brain was in serious trouble. . . .

"Huh," she said. "Well, *that's* new. I thought prostitution was still illegal."

"Far as I know, it still is," he agreed, feeling another little surge of relief. So he wasn't going nuts. Or at least he wasn't going nuts alone. "Hang on, though — it gets worse."

She sat there silently as he flipped back to the *Embezzlers* section, and then forward again to point out the *Murderers* heading. "I don't know what else is here," he told her. "This is as far as I got."

She looked up, an odd expression on her face. "You *do* realize, I hope, that this is nothing but an overly elaborate practical joke. This stuff can't really be in a real phone book."

"Well . . . sure," he floundered. "I mean, I know that the phone company wouldn't —"

She was still giving him that look. "Radley," she said warningly. "Come on, now, let's not slide off reality into the cable end of the channel selector. No one makes lists of prostitutes and embezzlers and murderers. And even if someone did, they *certainly* wouldn't try to hide them inside a city directory."

"Yes, I know, Alison. But — well, look here." He pulled the yellow bag over and slid it into her hand. "Feel it. Does it feel like plastic to you? Or like anything else you've ever touched?"

Alison shrugged. "They make thousands of different

kinds of plastics these days —"

"All right then, look here." He cut her off, lifting up the end of the phone book. "Here — at the binding. I'm a printer — I *know* how binding is done. These pages haven't just been slipped in somehow — they were bound in at the same time as all the others. How would someone have done *that?*"

"It's a joke, Radley," Alison insisted. "It has to be. All the phone books can't have — Well, look, it's easy enough to check. Let me go downstairs and get mine while you get the salad going."

Her apartment was just two floors down, and he'd barely gotten the vegetables out of the fridge and lined them up on the counter by the time she'd returned. "Okay, here we go," she said, sitting down at the table again and opening her copy of the phone book. "Prostitutes . . . nope, not here. Embezzlers . . . nope. Murderers . . . still nope." She offered it to him.

He took it and gave it a quick inspection of his own. She was right; none of the strange headings seemed to be there. "But how could anyone have gotten the extra pages bound in?" he demanded putting it down and gesturing to his copy. "I mean, all you have to do is just look at the binding."

"I know." Alison shook her head, running a finger thoughtfully across the lower edge of the binding. "Well . . . I *said* it was overly elaborate. Maybe someone who knows you works where they print these things, and he got hold of the orig — oh, my *God!*"

Radley jumped a foot backwards, about half the distance Alison and her chair traveled. "What?" he snapped, eyes darting all around.

She was panting, her breath coming in short, hyperventilating gasps. "The . . . the page. The listing . . ."

Radley dropped his eyes to the phone book. Nothing looked any different. "What? What'd you see?"

"The murderer listing," she whispered. "I was looking at it and . . . and it got longer."

He stared at the page, a cold hand working its way down his windpipe. "What do you mean, it got longer?" he asked carefully. "You mean like someone . . . just got added to the list?"

Allison didn't answer. Radley broke his gaze away from the page and looked at her. Her face was white, her breath coming slower but starting to shake now, her eyes wide on the book. "Alison?" he asked. "You okay?"

"It's from the devil," she hissed. Her right hand, gripping the table white-knuckled, suddenly let go its grip, darting up to trace a quick cross across her chest. "You've got to destroy it, Radley," she said. Abruptly, she looked up at him. "Right now. You've got to —" she twisted her head, looking all around the room — "you've got to burn it," she said, jabbing a finger toward the tiny fireplace in the living room. "Right now; right there in the fireplace." She turned back to the phone book, and with just a slight hesitation scooped it up. "Come on —"

"Wait a minute, Alison, wait a minute," Radley said, grabbing her hands and forcing them and the phone book back down onto the table. "Let's not do anything rash, huh? I mean —"

"Anything *rash?* This thing is a tool of the *devil.*"

"That's what I mean," he said. "Going off half-cocked. Who says this is from the devil? Who says —"

"Who says it's from the *devil?*" She stared at him, wide-eyed. "Radley, just where do you think this thing came from, the phone company?"

"So who says it didn't come from the other direction?"

Radley countered. "Maybe it was given to me by an angel — ever think of *that?*"

"Oh, sure," Alison snorted. "Right. An angel left you this — this — voyeur's delight."

Radley frowned at her. "What in the world are you talking about? These people are *criminals,* Alison. They've given up their right of privacy."

"Since when?" she shot back. "No one gives up any of their rights until they're convicted."

"But —" he floundered.

"And anyway," she added, "who says any of these people really *are* murderers?"

Radley looked down at the book. "But if they're not, why are they listed here?"

"Will you listen to yourself?" Alison demanded. "Five minutes ago you were wondering how this thing could exist; now you're treating what it says like it was gospel. You have no proof that any of these people have ever committed *any* crime, let alone killed anyone. For all you know, this whole thing could be nothing more than some devil's scheme to make you even more paranoid than you are already."

"I am *not* paranoid," Radley growled. "This city's dangerous — any big city is. That's not paranoia, it's just plain, simple truth." He pointed at the book. "All this does is confirm what the TV and papers already say."

For a long moment Alison just stared at him, her expression a mixture of anger and fear. "All right, Radley," she said at last. "I'll meet you halfway. Let's put it to the test. If there really was a murder tonight at" — she looked up at the kitchen wall clock — "about six-twenty, then it ought to be on the eleven o'clock news. Right?"

Radley considered. "Well . . . sometimes murders don't get noticed for a while. But, yeah, probably it'll be on tonight."

"All right." Alison took a deep breath. "If there *was* a murder, I'll concede that maybe there's something to all of this." She locked eyes with him. "But if there *wasn't* any murder . . . will you agree to burn the book?"

Radley swallowed. The possibilities were only just starting to occur to him, but already he'd seen enough to recognize the potential of this thing. The potential for criminal justice, for public service —

"Radley?" Alison prompted.

He looked at her, gritted his teeth. "We'll check the news," he told her. "But if the murder isn't there, we're not going to burn anything until tomorrow night, after we have a chance to check the papers."

Alison hesitated, then nodded. Reluctantly, Radley thought. "All right." Standing up, she picked up the book, closed it with her thumb marking the place. "You finish the salad. I'll be back in a couple of minutes."

"Where are you going?" Radley frowned, his eyes on the book as she tucked it under her arm.

"Down to the grocery on the corner — they've got a copy machine over by the ice chest."

"What do you need to copy it for?" Radley asked. "If the police release a suspect's name, we can just look it up —"

"We already know the book can change."

"Oh . . . Right."

He stood there, irresolute, as she headed for the door. Then, abruptly, the paralysis vanished, and in five quick strides he caught up with her. "I'll come with you," he said, gently but firmly taking the book from her hands. "The salad can wait."

It took several minutes, and a lot of quarters, for them to find out that the book wouldn't copy.

Not on any light/dark setting. Not on any reduction or enlargement setting. Not the white pages, not the Community Service pages, not the Yellow Pages, not the covers.

Not at all.

They returned to the apartment. The chicken was by now stone-cold, so while Radley threw together a passable salad, Alison ran the chicken, mashed potatoes, and gravy through the microwave. By unspoken but mutual consent they didn't mention the book during dinner.

Nor did they talk about it afterwards as they cleaned up the dishes and played a few hands of gin rummy. At eight, when prime time rolled around, they sat together on Radley's old couch and watched TV.

Radley wouldn't remember afterwards much about what they'd watched. Part of him waited eagerly for the show to be broken into by the announcement of what he was beginning to regard as "his" murder. The rest of him was preoccupied with Alison, and the abnormal way she sat beside him the whole time. Not snuggled up against him like she usually was when they watched TV, but sitting straight and stiff and not quite touching him.

Maybe, he thought, she was waiting for the show to be broken into, too.

But it wasn't, and the 'tween-show local newsbreak didn't mention any murders, and by the time the eleven o'clock news came on Radley had almost begun to give up.

The lead story was about an international plane crash. The second story was his murder.

"Authorities are looking for this man for questioning in connection with the crime," the well-scrubbed newswoman with the intense eyes said as the film of the murder scene was replaced by a mug shot of a thin, mean-looking man. "Marvin Lake worked at the same firm with the victim before he was fired last week, and had threatened Mr. Cordler several times in the past few months. Police are asking anyone with information about his whereabouts to contact them."

The picture shifted again, and her co-anchor took over with a story about a looming transit strike. Bracing himself, Radley turned to Alison.

To find her already gazing at him, her eyes looking haunted. "I suppose," he said, "we'd better go check the book."

She didn't reply. Getting up, Radley went into the kitchen and returned with the phone book. He had marked the *Murderers* listing with the yellow non-plastic bag. . . . "He's here," Radley said, his voice sounding distant in his ears. "Marvin Lake." He leaned over to offer Alison a look.

She shrank back from the book. "I don't want to see it," she said, her voice as tight as her face.

Radley sighed, eyes searching out the entry again. Address, phone number . . .

"Wait a minute," he muttered to himself, flipping back to the white pages. L, La, Lak . . . there it was: Marvin Lake. Address . . . "It's not the same address," he said, feeling an odd excitement seeping through the sense of unreality. "Not even close."

"So?" Alison said.

"Well, don't you see?" he asked, looking up at her. "The white pages must be his home address; *this* one" — he jabbed at the Yellow Pages listing — "must be where he is right now."

Alison looked at him. "Radley . . . if you're thinking what I think you're thinking . . . please don't."

"Why not?" he demanded. "The guy's a murderer."

"That hasn't been proved yet."

"The police think he's guilty."

"That's not what the report said," she insisted. "All they said was that they wanted to question him."

"Then why is he *here?*" Radley held out the open phone book.

"Maybe because you *want* him to be there," Allison shot back. "You ever think of *that?* Maybe that thing is just somehow creating the listings you want to see there."

Radley glared at her. "Well, there's one way to find out, isn't there?"

"Radley —"

Turning his back on her, he stepped back into the kitchen, turning to the front of the phone book. The police non-emergency number . . . there it was. Picking up the phone, he punched in the digits.

The voice answered on the seventh ring. "Police."

"Ah — yes, I just heard the news about the Cordler murder," Radley said, feeling suddenly tongue-tied. "I think I may have an idea where Marvin Lake is."

"One moment."

The phone went dead, and Radley took a deep breath. Several deep breaths, in fact, before the phone clicked again. "This is Detective Abrams," a new voice said. "Can I help you?"

"Ah — yes, sir. I think I know where Marvin Lake is."

"And that is . . . ?"

"Uh —" Radley flipped back to where his thumb marked the place. A sudden fear twisted his stomach, that the whole *Murderers* listing might have simply vanished, leaving him looking like a fool.

But it hadn't. "Forty-seven thirty West Fifty-second," he said, reading off the address.

"Uh-huh," Abrams grunted. "Would you mind telling me your name?"

"Ah — I'd rather not. I don't really want any of the spotlight."

"Yeah," Abrams said. "Did you actually see Lake at this address?"

This was starting to get awkward. "No, I didn't," Radley said, searching desperately for something that would sound convincing. "But I heard it from a — well, a pretty reliable source," he ended lamely.

"Yeah," Abrams said again. He didn't sound especially convinced. "Thanks for the information."

"You're —" The phone clicked again. "Welcome," Radley finished with a sigh. Hanging up, he closed the phone book onto his thumb again and turned back to face Alison.

She was still sitting on the couch, staring at him over the back. "Well?"

He shrugged. "I don't know. Maybe they won't bother to check it out."

She stared into his face a moment longer. Then, dropping her gaze, she got to her feet. "It's getting late," she said over her shoulder as she started for the door. "I'll talk to you tomorrow."

He took a step toward her. "Alison —"

"Good night, Radley," she called, undoing the locks. A minute later, she was gone.

For a long moment he just stood there, staring at the door, an unpleasant mixture of conflicting emotions swirling through his brain and stomach. "Come on, Alison," he said quietly to the empty room. "If this works, think of what it'll mean for cleaning up this city."

The empty room didn't answer. Sighing, he walked to

the door and refastened the deadbolts. She was right, after all; it *was* late, and he needed to be at work by seven.

He looked down at the phone book still clutched in his hands. On the other hand, Pete would be in by seven, too, and it didn't hardly take two of them to get the place ready for business.

And he really ought to take the time to sit down with the book and find out just exactly what this miracle was that had been dropped on his doorstep.

It was nearly one-thirty before he went to bed . . . but by the time he did, he'd made lists of every murderer, arsonist, and rapist in the book.

The next time one of those listings changed, he wouldn't have to wait for the news reports to find out who was guilty.

He got to the shop just before the seven-thirty opening time, feeling groggy but strangely exhilarated.

"Morning, Mr. Grussing." Pete Barnabee nodded solemnly from up at the counter as Radley closed the back door behind him. "How you doing?"

"I'm fine, Pete," Radley told him. "Yourself?"

"Pretty tolerable, thank you."

It was the same set of greetings, with only minor variations, that they'd exchanged every morning since Radley had first hired Pete two months ago. "So. The place ready for business?" he asked the other.

"All set," Pete confirmed. "You seen the new phone book yet?"

"Yeah — mine came yesterday," Radley nodded, resisting the urge to tell Pete about the strange Yellow Pages that had come with his. "The new ad looks pretty good, doesn't it?"

"Best of the bunch," Pete said. "Oughta bring in whole

stacks of new business."

"Let's hope so." Radley looked at his watch. "Well, time to let the crowds in," he said, walking around the counter and unlocking the front door. "Incidentally, you didn't happen to catch any news this morning, did you?" he added as he turned the "Closed" sign around.

"Yeah, I did," Pete answered. "They didn't mention our ad, though."

"Very funny. I was just wondering if the cops found that guy they were looking for in the Cordler murder."

"Oh, yeah, they did," Pete nodded. "Marvin Lake or something, right? Yeah, they found him holed up somewhere on West Fifty-second last night."

Radley felt a tight smile crease his cheeks. "Did they, now?" he murmured, half to himself. "Well, well, *well.*"

Pete cocked an eyebrow at him. "You know the guy?"

"Me? No. Why do you ask?"

Pete shrugged. "I dunno. You just seem . . ." He shrugged again.

Again, Radley was tempted. But he really didn't know Pete well enough to trust him with a secret like this. "I'm just happy that scum like that is off the street," he said instead. "That's all."

"Oh, he's still on the street," Pete said, squatting down to fuss with the loading tray on one of the presses. "Made bail and walked right out."

Radley made a face. That figured. The stupid leaky criminal justice system. "They'll get him again."

"Maybe. Maybe not. You don't get many volunteer stoolies after the first one bites it."

Radley stared at him, his throat tightening. "What are you talking about?"

"Oh, it's just that an hour after Lake walked out of the

police station the guy who lent him that apartment turned up dead. Shot twice in the face." Pete straightened up, brushed off his hands briskly. "Ready for me to start on the Hammerstein job?"

Somehow, Radley made it through the morning. At lunchtime he rushed home.

"Detective Abrams," he told the person who answered the phone. "Tell him it's the guy who gave him Marvin Lake's address last night."

"One moment." The line went on hold.

Wedging the phone between shoulder and ear, Radley hauled the phone book onto the table and opened it to the Yellow Pages. The M's . . . there. Mo, Mu —

"This is Abrams." The other man sounded tired.

"This is Ra — the guy who told you where Marvin Lake was last night," Radley said. He had the *Murderers* listing now. Running a finger down it . . .

"Yeah, I recognize the voice," Abrams grunted. "You know where he's gone?"

Radley opened his mouth . . . and froze. The Marvin Lake listing was gone.

"You still there?" Abrams prompted.

"Uh . . . yeah. Yeah. Uh . . ." Frantically, Radley scanned the listing, wondering if he'd somehow been looking at the wrong place. But the name wasn't under the L's, or under the M's, or anywhere else.

It was just gone.

"Look, you got something to say or don't you?" Abrams growled. "If you do, spit it out. If you don't, quit wasting everyone's time and get off the phone, okay?"

"I'm sorry . . ." Radley managed, staring at the spot where the Marvin Lake listing should have been. "I thought

— well, I'm sorry, that's all."

"Yeah. We're all sorry for something." Abrams sounded slightly disgusted. "Next time just write me a postcard okay?" Without waiting for an answer, he hung up.

Blindly, Radley groped for the hook and hung up the handset, his eyes still on the page. "This," he announced to himself, "is crazy. It's *crazy*. How can it be here one day and gone the —"

And right in mid-sentence, it hit him. "Oh, real smart, Radley," he muttered. "What are you using for brains, anyway, oatmeal? Of *course* Marvin Lake's not here any-more — if *he* had any brains he'll have left town hours ago. And soon as he leaves town . . ."

He sighed and closed the book, the all-too familiar tastes of embarrassment and frustration souring his mouth. "Doesn't matter," he told himself firmly. "Okay. So this one got away. Fine. But the next one won't. There's still gotta be a way to use this thing. All you have to do is find it."

He returned to the shop and got back to work.

If the new display ad had helped at all, it wasn't obvious from the business load. For Radley the day turned out to be an offset copy of the previous one, with the added secret frustration of knowing that a double murderer had slipped through his fingers.

And then he got home, to find Alison waiting for him.

"Did you see this?" she asked when they were safe be-hind the triple-locked door. The article the newspaper was folded to . . .

"I heard about it, yeah," he said. "Tried to call in Marvin Lake's new address to the police on my lunch hour, but the listing's gone. Best guess is he skipped town."

"So it didn't really do any good, did it?"

"It did a lot of good," he countered. "It showed that what the book says is true."

"Not really. We still don't *know* that Marvin Lake killed anybody."

"We don't? What about that guy?" He jabbed a finger at her newspaper. "If he didn't kill Cordler, why would he kill the guy who hid him from the cops?"

"We don't know he did *that*, either," she retorted. "Face it Radley — all you have there is hearsay. And not very good hearsay, either."

"It's good enough for me," he said doggedly. "Half the time people get away with crimes because the police don't know who to concentrate their investigations on. Well, this is just what we need to change that."

"And all thanks to Radley Grussing, Super Stoolie."

"Sneer all you like," Radley growled. "This is *truth*, Alison — you know it as well as I do."

"It's not truth," she snapped back. "It may be *true*, but it's not *truth*."

"Oh, well, *that* makes sense," he said, with more sarcasm than he'd really intended. "I can hardly wait to hear what the difference is."

She sighed, all the tension seeming to drain out of her. "I don't know," she said, her voice sounding suddenly tired. "All I know is that that book is wrong. Somehow, it's *wrong*." She took a deep breath. "This isn't good for you, Radley. Isn't good for us. People like you and me weren't meant to know things like this. Please, *please* destroy it."

He looked at her . . . and slowly it dawned on him that his whole relationship with Alison was squatting square on the line here. "Alison, I can't just throw this away," he said gently. "Can't you see what we've got here? We've got the chance to clean away some of the filth that's clogging the streets of this city."

"And to fluff up Radley Grussing's ego in the process?"

He winced. "That's not fair," he said stiffly. "I'm not trying to make a name for myself here."

"But you like the power." She stared him straight in the eye. "Admit it, Radley — you *like* knowing these people's darkest secrets."

Radley clenched his teeth. "I don't think this discussion is getting us anywhere." He turned away.

"Will you destroy the book?" she asked bluntly from behind him.

He couldn't face her. "I can't," he said over his shoulder. "I'm sorry, Alison . . . but I just *can't*."

For a long moment she was silent. Then, without a word, she moved away from him, and he turned back around in time to see her collect her purse and jacket from the couch and head for the door. "Let me walk you downstairs," Radley called after her as she unlocked the deadbolts.

"I don't think I'll get lost," she said shortly.

"Yes, but —" He stopped.

She frowned over her shoulder at him. "But *what?*"

"I just thought that . . . I mean, there are a lot of rapists running loose in this city. . . ."

She gazed at him, something like pain or pity or fear in her eyes. "You see?" she said softly. "It's started already." Opening the door, she left.

Radley exhaled noisily between his teeth. "Nothing's started," he told the closed door. "I'm just being cautious. That's hardly a crime."

The words sounded hollow in his ears, and for a minute he just stood there, wondering if maybe she was right.

"No," he told himself firmly. "I can handle this. I *can*."

Turning back to the kitchen, he pulled a frozen dinner out of the refrigerator and popped it into the microwave. Then, pulling a notebook from the phone shelf, he flipped it open and got out a pen. Time to compare the Book's listings of murderers, arsonists, and rapists against the lists he'd made last night. See who, if anyone, had sold their souls to the devil in the past fourteen hours.

According to the papers, there had been two gang killings in the city that day, both of them drive-by shootings. Both apparently by repeaters, unfortunately, because no new names had appeared in the *Murderers* listing. The *Arsonists* listing hadn't changed since last night, either.

On the *Rapists* list, though, he hit paydirt.

The phone rang six times. Then: "Hello?"

A woman's voice. Radley gripped the phone a little tighter. He'd hoped the man lived alone. "James Whittington, please," he said.

"May I ask who's calling?"

A secretary, then, not a wife? A thin straw, but Radley found himself clutching it hard. "Tell him I'd like to discuss this afternoon's activities with him," he instructed her. "He'll understand."

There was a short silence. "Just a minute." Then came the sound of a hand covering the mouthpiece, and a brief and heavily muffled conversation. A moment later, the hand was removed. Radley waited, and after nearly ten seconds a man's voice came on. "Hello?"

"Is this James Whittington?"

"Yes. Who is this?"

"Someone who knows what you did this afternoon," Radley told him. "You raped a woman."

There was just the briefest pause. "If this is supposed to be a joke, it's not especially funny."

"It's no joke," Radley said, letting his voice harden. "You know it and I know it, so let's cut the innocent act."

"Oh, the tough type, huh?" Whittington sneered. "Making anonymous calls and vague accusations — that's *real* tough. I don't suppose you've got anything more concrete. A name, for instance?"

"I don't know her name," Radley admitted, feeling sweat beading up on his forehead. This wasn't going at all the way he'd expected. "But I'm sure the police won't have too much trouble rooting out little details like that."

"I have no idea what the hell you're talking about," Whittington growled.

"No?" Radley asked. "Then why are you still listening?"

"Why are *you* still talking?" Whittington countered. "You think you can shake me down or something?"

"I don't want any money," Radley said, feeling like a blue-ribbon idiot. Somehow, he'd thought that a flat-out accusation like this would make Whittington crumble and blurt out a confession. He should have just called the police in the first place. "I just wanted to talk to you," he added uncomfortably. "I suppose I wanted to see what kind of man would rape a woman —"

"I didn't rape anyone."

"Yeah. Right. I guess there's nothing to do now but just go ahead and tell the cops what I know. Sorry to have ruined your evening." He started to hang up.

"Wait a second," Whittington's voice came faintly from the receiver.

Radley hesitated, then put the handset back to his ear. "What?"

There was a long, painful pause. "Look," the other man

said at last. "I don't know what she told you, but it wasn't rape. It *wasn't*. Hell, *she* was the one who hit on *me*. What was I supposed to do, turn her down?"

Radley frowned, a sudden surge of misgiving churning through his stomach. Could the Book have been wrong? He opened his mouth —

"*Damn* you."

He jumped. It was a woman's voice — the same voice that had originally answered the phone. Listening in on an extension.

Whittington swore under his breath. "Mave, get the hell off the phone."

"No!" the woman said, her voice suddenly hard and ugly. "No. Enough is enough — damn it all, can't you even drive to the airport and back without screwing someone? Oh, God . . . *Traci?*"

"Mave, shut the hell up —"

"Your own *niece?*" the woman snarled. "God, you make me *sick.*"

"I said *shut up!*" Whittington snarled back. "She hit on *me,* damn it —"

"She's *sixteen years old!*" the woman screamed. "What the hell does she know about bastards like you?"

Radley didn't wait to hear any more. Quickly, quietly, he hung up on the rage boiling out of his phone.

For a minute he just sat there at his table, his whole body shaking with reaction. Then, almost reluctantly, he reached for the Book, still open to the *Rapists* listings, and turned to the end. And sure enough, there it was:

Rapists, Statutory — See Rapists.

Slowly, he closed the Book. "It was still a crime," he reminded himself. "Even if she really *did* consent. It was still a crime."

But not nearly the crime he'd thought it was.

He took a deep breath, exhaled it slowly. The tight sensation in his chest refused to go away. A marriage obviously on the brink, one that probably would have gone over the edge eventually anyway. But if his call hadn't given it this particular push . . .

He swallowed hard, staring at the Book. The solitude of his apartment suddenly had become loneliness. "I wish Alison was here," he murmured. He reached for the phone —

And stopped. Because when she'd finished sympathizing with him, she would once again tell him to burn the Book.

"I can't do that," he told himself firmly. "She can play with words all she wants to. The stuff in the Book is *true;* and if it's true then it's *truth.* Period."

A flicker of righteousness briefly colored his thoughts. But it faded quickly, and when it was gone, the loneliness was still there.

He sat there for a long time, staring at nothing in particular. Then, with another sigh, he hitched his chair closer to the kitchen table and pulled the Book and notebook over to him. There were a lot of criminals whose names he hadn't yet copied down. With the whole evening now stretching out before him, he ought to be able to make a sizeable dent in that number before bedtime.

He arrived at the shop a few minutes before eight the next morning, his eyelids heavy with too little sleep and too many nightmares. Never before had he realized just how many types of crime there were in the world. Nor had he realized how many people were out there committing them.

Business was noticeably better than it had been the previous few weeks, but Radley hardly noticed. With the evil of the city roiling in his mind's eye like a huge black thunder-cloud, the petty details of printing letterhead paper and business cards seemed absurdly unimportant. Time and again he had to drag his thoughts away from the blackness of the thundercloud back to what he was doing — more often than not, finding a bemused-looking customer standing there peering at him.

Fortunately, most of them accepted his excuse that he hadn't been sleeping well lately. Even more fortunately, Pete knew his way around well enough to take up the slack.

Partly from guilt, partly because he wanted to give his attention over to the Book when he went home, Radley stayed for an hour after the shop closed, getting some of the next day's work set up. By the time he left, rush hour was over, leaving the streets and sidewalks about as empty as they ever got.

It was a quiet walk home. Quiet, but hardly peaceful. Perhaps it was merely the relative lack of traffic, the fact that Radley wasn't used to walking down these streets without having to change his direction every five steps to avoid another person. Or perhaps it was merely his own fatigue, magnifying the caution he'd always felt about life here.

Or perhaps Alison had been right. Perhaps it *was* the Book that was bothering him. The Book, and the page after page of *Muggers* he'd leafed through that first night.

It was an unnerving experience, and by the time he reached his building he was seriously considering whether to start carrying a gun to work with him. But as soon as he left the public sidewalk, the sense of imminent danger began to lift; and by the time he was safely behind his deadbolts he could almost laugh at how strongly a runaway imagination could make him feel.

Still, he waited until he'd finished dinner and had a beer in his hand before hauling out the Book, the newspaper, and his notebook and beginning the evening's perusal.

There had been two more murders — again, apparently by repeaters, since there were no new names under the appropriate listing in the Book. Ditto with rapists and armed robbers. The *Muggers* listing had increased by eleven names, but after wasting half an hour comparing lists it finally dawned on him that isolating the new names wouldn't do anything to let him link a particular person to a particular crime. The *Burglars* listing, increased by three, presented the same problem.

"Growing like a weed," he muttered to himself, flipping back and forth through the Book. "Just like a weed. How in blazes are we ever going to stop it?"

It was nearly nine o'clock when he finally went back to the *Embezzlers* listing . . . and found what he was looking for.

A single new name.

And what was more, a name Radley couldn't find mentioned anywhere in the newspaper. Which made sense; a crime like embezzlement could go unnoticed for weeks or even months.

Radley had tried informing on a murderer, and had wound up making matters worse. He'd tried wangling information out of a rapist, with similar results.

Perhaps he could become a conscience.

The phone was picked up on the third ring. "Hello?" a cool, MBA-type voice answered.

"Harry Farandell, please," Radley said.

"Speaking," the other man acknowledged. "Who's this?"

"Someone who wants to help you get off the path you're on before it's too late," Radley told him. "You see, I know

80

that you embezzled some money today."

There was a long silence. "I don't know what you're talking about," Farandell said at last.

Almost the same words, Radley remembered, that James Whittington had used in denying his rape. "I'm not a policeman, Mr. Farandell," Radley told him. "I'm not with your company, either. I could call both of them, of course, but I'd really rather not."

"Oh, I'm sure," Farandell responded bitterly. "And how much, may I ask, is all this altruism going to cost me?"

"Nothing at all," Radley assured him. "I don't want any of the money you stole. I want you to put it back."

"What?"

"You heard me. Chances are no one knows yet what you've done. You replace the money now and no one ever will."

Another long silence. "I can't," Farandell said at last.

"Why not? You already spent it or something?"

"You don't understand," Farandell sighed.

"Look, do you still have the money, or don't you?" Radley asked.

"Yes. Yes, I've still got it. But — look, we can work something out. I'll make a deal with you; any deal you want."

"No deals, Mr. Farandell," Radley said firmly. "I'm trying to stop crime, not add to it. Return the money, or else I go to the police. You've got forty-eight hours to decide which it'll be."

He hung up. For a moment he wondered if he should have given Farandell such a lenient deadline. If the guy skipped town . . . but no. It wasn't like he was facing a murder charge or something equally serious. And anyway, it could easily take a day or two for him to slip the money back without anyone noticing.

And when he had done so, it would be as if the crime had never happened.

"You see?" Radley told himself as he turned to a fresh page in the notebook. "There *is* a way to use this. Tool of the devil, my foot."

The warm feeling lasted the rest of the evening, even through the writer's cramp he got from tallying yet more names in his notebook. It lasted, in fact, until the next morning.

When the TV news announced that financier Harry Farandell had committed suicide.

Business was even better that day than it had been the day before. But again Radley hardly noticed. He worked mechanically, letting Pete take most of the load, coming out of his own dark thoughts only to listen to the periodic updates on the Farandell suicide that the radio newscasts sprinkled through the day. By late afternoon it was apparent that Farandell's financial empire, far from being in serious trouble, had merely had a short-term cash-flow problem. In such cases, the commentators said, the standard practice was to take funds from a healthy institution to prop up the ailing one. Such transfers, though decidedly illegal, were seldom caught by the regulators, and the commentators couldn't understand why Farandell hadn't simply done that instead.

Twice during the long day Radley almost picked up the phone to call Alison. But both times he put the handset down undialed. He knew, after all, what she would say.

He made sure to leave on time that evening, to get home during rush hour when there were lots of people on the streets. All the way up the stairs he swore he would leave the Book where it was for the rest of the night, and for the first hour he held firmly to that resolution. But with dinner eaten, the dishes washed, and the newspaper read, the evening seemed to stretch out endlessly before him.

Besides, there had been another murder in the city. Taking a quick look at his list wouldn't hurt.

There were no new names on the listing, which meant either that the murderer was again a repeater or else that he'd already left town. The paper had also reported a mysterious fire over on the east side that the police suspected was arson; but the *Arsonists* listing was also no longer than it had been the night before.

"You ought to close it now," he told himself. But even as he agreed that he ought to, he found himself leafing through the pages. All the various crimes; all the ways people had found throughout the ages of inflicting pain and suffering on each other. He'd spent he didn't know how many hours looking through the Book and writing down names, and yet he could see that he'd hardly scratched the surface. The city was dying, being eaten away from beneath by its own inhabitants.

He'd reached the T's now, and the eight pages under the *Thieves* heading. Compared to some of the others in the Book it was a fairly minor crime, and he'd never gotten around to making a list of the names there. "And even if I did," he reminded himself, "it wouldn't do any good. I bet we get twenty new thieves every day around here." He started to turn the page, eyes glancing idly across the listings —

And stopped. There, at the top of the second column, was a very familiar name. A familiar name, with a familiar address and phone number accompanying it.

Pete Barnabee.

Radley stared at it, heart thudding in his chest. No. No, it couldn't be. Not Pete. Not the man —

Whom he'd hired only a couple of months ago. Without really knowing all that much about him . . .

"No wonder we've been losing money," he murmured to himself. Abruptly, he got to his feet. "Wait a minute," he cautioned himself even as he grabbed for his coat. "Don't jump to any conclusions here, all right? Maybe he stole something from someone else, a long time ago."

"Fine," he answered tartly, unlocking the deadbolts with quick flicks of his wrist. "Maybe he did. There's still only one way to find out for sure."

There were more people on the streets now than there had been on his walk through the dinnertime calm the night before: people coming home from early-evening entertainment or just heading out for later-night versions. Radley hardly noticed them as he strode back to the print shop, running the inventory lists through his mind as best he could while he walked. There were any number of small items — pens and paper and such — that he wouldn't particularly miss even if Pete had been pilfering them ever since starting work there. Unfortunately, there were also some very expensive tools and machines that he could ill afford to lose.

And he'd already discovered that *Thieves, Petty* and *Thieves, Grand* were both included under the *Thieves* heading.

He reached the shop and let himself in the back door. The first part of the check was easy, and it took only a few minutes to confirm that the major machines were still there and still intact. The next part would be far more tedious. Digging the latest inventory list out of the files, he got to work.

It was after midnight when he finally put up the list with a sigh — a sigh that hissed both relief and annoyance into his ears. "See?" he told himself as he trudged back to the door. "Whatever Pete did, he did it somewhere else. Unless," he amended, "he's just been stealing pencils and label stickers."

But checking all of those would take hours . . . and for now, at least, he was far too tired to bother. "But I *will* check them out eventually," he decided. "I mean, I don't really care about stuff like that, but if he'll steal pencils, who's to say he won't back a truck up here someday and take all the copiers?"

It was a question that sent a shiver up his back. If that happened, he would be out of business. Period.

He headed toward home, the awful thought of it churning through his mind . . . and, preoccupied with the defense of his property, he never even heard the mugger coming.

He just barely felt the crushing blow on the back of his head.

He came to gradually, through a haze of throbbing pain, to find himself staring up at a soft pastel ceiling. The forcibly clean smell he'd always associated with hospitals curled his nostrils. . . . "Hello?" he called tentatively.

There was a moment of silence. Then, suddenly, there was a young woman leaning over him. "Ah — you're back with us," she said, peering into each of his eyes in turn. "I'm Doctor Sanderson. How do you feel?"

"My head hurts," Radley told her. "Otherwise . . . okay, I guess. What happened?"

"Best guess is that you were mugged," she told him. "Apparently by someone who doesn't like long conversations with his victims. You were lucky, as these things go: no concussion, no bone or nerve damage, only minor bleeding. You didn't even crack your chin when you fell."

Reflexively, Radley reached up to rub his chin. Bristly, but otherwise undamaged. "Can I go home?"

Sanderson nodded. "Sure. You'll have to call someone to get you, though — your friend didn't wait."

"Friend?" Radley frowned. The crinkling of forehead skin gave an extra throb to his headache.

"Fellow who brought you in. Black man — medium build, slightly balding. Carried you about five blocks to get you here — sweating pretty hard by that time, I'll tell you." She frowned in turn. "He told the E/R people you needed help — we just assumed he was a friend or neighbor or something."

Radley started to shake his head, thought better of it. "Doesn't sound like anyone I know," he said. "I certainly wasn't with anyone when it happened."

Sanderson shrugged slightly. "Good Samaritan, then. A vanishing breed, but you still get them sometimes. Anyway. Your shoes are under the gurney there; come on down to the nurses' station when you're ready and we'll run you through the paperwork."

He thought about calling Alison to come get him, but decided he didn't really want to wake her up at this time of night. Especially not when he'd have to explain why he'd been out so late.

With his wallet gone, he had no money for a cab, but a tired-eyed policeman who had brought in a pair of prostitutes gave him a lift home. What the blow on the head had started, the long trek up the steps to his apartment finished, and he barely made it to his bed before collapsing.

★ ★ ★ ★ ★

His headache was mostly gone when he awoke. Along with most of the day.

"Yeah, I figured you were sick or something when you didn't show up this morning," Pete said when he called the print shop. "Didn't expect it was something like *this*, though. You okay?"

"Yeah, I'm fine," Radley assured him, a wave of renewed shame warming his face. How could he ever have thought someone with Pete's loyalty would betray him? "Let me shower and change and I'll come on down."

"You don't need to do that," Pete said. "Not hardly worth coming in now, anyway. If I may say so, it don't sound to me like you oughta be running 'round yet, and I can handle things here okay." There was a faintly audible sniff/snort, and Radley could visualize the other man smiling. "And I really don't wanna have to carry you all the way home if you fall apart on me."

"There's that," Radley conceded. "I guess you're right. Well . . . I'll see you in the morning, then."

"Only if you feel like it. Really — I can handle things until you're well. Oops — gotta go. A customer just came in."

"Okay. Bye."

He hung up and gingerly felt the lump on the back of his head. Yes, Pete might have had to carry him home, at that. *That* little outing had sure gone sour.

As had his attempt to catch a murderer. And his attempt to solve a rape. And his attempt to stop an embezzlement.

In fact, everything the Book had given him had gone bad. One way or another, it had all gone bad.

"But it's truth," he gritted. "I mean, it *is*. How can truth be bad?"

87

He had no answer. With a sigh, he stood up from the kitchen chair. The sudden movement made his head throb, and he sat down again quickly. Yes, Pete might indeed have wound up carrying him.

Like someone else had already had to do.

Radley flushed with shame. In his mind's eye, he saw a medium-build black man, probably staggering under Radley's weight by the time he reached the hospital. Quietly helping to clean up the mess Radley had made of himself.

"I wish they'd gotten his name," he muttered to himself. "I'll never get a chance to thank him."

He looked down at the Book . . . and a sudden thought struck him. If the Book contained the names of all the criminals in town, why not the names of all the Good Samaritans, too?

He opened to the Yellow Pages, feeling a renewed sense of excitement. Perhaps this, he realized suddenly, was what the Book was really for. Not a tool for tracking down and punishing the guilty, but a means of finding and rewarding the good. The G's . . . there they were. Ge, Gl, Go . . .

There was no *Good Samaritans* listing.

Nor was there an *Altruists* listing. Nor were there listings for benefactor, philanthropist, hero, or patriot. Or for good example, salt of the earth, angel, or saint.

There was nothing.

He thought about it for a long time. Then, with only a slight hesitation, he picked up the phone.

Alison answered on the fourth ring. "Hello?"

"It's me," Radley told her. "Listen." He took a careful breath. "I know the difference now. You know — the difference between *true* and *truth?*"

"Yes?" she said, her voice wary.

"Yeah. *True* is a group of facts — any facts, in any combination. *Truth* is *all* the facts. Both sides of the story. The bad *and* the good."

She seemed to digest that. "Yes, I think you're right. So what does that mean?"

He bit at his lip. She'd been right, he could admit now; he *had* enjoyed the knowledge and power the Book had given him. "So," he said, "I was wondering if you'd like to come up. It's . . . well, you know, it's kind of a chilly night."

The Book burned with an eerie blue flame, and its non-plastic bag burned green. Together, they were quite spectacular.

The Broccoli Factor

"So," Tom Banning said, his voice muffled by the coffee cup hovering just below mustache level. "How's life in the hot lane?"

"Don't ask," Billy Hayes sighed, spooning the last few chunks of ice from his water glass into his own mug. The Institute's cafeteria invariably served their coffee at a temperature which, in his opinion, was just short of the melting point of lead. "The last confinement scheme officially went down the gutter this morning, and we're right back on square one."

Banning slurped some coffee and shook his head. "Remember the good old days when fusion power was going to be just around the corner?"

"Yeah," Hayes retorted. "That was maybe twenty years before artificial intelligence was going to be just around the corner."

Banning grimaced. "Talk about job security."

Hayes nodded, and for a minute they sat silently, each contemplating in his own way the perversity of the Universe. "So what's the trouble this time?" Banning asked at last.

"Oh, the usual," Hayes shrugged. "We can get the plasma hot enough, but we can't figure out how to keep it confined long enough in the center of the vacuum chamber. Every time we reconfigure the fields to eliminate one instability — Blooie! — another one crops up, drives the plasma out to the wall, and that's that."

"Computer design doesn't help?"

"Not so far. I don't suppose you've got JUNIOR to the point of understanding plasma physics yet?"

"Don't rub it in," Banning growled.

"Sorry," Hayes apologized. "Still stuck at the two-year-old intelligence level, eh?"

Banning glared down into his coffee. "We got him to the level of a six-month-old exactly eight months after the breakthrough. Six months later he was a year old. It took just *two* more months to get him where he is now . . . and we haven't gotten him to budge since."

Hayes nodded. He'd heard the litany a hundred times in the past four years — just as Banning had spent endless lunch breaks listening to *his* litany. *Just a couple of broken old men,* he thought sourly. *Flat up against the wall of the Universe, without an exit sign in sight.* "At least you don't have to worry about funding," he offered.

"Not from congressional committees, no," Banning agreed darkly. "But on the other hand, *you* don't have the entire Japanese computer industry breathing down your neck."

Hayes sighed. "A pity you can't at least get him to the three-year-old level. My grandson just turned three, and he loves to tinker with mechanical toys. Give a three-year-old AI the magnetohydrodynamic equations and it might just come up with something."

"Be thankful JUNIOR's not still at the six month level," Banning said dryly. "He'd take your equations and chew them to a pulp."

"Gum them to a pulp, you mean," Hayes corrected him. "Six-month-olds don't have any teeth."

"Just like sixty-year-olds," Banning said, snorting a chuckle as he readjusted his upper plate. "You suppose the secret of the Universe is that life is round?"

" 'Pi are round; *cornbread* are square,' " Hayes said, quoting the hairy old joke from his youth. It was one of the chestnuts he brought out periodically to try on ever-younger sets of new Institute employees, who were generally unanimous in failing to see any humor in it. "And on that note, I guess lunch is over," he added.

"Yeah," Banning agreed with a sigh. "Back to uselessly banging our heads."

"Six-month-olds do *that* a lot, too," Hayes said. "Mostly when they're crawling under coffee tables."

"Haven't programmed a coffee table into JUNIOR's environment," Banning said as they headed for the cafeteria door. "Maybe I ought to try it."

"Yeah — it'd be interesting to hear what a computer sounds like when it cries. Well, happy hunting."

Four hours later Banning's private line rang. "Hello?"

"It's Billy," Hayes identified himself. "Listen, you said earlier that JUNIOR's environment can be programmed. "Can JUNIOR himself be programmed, too?"

"Sure," Banning said, frowning. "You can dump any peripheral stuff into him —"

"Without affecting his intelligence?"

"Such as it is, sure."

"Can you lend him to me? Say, for six hours?"

"Take all the time you want," Banning sniffed. "Adopt him, for all I care. I'm thinking of quitting and joining a monastery, anyway."

"Yeah, well, don't invest in rosary beads just yet," Hayes told him. "Your idiot savant computer may just be good for something, after all."

The red glow on the monitor faded, and Banning shook

his head in wonderment. "I'll be damned. You did it. You really and truly *did* it."

"We sure did," Hayes nodded. "Me and JUNIOR."

"I'll be damned," Banning repeated, reverently. "After all these years. Real, genuine fusion."

"It's the fluctuating confinement fields that broke the deadlock," Banning told him, tapping the printout still snaking its way out of the printer. "JUNIOR has to alter them every ten microseconds or so to keep the plasma confined, but that appears to be well within his capabilities."

"Capabilities, yes. Sophistication, no." Banning fixed him with a puzzled and slightly ominous look. "Come on, Billy; I came to see your triumph, like you asked, and I agree you're a genius. So now level with me — because if you got JUNIOR past the two-year-old level last month and didn't tell me about it then, I swear I'm going to strangle you."

Hayes shook his head. "No such luck, I'm afraid. JUNIOR's no further along than he was when you loaned him to me."

"Then kindly explain *that*," Banning demanded, waving at the fusion test chamber. "JUNIOR can't possibly have the intelligence or expertise that demonstration showed."

"Ah — but you underestimate two-year-olds," Hayes waggled a warning finger at him. "All I had to do was find the proper age-specific behavior pattern and figure out how to adapt it."

Banning blinked. "You've lost me."

"Oh, come on, Tom, you've seen it yourself. What does a kid JUNIOR's age do when you make him eat something he doesn't like? He pushes it around with his teeth and the tip of his tongue, trying like the devil to swallow it *without letting any of it touch the sides of his mouth*."

Banning's eyes went wide. "Are you saying . . . ?"

"That's right," Hayes nodded. "I tied JUNIOR into the test chamber . . . and then programmed him to hate the taste of plasma."

Banning looked at the printout. "When the Nobel committee phones you," he said, "I want dibs on half the prize money."

"You got it."

The Art of War

You know how it ended, of course. Or at least you know the official version of how it ended, which isn't quite the same. I imagine all the parties involved would have preferred to completely bury that first incident; I know for my part that I was instructed in no uncertain terms to keep quiet about what I knew. But you can't completely hush up a debacle that cost sixty-three men their lives. Especially not when one of them was a Supreme Convocant of the United Ethnos of Humanity.

So you know more or less how it ended. It's time you learned how it began.

It began with my eighteenth birthday, and my parents' desire to do something really special for my nineteenth year. The Year of YouthJourneying, we called it on New Ararat: a brief interval between the end of Institute and the beginning of life as adults. Most of my friends were going the traditional routes: taking career-sample apprenticeships, joining volunteer groups, doing YouthJourney tours around New Ararat, or — for the more adventuresome — signing aboard starfreighters to travel the whole sector.

My parents outdid them all. Somehow, I still don't know how, they wangled me a one-year appointment as aide to Magnell Sutherlan, Convocant from New Ararat to the Supreme Convocation of the UnEthHu. My friends were all kelly green with envy; naturally, I milked it shamelessly for all it was worth.

It didn't take long for the shine to wear off, though. Zurich was crowded and noisy, with a crime rate probably a thousand times that of our whole district back home. The Convocation Complex itself was huge, practically impossible not to get lost in, and populated by some of the most snidely condescending people I'd ever met. And Convocant Sutherlan, far from being a respected, sharp-edged lawmaker the way the newspages always portrayed him, was old, tired, and completely detached from what was going on. Just treading water, really, until this final term was over and he could go home.

It was not exactly an atmosphere that bred enthusiasm. As a result, whenever there was travel to be done — whether secure document delivery, repre-meetings, or personal errands — I was always the first of Sutherlan's aide corps to volunteer. A fair percentage of those first few months were spent crisscrossing Earth in a suborbital or hopping between various planets of the UnEthHu in one or another of Sutherlan's official half-wings.

And so it was that, four months into my tenure, I found myself two hundred parsecs from Earth on the Kailth world of Quibsh.

Everyone in the UnEthHu knows where Quibsh is now, of course, but back then even most professional politicians had never heard of the place. No real surprise; Quibsh was a fairly useless border world, with an unimpressive list of resources and an outer crust that was a staggering collection of tectonic instabilities. The Kailth had put a couple of minor military outposts there to watch over a population of a few million hardy colonists, about half of whom resided in a single city in one of the more fertile valleys. The Kailth and UnEthHu had made contact about ten years previously, but with the Dynad's main attention focused on the ongoing Pindorshi trade disputes, we hadn't given the

Kailth much more than passing notice.

The diplomatic corps had installed a one-man consulate in the main Quibsh city, where I was supposed to pick up some research documents Convocant Sutherlan had ordered as a favor to a constituent. The pilotcomp landed the half-wing behind the consulate — it had its own drop beacon — and I presented my ID and request to the consular agent, a wrinkled man named Clave Verst who, like Sutherlan, seemed to be marking time until retirement. He got me the documents, and I was preparing to head back to the half-wing when I took a second look at the request form and noticed a hand-written note asking me to also bring back a case of Kailth mixed cooking brandies. There wasn't a single shell of the stuff to be had in the consulate, the nearest potables dealer was a kilometer away, and Verst made it abundantly clear he wasn't about to waste his own time on such a frivolous errand. So, armed with a fistful of detailed instructions and a stomachful of queasiness, I headed out alone.

The spider-web maze of streets was surprisingly crowded — I thought more than once that the entire population must have decided to go out walking or driving that afternoon — but I'd bumped shoulders with other species before and it wasn't as bad as I'd been afraid it would be. For a small fraction of the pedestrians I seemed to be a minor curiosity; for the rest, I was something to be ignored completely.

I had just turned what I hoped was the last corner when I spotted Tawni.

She was probably the last thing I would have expected to see out there among all those lizard-skinned, bumblebee-faced Kailth. A human woman, of medium height and slender build, with an exotically cut cascade of black hair that at the moment was obscuring most of her face as she leaned into the open engine compartment of what looked like an ancient Pemberkif Scroller. The vehicle was parked beside the curb, or else had summarily died there. On all sides, completely oblivious to her plight, streams of Kailth shuffled past, breaking around her like a river around a rock.

Protocol probably dictated that I call back to the consulate, report the situation, and then continue on with my errand while Verst handled it. But she was a human, and in trouble, and I was an aide to a UnEthHu Convocant. More importantly, I was nineteen, and what I could see of her looked pretty attractive. Working my way through the traffic, I headed over.

I got through the last rivulet of pedestrians and stepped to her side. "Having some trouble?" I asked inanely.

She looked up, giving me my first look at a face that more than met my expectations: young and beautiful, in a dark and distinctly exotic way, though at the moment she was almost at the point of tears from the frustration of her situation. A delicate line — scar or tattoo, I couldn't tell which — arched almost invisibly from the bridge of her nose over her right eyebrow, curving around her cheekbone and past the corner of her lip to disappear into the dimple at the point of her chin. From one of the frontier Ridgeline worlds, I guessed, where humanity's races had been mixed in unusual combinations and body ornamentation could get a little bizarre.

And where, I belatedly remembered, Anglish was not always the language of choice. For a second she just gazed up at me, her face not seeming to register my question; and I was trying to figure out a Plan B when my words suddenly seemed to click. "Yes," she said. Her accent was soft and delicate and as exotic as the rest of her. "Can you help me?"

"I can try," I said, peering into the engine compartment. It was a Scroller, all right, though from the looks of it whoever had traded it to her had gotten the better end of the deal. I was just reaching in to check the motivor cables when, out of the corner of my eye, I noticed the pedestrian stream falter and looked up to see what was going on.

Rounding another corner, heading across the intersection, were a pair of Kailth warriors.

I'd seen pictures of Kailth warriors at the Convocation Complex, vids secretly taken by SkyForce Intelligence at the Chompre and TyTiernian pacifications near the edges of the Kailthaermil Empire. We hadn't tangled with them yet ourselves, but there was a widespread feeling in the Complex back rooms that it was just a matter of time before we did. The Kailth controlled a lot of territory, with a fair number of non-Kailth under their control, and that almost always spelled trouble.

Besides which — the more cynical argument went — the Pindorshi situation wouldn't last forever, and wars and conflicts were too politically useful for politicians to stay away from them for long.

Watching the SkyForce reports in the safety of a Zurich screening room, I had hoped those cynics were wrong. Standing there in the middle of a Quibsh street, I desperately hoped they were wrong. On telephoto vids, Kailth warriors were impressive; up close and personal, they were damn near terrifying. Armored up to their headcrests in full combat suits, walking in lockstep, they were straight out of a xenophobic newspage docu-diatribe. Or straight out of hell.

The two warriors spotted me at roughly the same time I spotted them, and in perfect unison they shifted direction toward us. Instinctively, I moved closer to the girl — some chivalric idea about sticking together, I suppose — and I threw her a quick glance to see how she was handling this.

And paused for a longer look. She was gazing at the warriors, but the look on her face wasn't the knee-shaking trepidation I was feeling. She was smiling, the tension lines in her face already starting to smooth out.

It was a look of relief. Maybe even adoration.

"You," one of the Kailth said in passable Anglish. "Human male. What are you doing?"

My tongue tangled momentarily over my teeth. "I — she's having trouble with her Scroller," I managed. "I stopped to help."

He held out his right hand. "Identify."

I fumbled out my ID folder and handed it over, wondering nervously whether a UnEthHu Convocation ID would be an asset or a liability here. My eyes drifted to the lumpy black weapon strapped to his left side, not much bigger than the 5mm slugkicker pistol I used to plink targets with when I was a kid. At its highest setting, this particular sidearm could allegedly drop a two-story brick building with a single shot.

The warrior studied the ID for what seemed like an inordinately long time. Then, closing it, he handed it back and turned his insectine gaze on the woman. "Does he bother you, Citizen-Three?" he demanded.

"Not at all, Warrior-Citizen-One," she said, bowing her head. "It is as he said: he paused to help me."

I stared at her, suddenly almost oblivious to the warriors. *Citizen-Three?*

"Do you wish our assistance?" the warrior continued.

The girl looked at me. "No," she said. "I will be fine. Thank you for your concern."

The warrior threw one more long look at me. Then, in lockstep once more, the two of them passed us by and disappeared down another street.

I looked at the girl, my stomach churning. "He called you Citizen-Three," I said. "Citizen-Three of what?"

"Of the Kailthaermil Empire," she said, as if it was obvious. "I and my people are third-citizens." She reached up and touched the tattoo line on her face.

"Your people," I said, dimly realizing I was starting to blither like an idiot. But I couldn't help it. "But you're human. Aren't you?"

"Yes," she said. "My people were saved from invaders by the Kailthaermil many years ago. For that we will forever be grateful to them."

I frowned harder . . . and then, with a sudden jolt, I got it.

She and her people were verlorens.

"Would you be willing," I asked carefully, "to take me to your people?"

For the first time a shadow of uncertainty seemed to cross her face. But then the shadow passed, and she smiled. "Of course," she said.

"Thank you." I cleared my throat. "By the way, my name's Stane Markand."

"Stane Markand," she repeated, bowing her head as she had toward the Kailth warriors. "I am Tawnikakalina."

"Tawnikakalina," I said. It didn't sound nearly as melodious as when she said it. But with any luck, I figured I might just have a chance to practice.

We spent the next half hour kluge-rigging the Scroller back to health, then nursing it over to the consulate. There I had it loaded aboard my half-wing, informing the pilotcomp and Consular Agent Verst that I'd be making one more stop on Quibsh and postponing my departure from the planet for a day or two. The pilotcomp, programmed with flexibility in mind, took the change in plans in stride. Verst obviously couldn't have cared less.

It was about two hundred kilometers to where Tawni's people had been settled in a scattering of small villages beneath a line of squat volcanoes. We put down on a section of lava flow near Tawni's village, and by the time we had the Scroller rolled out, a small mob of her people had gathered around the half-wing to see what was going on. She explained the situation to them in a few musical sentences, and with a dozen enthusiastic young men pushing the Scroller ahead of them, we all went down to her village.

I don't know how widespread the term *verloren* ever became around the UnEthHu. It was mostly an academic word, borrowed from the Old German word for *lost,* that was used to describe the phenomenon of Earth-born human beings or their relics discovered dozens or even hundreds of parsecs away from Earth with no apparent way for them to have gotten there. Genetic and linguistic studies were inconclusive, but they suggested that the original ancestors of the groups had left Earth some six to ten thousand years earlier. Whether the colonies had been deliberately planted by some unknown starfaring race, or whether the verlorens were the equivalent of white rats discarded after an experiment, no one knew.

There were thirty-one known archaeological digs that showed evidence of a long-past human presence, another dozen or so scatterings of primitive humans at Iron Age level or below, and three genuinely thriving verloren societies. With Tawni's people, I'd apparently discovered a fourth.

"Our history on Sagtt'a goes back to the Great Rain of Fire," she explained as she showed me around her village. "Our ancestors sought refuge from the fire inside a strange mountain. When they came out, the land and the stars had changed."

I nodded. Two of the other verloren cultures also had a Rain of Fire in their histories. "That must be when you were taken from Earth."

"Yes, though it was many generations before we realized what had actually happened," Tawni said. "Not until after the first invasion."

"The Kailth?"

She shook her head, her hair shimmering in the sunlight with the movement. "No, the invaders were called the Orraci Matai," she said. "Large creatures with many fish-like fins. They occupied Sagtt'a for four generations before they were overthrown by the Xa, who ruled us for thirty years before they were in turn overthrown by the Phashiskar. They stayed three generations before they were conquered by the Baal'ariai, in a terrible battle that killed a quarter of our people."

It was an old, old pattern: innocent people caught in a trade route or strategic power position, being fought over by every ambitious empire-builder who came along. "So the Kailth are just the latest batch of conquerors?"

"The Kailthaermil are not conquerors," she said. "They are liberators. They forced the Aoeemme from Sagtt'a, but then pulled their own warriors back to orbiting stations and proclaimed that our people were once again free to rule ourselves."

"Ah." Another old pattern, though one that was far less frequently seen: conquerors who were smart enough to allow local self-rule in exchange for cooperation and the payment of tribute. It was more efficient than trying to run everything directly, and you could always go in and stomp them if they tried pushing their autonomy too far. "This was in exchange for certain rules of conduct from your society?"

"All societies have rules of conduct," she pointed out.

"Of course," I said. "How much tribute do you pay each year?"

She stopped and frowned up at me. "Why do you persist in thinking ill of the Kailthaermil?" she asked. "Have they done ill to you?"

"Well, no, not exactly," I had to admit. "Actually, we don't know all that much about them yet. But we know they've conquered a large number of other races and peoples, and we've seen enough conquerors to know how they usually behave."

"But you do not know the Kailthaermil," she insisted. "They do not demand our lives or our property. Only some of our artwork. And for this they give us safety."

Aha, I thought, there it is. Artwork. "What artwork?" I asked.

She pointed toward a squat volcano with a wide crater. "I will show you. Come."

I was not, to say the least, thrilled at the prospect of climbing into a volcano crater, particularly one that was smoldering restlessly with sulfur and the occasional burst of steam from some vent or other. Tawni's people obviously felt differently: there were already five others moving briskly around the crater at various tasks as we entered through a gap in the side of the cone.

"This is our curing chamber," Tawni said at my side. "Over there —" she pointed to a rough shelf along one side of the wall — "are our calices."

I stared at them, forgetting the sulfur corroding my lungs, forgetting even that I was standing inside a volcano. The calices were that riveting. Roughly spherical in shape, about twenty centimeters across each, they were composed of intricate twistings of brilliant gold metal fibers interwoven with equally slender twistings of some richly dark-red material. There were eight of them lined up on the shelf, with the kind of small variations that said they were individually handmade.

"Come," Tawni said softly, taking my arm. "Come and see."

We walked across the uneven rock to the shelf. Up close, I could see that the dark red strands were some kind of wood or plant fiber, not quite as flexible as the metal wires but with a stiffness that introduced a textural counterpoint into the design. At the very center of the woven threads was some kind of crystalline core that reflected the gold and red that swirled around it, as well as adding a pale blue-white to the color scheme.

It took me a while to find my voice. "They're beautiful," I said. My voice came out a husky whisper.

"Thank you," Tawni said. She took a step closer to the shelf and gently ran a hand down around the top of one of them. "They are unique, Stane, among all the worlds. Or at least those worlds visited by the Kailthaermil. The wood is from a tree that grows in only five places on Sagtt'a, and the crystals and metal are nearly as rare. Each calix can take a crafter a year to create."

She lowered her hand, almost reluctantly. "But the result is so beautiful. So very beautiful."

I nodded. "And this is what the Kailth take as their tribute?"

"They take a few," Tawni said. "No more than a tenth

of those we make." Her face took on a slightly stubborn expression. "And for this small price they give us protection from all who would invade us, and leave us otherwise in peace. Do you still wish to speak ill of them?"

As tributes went, I had to admit, this was a pretty minor one. "No," I conceded.

"Good." The stubbornness vanished and she smiled, the sun coming out from behind a threatening storm cloud. "Then let us go back to the village. The Elders will wish to speak with you."

I wound up spending nearly two days in Tawni's village. Her people were amazingly open and trusting, willing to let me see anything I wanted and to answer any question I could think to ask. This group had only recently been brought to Quibsh from their world of Sagtt'a, I learned, though the Kailth had previously set up other human colonies on worlds that had the necessary volcanic activity for the calix curing process. Among the six hundred people in this colony were twelve calix artisans and twenty apprentices, of whom Tawni was apparently one of the most promising.

It was clear that there was an enormous amount we needed to learn about these people, but it was equally clear that I had neither the time nor the expertise to handle the job. So after those two days, I reluctantly told Tawni I had to leave. She thanked me again for rescuing her from her balky Scroller — which the village mechanics still hadn't gotten working yet — extracted a promise from me to come back if I could, and offered me a parting gift.

A calix.

"No," I protested, holding the sculpture up to the sunlight. It wasn't nearly as heavy as I would have expected, with a pleasantly tingling sensation where I held it. "Tawni, I couldn't possibly take this. It wouldn't be right."

"Why not?" she asked, that stubborn look of hers threatening to cloud her face again. "You are my friend. Can a friend not give a friend a gift?"

"Of course," I said. "But won't the Kailth be angry with you?"

"Why would they?" she countered. "They will receive those they are due. They do not own all calices, Stane. Nor do they own us."

"I know, but —" I floundered. "But this is just too much. I didn't do enough for you to justify a gift like this."

"Do you then reduce friendship to a balance of plus and minus?" she asked quietly. "That does not sound like a friendship to be cherished."

I sighed. But she had me, and we both knew it. And to be honest, I didn't really want to give up the calix anyway. "All right," I said. "I accept, with thanks. And I *will* be sure to come visit you again some day."

It was a four-day voyage back to Earth. I spent a fair amount of that time dictating my report on this new verloren colony, adding my thoughts and impressions to the running record the half-wing's sensors had taken. I spent an equal amount of time studying the calix.

I'd seen right away, of course, the ethereal beauty that had been frozen into the sculpture. But it wasn't until I began spending time with the calix that I realized that there was far more to it than I'd realized. There was the metalwork, for starters: a filigree of threads far more intricate than it had appeared at first sight. I found I could spend hours just tracing various lines from start to finish with my eyes, then seeing if I could track them backwards again without getting sidetracked by one of the other loops or branchings.

The intertwined wood fibers were just as fascinating. Virtually never the same color twice, they had a varying texture that ranged from smooth and warm to sandpapery and oddly cool. After the first day, my searching hands found two spots on opposite sides that seemed to particularly fit my palms and fingertips, and from that point on I nearly always held the calix that way.

Then there was the crystal that peeked out from the center. Like the wood and metal, it never seemed to look quite the same way twice. From one angle it would look like nothing more esoteric than a lump of quartz; from another it might seem to be pale sapphire or diamond or even delicately stained glass. Sometimes even when I returned to the same angle the crystal would look different than it had before.

But the most enigmatic part of all was the way the calix hummed at me.

It was a day before I even noticed the sound, and two more before I finally figured out that what it was doing was resonating to the sound of my voice. Like everything else about the sculpture, it never seemed to react quite the same way twice, though I spent a good two hours at one point talking, humming, and singing as I tried to pin down a pattern. If there was one there, I never found it.

I reached Zurich, explained my delay to Convocant Sutherlan, filed my report, and sat back to wait for the inevitable flurry of attention that the discovery of a new verloren culture would surely stir up.

The inevitable didn't happen. Oh, there was a ripple of interest from the academic community, and a couple of government-endorsed artists stopped by to look briefly and condescendingly at the calix. But for the most part the Supreme Convocation could only come up with the political equivalent of a distracted pat on the head. With the Pindorshi situation still dominating the firstlines in the newspages, the Convocants were apparently not interested in anything so mundane as a long-lost human colony.

I can't tell you how frustrating it was, at least at first. This was, after all, probably the only shot I would ever have at interstellar fame. But gradually I began to realize that all this official indifference was probably for the best. The alternative would have meant a horde of Convocant aides and factfinders descending like locusts on Quibsh; and having worked with some of those aides, that wasn't something I would wish on anyone. Particularly not the friendly, naive people of Tawni's village.

So I did my best to philosophically put it behind me, decided to concentrate instead on finding a way to get back to Quibsh some day soon, and settled back to endure the remainder of my appointment.

Until the day, two weeks later, when Convocant Lantis Devaro came into the office.

The newspages painted Sutherlan as an elder statesman, and they lied. They painted Devaro as an aspiring future leader, and lied again, only in the opposite direction. To say Devaro was aspiring was like saying a Siltech Brahma bulldozer can push dirt around. Devaro was a charismatic man; clever, powerful, and almost pathologically ambitious. Rumor was that his ultimate goal was to challenge the blood-line tradition of the Dynad long enough to claim one of the two seats for himself, something that had never happened in two centuries of Dynad rule. The private backrooms consensus was that he had an even-money chance of making it.

I don't know what exactly he came to Sutherlan's office for that day. In hindsight, though, it was obviously just a pretext anyway. Even as he announced himself at the outer receptionist's station his eyes were surveying the aide room; and when he emerged from Sutherlan's private offices ten minutes later, he crossed directly to my desk.

"So," he said as I scrambled to my feet, "you're the one."

"Sir?" I asked, not entirely sure what he meant and not daring to make any assumptions.

"The young man who discovered that new verloren group," he amplified. "Good work, that and excellent follow-up."

"Thank you, sir," I said, trying not to stutter. Praise for underlings was almost unheard of in Convocant Sutherlan's office.

"You're quite welcome." Devaro nodded toward the calix, sitting on a corner of my desk where I placed it every morning when I came in. "I take it that's the sculpture you brought back?"

"Yes, sir," I said. "It's called a calix. Uh . . . would you like . . . ?"

"Thank you," he said, crossing around behind the desk. Sliding a hand beneath the calix — he was wearing informal daytime gloves, I noticed — he picked it up.

For a long moment he gazed at and into it. I stood silently, fighting the urge to plead with him to be careful. He turned it around one way and then the other, then set it back on its stand. "Interesting," he said, turning to me again. "Your report said the Kailth accept these as part of the verlorens' tribute."

"According to Tawni, it's all they take," I told him, breathing a little easier now that the calix was safe. "They must like art."

"Yes," he murmured, gazing at me with a thoughtful intensity that made me feel distinctly uncomfortable. "Interesting. Well, good day."

"Good day, Convocant Devaro," I said.

I watched him stride out, feeling the other aides' looks of envy on the back of my neck as I basked in the warm glow of triumph, small though it might be. Finally, someone in authority who'd actually noted and appreciated what I'd done.

The warm glow lasted the rest of the day, through the evening, and right up until I opened my eyes the next morning.

To find the calix gone from my night table.

There were four separate reception stations along the approach to Devaro's inner offices. I strode past all four of them without stopping, to the consternation of the various receptionists, and was about two steps ahead of Convocation Security when I shoved open the ornate doors and stomped into Devaro's presence.

"Ah — there you are," he said before I could even get a word out. "Come in; I've been expecting you."

"Where is it?" I demanded, starting toward him.

"It's perfectly safe," he assured me, his eyes shifting to a spot over my shoulder. "No, it's all right — let him be. And leave us."

I looked behind me, to see two guards reluctantly lower their tranglers and back out of the room. "Now," Devaro said as they closed the doors. "You seem upset."

"You had my calix stolen from my apartment," I said, turning back to glare at him. "Don't try to deny it."

His eyebrows lifted slightly, as if denial was the furthest thing from his mind. "I had it borrowed," he corrected. "I

113

wanted to run a few tests on it, and that seemed the quietest way to go about it."

My heart momentarily seized up. "What kind of tests? What are you doing to it?"

"It's perfectly safe," Devaro said again, standing up. From across the office a door opened and two white-jacketed women stepped into the room. "Don't worry, we'll return it to you soon. While we're waiting, we'd like to run some tests on you."

"What sort of tests?" I asked, eying the doctors warily.

"Painless ones, I assure you," Devaro said, crossing to me and taking my arm in a friendly but compelling grip. "You'll need to sign some forms first — the doctors will show you."

"But I'm supposed to be working," I protested as he led me over to the door where the doctors waited. "Convocant Sutherlan is expecting me to be at my desk —"

"I've already taken care of Convocant Sutherlan," Devaro said. "Come, now. You won't feel a thing."

I didn't, but that was probably only because the first thing they did when we got to the examination room was put me to sleep.

I woke to find myself lying on a rolltable moving down a deserted corridor. There was an empty growling in my stomach, an unpleasant tingling in my fingertips and fore-head, and a strange difficulty in focusing my eyes. One of the two doctors was riding along with me, watching my face as I came to, and I considered asking her where we were going. But I didn't feel like talking, and anyway her expression didn't encourage questions.

A few minutes later we passed through a door and I found myself back in Devaro's office. The Convocant was sitting in his chair, feet propped up informally, gazing at his desk display. "Ah — there you are," he said as the rolltable crossed to him. "That will be all, Doctor."

"Yes, sir," she said, waiting until the rolltable had come to a halt beside the desk before stepping off and disappearing back through the door.

"It's been a long day," Devaro commented. "How are you feeling?"

"A little groggy," I said, carefully sitting up on the edge of the rolltable. There was a moment of dizziness, but it passed quickly. "How long was I out?"

"As I said, all day," Devaro said, nodding toward his window. To my shock, I saw it was black with night. "It's a little after eight-thirty."

No wonder my stomach was growling. "Can I go home now?" I asked.

"You'll want to eat first," Devaro said. "I'm having some food sent up. Tell me, have you ever had a brainscan done before?"

"I don't think so," I said. "Is that what they did to me in there?"

"Oh, they did a little of everything," he said. "A complete brainscan, including a neural network mapping and a personality matrix profile. Do you always hold the calix at the same spots?"

"Usually," I said. "Not always. Why?"

"Did your friend Tawnikakalina ever tell you how she and her people learned Anglish?"

The abrupt changes of subject were starting to make my head hurt. "She didn't know," I told him. "All she knew was that the Kailth had some of her group learn the language when they decided to set up a colony on Quibsh."

Devaro's lip twisted in a grimace. "It was the Church,"

he said, spitting the word out like a curse. "One of those il-legal little under-the-table deals they're always making with alien governments. The Kailth apparently took a group of priestians in to Sagtt'a a few years ago to inspect the verloren colony."

"I see," I said, keeping my voice neutral. The Convoca-tion and Church were always going head-to-head on some-thing, usually with the Church taking the government to task for violating some basic humanitarian principle. The fact that the majority of UnEthHu citizens generally sup-ported the Church on those issues irritated the Convocants no end. "So then you already knew about those verlorens."

"Hardly," Devaro growled. "The Church hadn't deigned to tell us about them. I did some backtracking after your re-port came in and was able to put the pieces together. Tell me, how does the calix make you feel?"

Another abrupt change of topic. With an effort, I tried to think. "It's soothing, mostly. Helps me relax when I'm tense."

"Does it ever do the opposite?" he asked. "Invigorate you when you're tired?"

"Well . . ." I frowned. "Actually, yes. It does, some-times."

"In other words," Devaro said, his eyes hard on me, "it creates two completely opposite effects. Doesn't that strike you as a little strange?"

It *was* odd, come to think about it. "I suppose so," I said, a little lamely. "I guess I just assumed it was mirroring my moods somehow."

He smiled, a tight humorless expression. "Not mirroring them," he said softly. "Creating them."

The skin on the back of my neck began to crawl. "What do you mean?"

He reached over and swiveled his desk display around to face me. There was a graph there, with a bewildering array of multicolored curves. "We did a full analysis of the calix," he said. "Paying particular attention to the places where you say you always hold it. We took some five-micron core samples from the wood fibers there; and it turns out they have an interesting and distinctive substratum chemical composition."

His face hardened. "A composition which, after it's been run through the proper chemo-mathematical transforms, shows a remarkable resemblance to the neural network pattern we took from you today."

I didn't know what half those words meant. But they sounded ominous. "What does that mean?" I asked.

"It means that the 'gift' your friend Tawnikakalina gave you isn't a gift," he said bluntly. "It's a weapon."

I gazed out the window at the black sky over the city, my empty stomach feeling suddenly sick. A weapon. From Tawni? "No," I said, looking back at the Convocant. "No, I can't believe that, sir. Tawni wouldn't do something like that to me. She couldn't."

He snorted contemptuously. "This from your long and exhaustive experience with different cultures, no doubt?"

"No, but —"

"You'll be trying to tell me next that it's the Kailth who are behind it all," he went on. "And that the verloren artists themselves have no idea whatsoever what it is they've created with these calices of theirs."

I grimaced. I had indeed been wondering exactly along those lines. Hearing it put that way, it did sound vaguely ridiculous.

"No, it's a grand plot, all right," Devaro went on darkly. "And if the Kailth are taking ten percent of the verlorens' calices every year, they must be using them pretty extensively. Maybe as a prelude to all their conquests." He shook his head wonderingly. "Artwork used as a weapon. What an insidious concept."

I shook my head. "I'm sorry, but I still don't understand. What is the calix doing?"

Devaro sighed, swiveling his display back around toward him. "We don't know for sure. If we had a brainscan record for you prior to your trip to Quibsh — but we don't. All we have to go on is this." He waved a hand at the display. "And what this says is that, through your contact with the wood fibers, the calix is changing you into something that matches its own pre-set matrix. Turning you into God alone knows what."

The room seemed suddenly very cold. "But I don't feel any different," I protested. "I mean . . . I should feel *something*. Shouldn't I?"

He leaned back in his seat and steepled his fingertips together. "You ever try to cook a frog?" he asked. "Probably not. Doubt anyone has, really, but it makes a good story. They say that if you drop a live frog into a pot of boiling water, it'll hop right out again. But if you put it in cold water and slowly heat the pot to boiling, the frog just sits there until it cooks. It can't detect the slow temperature change. You see?"

I saw, all right. "Is that what the calix is doing? Slow-cooking me?"

He shrugged. "It's trying. Whether it's going to succeed . . . that we don't yet know."

The room fell silent again. I stared out the window, mentally taking inventory of my mind, the way you would poke around your skin checking for bruises. I still couldn't find anything that felt strange.

But then, maybe the calix hadn't heated the water up enough. Yet. "Why me?" I asked.

"A mistake, obviously," Devaro said. "The Kailth probably assumed you'd give the calix to Convocant Sutherlan instead of keeping it for yourself. Or else they thought you were more important than you really are, though how they could make that kind of blunder I don't know."

"So what do we do?" I asked. "Do we —" I hesitated "— destroy the calix?"

He eyed me closely. "Is that what you want?"

"I —" I broke off, the quick answer sticking unexpectedly in my throat. Of course we should destroy it — the thing was clearly dangerous. And yet, I felt oddly reluctant to make such a decision. It was such a magnificent piece of art.

And it had been a gift from Tawni.

"Actually, it's a moot point," Devaro said into my indecision. "I'm not sure destroying it would do any good. The places where you hold the calix have clearly had the greatest effect on you; but you said yourself you've touched other spots on it, so you've probably already picked up at least some of the programming embedded there."

Programming. The word sent a shiver up my back. "What are we going to do?"

"Three things," Devaro said. "First of all, we don't panic. You've been affected, but we're on to them now, so we can keep an eye on you. Second, we need to get more information on these calices in general." He cocked an eyebrow. "Which means you're going to have to go back to Quibsh and get us some more of them."

I felt my mouth drop open. "Back to Quibsh?"

"You have to," Devaro said, his voice quiet but compelling. "You've met the people there — you're the only one who can pretend it's just a social visit. Moreover, they gave you a calix, so it's reasonable you'd be back to buy more as gifts."

This was coming a little too fast. "Gifts?"

"Certainly." Devaro smiled slyly. "What better way to guarantee their cooperation than to tell them you want calices to give to prominent members of the Convocation?"

There was a tone at the door, and a rollcart came in with two covered dishes on it. "Ah — dinner has arrived," Devaro announced, standing up and pointing the rollcart toward one side of the room where a bench table was now unfolding itself from the wall. "Let's eat before it gets cold."

"Yes, sir," I said, sliding off the rolltable and heading over. The delectable aromas rising from the plates made my stomach hurt even more. "You said there were three things we were going to do."

"Yes, I did," he said, setting the plates onto opposite ends of the table. "The third thing is for us to learn exactly what the calix's programming does. Unfortunately, core samples and structural analyses can get us only so far. Which leaves only one practical approach."

I nodded. I'd already guessed this one. "You want me to keep the calix," I said. "And let it keep doing whatever it's doing to me."

"We'll start that phase as soon as you get back from Quibsh," Devaro said. "But don't worry, we'll be with you every step of the way. We'll take a complete brainscan once a week — more often if it seems justified — as well as monitoring your general health."

It made sense, I supposed. It was also about as unpleasant a prospect as I'd ever faced in my whole life. "What about my work?"

"This *is* your work from now on," Devaro said. "You're on my staff now — I made the arrangements with Sutherlan earlier today."

"I see," I said, walking over to the table. The aromas didn't smell quite so good anymore.

"You have to do this, Markand," Devaro said quietly. It was, as near as I could remember, the first time he'd ever called me by my name. "It's the only way we're going to get a handle on this Kailth plot. The only way to protect the UnEthHu."

I sighed. "Patriotism. You found my weak spot, all right."

"It's a weak spot many of us have," Devaro said. He gestured to the table. "Come; let's eat. We still have a great many things to discuss."

Four days later, I was back on Quibsh.

I'd spent the whole trip worrying about how I was going to hide from Tawni the sudden change in the way I now perceived her and her people. No longer as friends, but as enemies.

Fortunately, the issue never came up. I'd barely stepped out of the half-wing into the late afternoon sunlight when Tawni was there in front of me, all but knocking me over as she threw herself into an enthusiastic full-body hug, chattering away in my ear in an exuberant jumble of Anglish and her own language. When she finally broke free and took my hand a half dozen of her people had joined us, and amid a general flurry of greetings we all tromped together down to the village. By the time we got there, I found myself slipping back into the old friendly, easygoing mode.

But only on the surface. Beneath the smiles and pleasantries I was on nervous and cautious guard, seeing everything here with new eyes. Behind every verloren face I now searched for evidence of hidden cunning; beneath every word strained to hear a tell-tale echo of deceit.

And yet, even as I tried to keep Devaro's stern face in front of me as inspiration, I could feel doubts draining my resolve away. Either their deceit was so ingrained, so expertly hidden that I couldn't detect even a breath of it, or else Devaro's assessment about them was wrong. Perhaps they were indeed just as they appeared, open and honest and innocent. Perhaps they really *didn't* know what the calices did, or else the programming aspect was something the Kailth had covertly introduced into the original design.

Or perhaps it was that same programming that was the true source of my doubts. The calix, whispering to its frog that the water wasn't warm at all.

It was an hour before the last of the greeters drifted away. I was feeling a little squeamish about being alone with Tawni, not at all sure I could fake the friendship and affection I'd once felt for her. Which I still wanted to feel for her. Fortunately, that moment was put off by her wish to show me the changes that had taken place in the fruit tree grove bordering the village while we still had the afternoon light.

"I am so pleased you came back to see us," she commented as she led me along a twisting path between the trees. "You had said you might not be able to return for a long time."

"Things just happened to work out this way," I said, impressed in spite of my dour mood at what had happened to the grove. Once little more than branches and pale green leaves, the trees had exploded all over into brilliant, multicolored flowers.

"I'm glad they did," Tawni said, taking my arm. "I was

sorry to see you go."

"I was sorry to leave," I said, covering her hand with my own and feeling what was left of my resolve weakening again. Tawni was only my age, eighteen years old — surely she wasn't this accomplished a liar already. Besides, she was only an apprentice calix artisan. It would make sense for her leaders to hide the deeper secrets of their agenda from her until they'd confirmed both her skill and her dedication.

A small part of my mind told me that was rationalization. But suddenly I didn't really care. Tawni was there beside me, warm and affectionate, and there was simply no way I could believe she was my enemy. Whatever the Kailth had programmed the calix to do to me, I knew she would stand beside me in fighting it.

And if I lost that fight, that same small part reminded me soberly, at least Convocant Devaro would have the final data he wanted.

Speaking of Devaro, it was time I got down to the task he'd sent me here to do. "As a matter of fact," I said, "it was your parting gift that's responsible for me being back so soon."

"Then I am even more pleased I gave it to you," she said cheerfully. "How did this happen?"

"Well, of course I showed it to everyone in my office and around the Convocation," I said, a fresh twinge of guilt poking at me. I'd convinced myself that Tawni was on my side; and now here I was, lying to her. "They all thought it was beautiful, of course."

"I am honored."

"Anyway, some of them wanted to know how they could get one for themselves," I pushed ahead. "One of them — Convocant Devaro — asked me to come back and see if they were for sale."

"I am certain that can be arranged," Tawni said, turning us onto another path that led deeper into the grove. "Come, we will ask permission."

"Permission?" I asked, frowning, as she led us around a particularly bushy tree. "Who in here do we need to — ?"

I broke off, my breath catching in my throat as we stepped into a small clearing. In the center was a small cookstove, with something flat and gray sizzling on the grill-work at its top. Arranged in a neat circle around it were a half dozen sleepbags, with antenna-like posts sticking out of the ground beside each one.

And standing in a line between the ring of sleepbags and the cookstove, facing our direction, were six Kailth warriors.

I froze. It was probably the worst, most guilty-looking thing I could have done, but I couldn't help it. I froze right there to the spot, Tawni's grip on my arm bringing her up short as well. She blinked at me, obviously bewildered by my reaction, and tried to pull me forward —

"You," one of the Kailth said. "Human male. Come."

I wanted to run. Desperately. To run back to the half-wing and get the hell out of there.

But they were all wearing those lumpy sidearms, the ones that could bring down a two-story building with one shot. So instead I let Tawni pull me across the clearing to them.

"What do you wish here?" the warrior demanded when I was standing right in front of him.

"He is my friend, Warrior-Citizen-One," Tawni said. "He would like to purchase some of our calices."

There was a long moment of silence. "You were on Quibsh before," the warrior said at last. "You are a clerk to Convocant Magnell Sutherlan."

"Yes, that's right," I managed. "I mean, I was. I'm working for Convocant Lantis Devaro now."

"Why do you clerk now for Convocant Lantis Devaro?"

"He hired me away from Convocant Sutherlan." I had a flash of inspiration — "He was the only Convocant who was really interested in finding out more about Tawni's people. Since I'd met them, he thought I could be of help."

There was another silence. I felt the sweat collecting on my forehead, wondering if the Kailth was suspicious or merely having difficulty sorting through the Anglish. "Were you?" he asked.

Was I helpful? What exactly did he mean by that? "I tried to be," I stammered. "I — he did send me back here to see them."

"And to purchase their calices."

"Yes," I said, bracing myself. This was going to be risky, but it might just add the necessary bit of verisimilitude to my story. "He was very upset when I refused to sell him the one Tawni gave me," I told him. "I told him it was a gift, and that I wouldn't give it up under any circumstances."

The warrior eyed me, and I held my breath. If the possessiveness I really did feel for Tawni's calix was part of its programming, then the Kailth should conclude that it was doing its job and let me go about my business.

And apparently, it worked. "How many calices does Convocant Devaro wish to purchase?" the warrior asked.

I started breathing again. "He would like to buy three or four," I said. "Though that would depend on the price — he only gave me twenty thousand to spend. He wants to give them as gifts."

The warrior turned to his comrades and said something in the Kailth language. One of them answered, and for a moment they conversed back and forth. Then the first warrior turned back to face me. "He may have three," he announced. "They shall be gifts, without payment required."

Gifts. At least, I thought, the Kailth had the class not to require the UnEthHu to pay for its own destruction. "Thank you," I said. "You are most generous."

"The generosity is not for you," the warrior said. "Nor for Convocant Devaro. It is for this citizen-three who calls you friend."

It was a line, of course, something to allay any suspicions I might have about getting such valuable artwork for free. But just the same, it dug another sharp edge of guilt into me. Tawni had indeed called me a friend to her overlords, and here I was using her against them.

But then, the Kailth were using me as a pawn, too. It all came out even. Maybe.

Tawni bowed to them. "I am honored, Warrior-Citizen-One," she said. "Thank you."

"It is our pleasure," the warrior said. "You may take the human male to where he may choose."

She bowed again and pulled gently on my arm, and together we turned away and left the clearing. It wasn't until we were out of the grove and heading up the slope of the volcano that she spoke. "You still think ill of the Kailthaermil," she said quietly.

My first impulse was to deny it. But I'd done enough lying for one day. "I don't trust them, Tawni," I told her. "They're conquerors. Who's to say they aren't going to take a shot at the UnEthHu next?"

"But you are not like the others they have fought against," Tawni said. "You do not enslave other peoples, nor do you seek to impose your will on them."

That was true enough, I supposed. Preoccupied with our own internal squabblings, the UnEthHu generally ignored the alien races we came across except to get them involved in the arcane labyrinth of our commerce. "You weren't bothering anyone on Sagtt'a either," I pointed out. "Yet you have Kailth war platforms orbiting overhead."

"That is not the same," she insisted, shaking her head in exasperation. "The stations are there for our protection." She made a clicking sound in her throat. "You choose not to see. But someday you will. Someday the Kailthaermil will prove their true intentions."

"Yes," I murmured. "I'm sure they will. Tell me, what were those warriors doing in the grove?"

"They have brought a new shipment to us," Tawni said, still sounding a little cross with me. "They will stay another few days before departing, and prefer to sleep outdoors."

Bivouac practice? "Why in the grove?"

She shrugged. "I am told they enjoy the scent of the flowers."

I stared at her. "You're kidding."

"Why should I be?" she countered, throwing a puzzled look up at me. "Can Kailthaermil not enjoy the small things of life as well as you or I?"

"I suppose so," I conceded. "It's just not something I would have pictured warriors doing."

"The Kailthaermil are not like other warriors," Tawni said. "Someday you will see."

We reached the volcano and went in through the crack in the cone . . . and for the second time that day I found myself stopping short in shock. There on the wall shelves, where a few weeks ago there had been only eight calices, were now nearly fifty of the sculptures. "Tawni — those calices," I said stupidly, pointing at them. "Where did they come from?"

"That is what the Kailthaermil brought," she said, as if it

was obvious. "They believe this volcano to have unusually good curing characteristics. They have decided to test this by bringing calices here from other artisan colonies."

"I see," I said, getting my feet moving again. "You've never told me how long the curing process takes."

"They will cure for fifteen days," she said. "When they are done, the Kailthaermil will bring more in. They say the complete test will require a hundred days and three hundred calices."

"I see," I said, gazing uneasily at the glittering sculptures. Three hundred calices, suddenly and conveniently moved here to a minor border world.

A border world which the Dynad and Convocation just happened to be paying virtually no attention to. Coincidence? Or could the Kailth plan be further along than Devaro realized?

"Will you choose your three calices now?" Tawni asked as I hesitated. "Or shall we spend a pleasant evening together first, and a night of sleep with the others, and you may choose in the morning?"

With an effort, I shook off the sense of dread. If the Kailth were planning these calices for a prelude to invasion . . .

But what difference could a single night make? Besides, it occurred to me that if Devaro proved the calices were weapons, this would likely be my last trip back here.

My last chance to see Tawni.

"Morning will be soon enough," I told her, turning us around again. "Let's go back."

In the morning I selected my three calices, wearing gloves while handling them as Devaro had instructed, and in a flurry of good-byes and farewell hugs I left Quibsh.

Devaro was grimly pleased with my report and his new prizes. "Three hundred of them, you say," he commented, gazing at the three calices lined up on his desk. "Interesting. Did any of the other verlorens seem upset that Tawnikakalina told you about that?"

"I didn't hear her mention it to anyone," I said. "I know I didn't say anything. But don't forget the Kailth themselves sent me to the volcano to pick out your gifts."

"Waving the red flag under our noses," Devaro grunted, running a gloved finger thoughtfully along one of the metal strands in the middle calix. "Or else Tawnikakalina and the Kailth both assumed you were sufficiently under your own calix's influence that they could do or say anything in your presence without you noticing."

I shifted my shoulders uncomfortably beneath my jacket. In Tawni's presence I couldn't think of her as a threat. In Devaro's, I couldn't seem to think of her as anything but. "Could they have been right?" I asked. "Could the calix have made me forget something significant?"

"If so, it won't be forgotten for long," Devaro said. "I've scheduled you for another brainscan for tomorrow morning. If there are any suppressed memories from the trip, they'll dig them out."

"A brainscan can do that?" I asked uneasily. That wasn't what they'd told us about brainscans in Institute bio class.

"Of course," Devaro said. "We can pull out strong or recent memories, personality tendencies — everything that makes you who you are. That's why it's called *complete*." He lifted an eyebrow sardonically. "Why, is there something about this last trip to Quibsh you don't want me knowing about?"

"Well, no, of course not," I said, suddenly feeling even more uncomfortable. My conversations with Tawni — and the more private times with her — all of that was going to be accessible to them? "It's just that — I mean —"

"This is war, Markand," he said coldly, cutting off my fumbling protest. "Or it will be soon enough. I don't know what you did with Tawnikakalina out there, and I don't especially care. All that matters is the defense of the UnEthHu."

"I understand, sir," I said, feeling abashed. "And I didn't do anything with her. What I mean is —"

"That's all for now," he cut me off again. "Be in the examination room at seven o'clock tomorrow morning, ready to go."

And I was dismissed. "Yes, sir," I murmured.

He was gazing thoughtfully at the three calices as I left the room.

The brainscan the next morning was just as unpleasant as the first one had been. So was the next one, a week later, and the one the week after that.

Devaro had me into his office after each test to talk about the results. But as I think back on those conversations, I realize that he never really told me very much about what the doctors had learned. Nor did he say anything about the parallel tests they were performing on my calix. I assumed they were taking more of the five-micron core samples he'd mentioned, but I wasn't able to see any marks on the calix and he never actually said for sure.

Gradually, my life settled into a steady if somewhat monotonous routine. I worked in Devaro's outer office during the day, sifting reports and compiling data for him like the junior aide that I was. Evenings were spent alone at my apartment, giving myself over to the calix and letting it do whatever it was doing to me. Oddly enough, though I'd expected to feel a certain trepidation as I handled the sculpture, that didn't happen. It still soothed me when I was tense or depressed, invigorated me when I felt listless, and generally felt more like a friend than anyone I'd yet come across in Zurich.

And late at night, in bed, I would gaze at the lights flickering across the ceiling and think about Tawni and her village. Wondering endlessly how such an open and friendly people could be doing all this.

But there was never any answer. And the night after my sixth brainscan I finally realized that there never would be. Not as long as I was trying to solve the puzzle with my own limited knowledge and experience. What I needed was more information, or a fresh perspective.

And once I realized that, I knew there was only one place I could go.

I called Devaro's chief of staff the next morning and, pleading illness, arranged to take two days off. An hour after that, I was on the magtrans heading south.

And three hours after that I was walking into the *Ponte Empyreal* in Rome. The heart, soul, and organizational center of the Church.

They left me waiting in an anteroom of the inner sanctorum while word of my errand was taken inside. I sat there for nearly an hour, wondering if they were ignoring me or just drawing lots among the junior clerics to see which of them would have to come out and talk to me.

I couldn't have been more wrong.

"You must be Mr. Markand," the elderly, white-cloaked man said as he stepped briskly through the archway into the anteroom. "I'm sorry about the delay, but I was in conference and I've just now been told you were here."

"Oh, no problem, your Ministri, no problem," I said, scrambling to my feet and trying not to stutter. Some junior cleric, I'd been cynically expecting; but this was the man himself. First Ministri Jorgen Goribeldi, supreme head of the Church. "I've been perfectly fine here."

"Good," he said smiling easily as he waved me toward the hallway he'd emerged from. It was, I realized with some embarrassment, a reaction he was probably used to. "Come this way, please, and tell me what I can do for you."

"I should first apologize for the intrusion, your Ministri," I said as we set off together down the hallway. "I wasn't expecting them to bother you personally with this."

"That's quite all right," Goribeldi assured me. "I like meeting with people — it's too easy to get out of touch in here." He shrugged, a slight movement of his white cloak. "Besides, I'm one of the few people in the *Ponte Empyreal* at the moment who can help you with your questions about the Sagtt'a colony."

"Yes, sir," I said, feeling my heartbeat pick up. "Am I right, then, in assuming that the Church did indeed send a delegation there?"

"Certainly," he nodded. "At the direct invitation of the Kailth, I might add. They had noted the Church's passion for the well-being of humanity, and wanted to demonstrate their good-will by letting us visit the humans living under their dominion. We found no evidence of cruelty or oppression, by the way."

"Yes, I've talked to some of them," I agreed. "They seem to think of the Kailth as liberators."

"Apparently with a great deal of validity. So what exactly do you wish to know?"

"It's a little hard to put into words," I said hesitantly. "I guess my question boils down to whether they could be so

132

deeply under Kailth influence that they could appear open and honest to other people while at the same time actually being engaged in a kind of subversive warfare."

"In theory, of course they could," Goribeldi said. "Humanity has a tremendous capacity for rationalization and justification when it comes to doing evil against our brothers and sisters. They would hardly need to be under Kailth influence to do that. Or the influence of propagandists, megalomaniacal leaders, or Satan himself. It's a part of our fallen nature."

I nodded. "I see."

We had reached the end of the hallway now and a doorway flanked by a pair of brightly clad ceremonial guards. "But in this specific case," Goribeldi continued, pausing outside the door, "I would say any such worries are probably unfounded. Our delegation found the Sagtt'an society to be a strongly moral one, with a long tradition of ethical behavior. I'm sure they still have their share of people who can lie or steal with a straight face; but as a group, no, I don't think they could say one thing and do another. Not without it being obvious."

"All right," I said slowly. "But couldn't the group on Quibsh have been hand-picked by the Kailth for just that ability? Especially if it was drummed into them that the UnEthHu was their enemy?"

"I suppose that's possible," Goribeldi conceded, nodding to the guards. One of them reached over and released the old-fashioned latch, pushing the door open in front of us. "But I would still think it unlikely. Why don't you come in and I'll show you some of the relevant portions of the priestians' report."

We stepped together through the doorway. Goribeldi's private office, apparently, if the comfortably lived-in clutter was an indication. In the center of the room was a small conversation circle of silkhide-covered chairs and couches, to the right a programmable TV transceiver console, and to the left, beneath a wall of privacy-glazed windows, a large desk.

And sitting prominently on a corner of that desk was a calix.

I stopped short, my heart freezing inside me. "No," I whispered involuntarily.

"What is it?" Goribeldi asked, frowning at me.

I threw a quick glance at him, threw another out the door at my only escape route. But it was already too late. At my reaction the guards had suddenly stopped being ceremonial and were eying me like a pair of tigers already coiled to spring.

It was over. All over. And I had lost. The Kailth had gotten to First Ministri Goribeldi . . . and whatever the calix was supposed do to him had surely already been accomplished.

And knowing my suspicions about them, he certainly couldn't allow me to live. I would just disappear from the *Ponte Empyreal*, with no one ever knowing what had happened.

Goribeldi was still frowning at me. "The calix," I said, with the strange calmness of someone who has nothing left to lose. "A gift from the Sagtt'ans?"

"No," he said. "From your superior."

I blinked at him. "My superior? You mean . . . Convocant Devaro?"

"Yes, of course," he said, frowning a little harder. "He sent it here — oh, four or five weeks ago. A thank-you gift for my sending him a revised copy of our Sagtt'a report. Why, is there a problem?"

I looked at him, and the guards, and the calix. Then, as if moving in a dream, I walked over to the desk. Devaro had ordered me not to touch any of the three new calices on my way back from Quibsh, and I hadn't. But I'd had four days to study them en route, and I had.

Goribeldi was right. This was indeed one of them.

I turned back to face him, feeling vaguely light-headed. "But why?" I asked. "Why would he do this? It's a weapon."

Goribeldi shook his head. "I'm sorry, but I don't follow you."

"A weapon," I repeated. "It's programmed — programmed by touch. Whenever you hold it, it starts affecting you. It turns you from human into something else."

The guards took a step toward me. "Sir?" one of them murmured.

"No, no, it's all right," Goribeldi said, waving them back. "I'm not sure how you came to that conclusion, Mr. Markand, but you have it precisely backwards. The calix doesn't affect you. *You* affect *it*."

I stared at him. "What do you mean?"

"It's your presence that changes the calix, not the other way around," he said. "Your touch and voice affect the wood and crystal, altering the sculpture into a sort of echo of your own personality. A beautifully unique art form, far more individual than anything else you could possibly —"

"Wait a minute," I interrupted him, fighting hard to keep my balance as the universe seemed to tilt sideways beneath me. "You know this for a fact? I mean, it's been proven?"

"Of course," Goribeldi said. "The scientists in our delegation studied it thoroughly. In fact, 'calix' was actually the priestians' name for it, coming from an old term for the

Cup of Communion. Holding a reflection of your soul, as it were. I hadn't realized the Sagtt'ans had picked up on the name."

I looked back at the calix. "I'm sorry, your Ministri," I said, my face warm with a thoroughly unpleasant mixture of embarrassment and confusion. "I guess I —" I broke off, shaking my head. "I'm sorry."

"That's all right," Goribeldi said, waving the guards back to their posts. Apparently, he'd decided I wasn't crazy. Me, I wasn't so sure. "Come, let me show you the priestians' report."

I still wasn't sure half an hour later when he escorted me back to the anteroom and thanked me for coming. One thing I was sure of, though: the calices did indeed seem to behave exactly as he had said they did.

Which meant they weren't the weapons that Convocant Devaro had thought they were. Surely if he'd read the Church's report he already knew that.

But he'd had that report at least a month ago. If he had read it, why was he still subjecting me to weekly brainscans?

Unless he still wasn't convinced the calices were harmless. But in that case, why would he risk giving a potentially dangerous weapon to First Ministri Goribeldi?

I puzzled over it as I headed down the street toward the magtrans station. I was still puzzling, in fact, right up to the point where the two large men came up on either side of me and effortlessly stuffed me into a waiting car. There was the tingle of a stunner at my side, and the world went dark.

I awoke aboard a half-wing already driving through space. The two men who'd kidnapped me were aboard as well, the three of us apparently the only passengers. As jailers they initially seemed rather amateurish; aside from the control areas and their two cabins I had complete freedom of the ship. But after two days of searching for weapons or escape routes or even information, I came to realize they weren't so much amateurish as just casually efficient. They completely ignored my questions and occasional frustrated demands, and only spoke to each other in clipped sentences of a language I didn't recognize.

Finally, three days of flight, we came alongside an unmarked military-style full-wing floating quietly in space. A transfer tunnel was set up and I was sent through, where I was met by a pair of hard-faced men in SkyForce uniforms. No chattier than my jailers had been, they escorted me silently to the command observation balcony above and behind the bridge.

Waiting for me there, as I'd rather expected, was Convocant Devaro.

"So," he said without preamble. "Here you are."

"Yes, sir," I said. "Here we both are."

For a moment he studied my face. "You've figured it out, haven't you?" he said at last. "Something the priestians at the *Ponte Empyreal* said to you."

I looked past his shoulder through the balcony's twin-sectioned canopy. Directly ahead, the view over the bow of the full-wing showed that we were coming in toward a planetary darkside; ahead and below, I could see down into the bridge and the SkyForce officers and crewmen at their stations. "I saw the calix you gave to First Ministri Goribeldi," I said. "He told me it wasn't a weapon." I looked back at Devaro. "He was wrong, wasn't he."

Devaro shrugged. " 'Weapon' is an unfairly loaded term," he said. "I prefer to think of it as a tool."

"A tool which you're using to invade other people's privacy," I accused him. "Giving someone a calix is really no different than doing a brainscan on him. Except that he doesn't know it's been done. All you have to do is give the wood fibers enough time to adapt to his personality, then take your five-micron core samples and read his personality matrix right off them."

Devaro laughed, a short animal-like bark. "You make it sound so easy. You have no idea how much time and sweat went into developing the proper chemo-mathematical transforms to use."

"I think I have some idea," I said stiffly. "After all, I was your guinea pig in the whole thing. If you hadn't had my weekly brainscans to compare with the calix's chemical changes you'd never have been able to work out your precious transforms."

He shrugged carelessly. "Oh, we'd have managed. It just would have taken longer, and required us to get hold of a calix on our own. Your providential return from Quibsh merely made it simpler."

"Well, enjoy it while you can," I bit out. "When we get back to Earth, I'll see you in prison."

He lifted his eyebrows. "On what grounds? You signed a legal authorization before each of those brainscans."

"What about the calix you gave First Ministri Goribeldi?" I countered.

"A thank-you gift. Perfectly legal."

"Except when the gift's part of an illegal brainscan."

"What illegal brainscan?" Devaro countered calmly. "A brainscan is performed with a Politayne-Chu neural mapmaker or the equivalent. There's no such device in a calix."

"You're splitting hairs."

"I'm staying precisely within the letter of the law," Devaro corrected. "That's all that counts."

I glared at him. But even as I did so, I could feel my position eroding out from under my feet like loose sand. I had no idea how the brainscan laws were worded, but I had no doubt that Devaro had studied them thoroughly. "So where within the letter of the law does destruction of the Church come?" I demanded. "I presume you *are* planning its destruction?"

"Eventually," Devaro said off-handedly. "But that's a long way in the future. There are other more urgent matters that need to be attended to first."

"Such as?"

"Such as the threat posed to the UnEthHu by the Kailthaermil Empire," he said, his voice suddenly hard. "And our moral responsibility to protect fellow human beings wherever they might be found."

I blinked. "What are you talking about?"

"Your verlorens of course," he said. "Conquered and enslaved by the Kailth, along with dozens, perhaps hundreds, of other races. The UnEthHu has stood by idly for ten years now. It's time we took a stand against such tyranny."

I glanced at the dark planetary surface now rolling by beneath us, a dark suspicion digging into my stomach. "This is Quibsh, isn't it?" I said. "You're going to attack Quibsh."

"We're not *attacking* anyone," Devaro said. "We're liberating a human colony from alien overlords."

"And while you're liberating them, you'll also liberate their collection of calices?"

"The calices are evidence of their enslavement," Devaro said evenly. "Fabulous works of art, routinely and ruthlessly stolen from them by their alien overlords."

"Which you'll no doubt be giving to other high-ranking UnEthHu and Church officials," I said, a bitter taste in my mouth. "And senior SkyForce officers —"

I stopped short, suddenly remembering where we were. On an unmarked military full-wing with SkyForce personnel aboard . . . "You used a calix to blackmail the *SkyForce?*"

"Don't be absurd," Devaro sniffed. "A Supreme Convocant hardly needs to stoop to anything as crude as blackmail. Let's just say that when I presented my request to Admiral Gates, I knew the right words to use to persuade him to my point of view."

"Yes, I suppose you did," I said, thinking back over all the conversations I'd had with Devaro during the past few weeks. How he had always somehow managed to say just the right things to keep my suspicions of Tawni alive, even against the evidence of my own eyes and heart. At times, usually late at night, I'd wondered at my inability to make my own decisions and stick to them. Now, too late, I understood what he'd done to me.

The intercom twittered. "We're approaching the target site, Convocant," a voice said.

"I'll be right there," Devaro said. "You're welcome to stay here," he added to me as he stepped over to the lift plate leading to the bridge below.

"This could start a war," I warned quietly. Trying, I suppose, one last time. "Are a few calices worth that much to you?"

"The calices are power," he said simply. "If you haven't already figured out what that means, you're either too naive or too stupid for me to explain it to you now." He shrugged. "Besides, I've already told you that war with the Kailth is inevitable. If it starts here, so be it."

He touched the control and dropped away through the floor. The opening sealed again, and I was alone.

I walked over to the canopy, a hundred painful thoughts

and useless plans and bitter self-recriminations chasing themselves through my mind. Devaro was on the move, with his long sought-after seat on the Dynad in his sights. Only now he had a secret weapon that might just get it for him.

And I'd been the one who'd given it to him. That was what galled the most. Not only had my brainscans provided the key to his scheme, but I'd even trotted obediently out to Quibsh and gotten him the extra calices he wanted.

He'd used one of them to talk a SkyForce admiral out of a military full-wing and crew. Another was waiting like a hidden time bomb for an eventual attack against the unwanted moral criticisms of the Church. I was afraid to wonder whom he'd given the third one to.

I stepped up to the canopy. We were approaching the terminator now, the hazy line marking dawn on the planet below. Just into the lighted area I could see the familiar chain of volcanoes that bordered the little group of verloren villages.

A motion below me caught my attention, and I looked down into the bridge. Devaro and two of the officers were gazing to the right; even as I watched, one of them shoved the Convocant into one of the chairs. Frowning, wondering what they were looking at, I leaned my head against the canopy and peered in that direction —

And was slammed bodily against the curved plastic as the full-wing abruptly skidded into a hard right-hand turn.

I peeled myself off the canopy and dived toward one of the balcony's chairs, grabbing the safety straps and pulling myself into it. Ahead now I could see what had gotten everyone so riled up: a pair of aircraft heading our way. I tried to figure out if the direction was right for them to be coming from one of the Kailth bases, but I was so turned around now I didn't know which way was which. I threw another glance down at the bridge —

And flinched back as, at the edge of my vision, a burst of fire flashed out from the full-wing's bow.

I looked up again. The missile was heading straight toward the incoming aircraft, its drive blazing like a miniature sun against the lightening sky. I held my breath, thinking of those awesome Kailth weapons, and waited for the aircraft to return the fire.

But they didn't. Instead, they merely broke formation, veering off sharply to either side. The missile split in response, one half targeting each of them, and the race for survival was on. One of the aircraft vanished into the darkness behind us as our full-wing swung back around toward the terminator line ahead. The other aircraft was driving directly away from us toward the rising sun, the missile rapidly overtaking it. I scanned the ground ahead, trying to reorient myself —

And suddenly I jabbed at the chair's intercom switch. "Convocant Devaro! That aircraft — it's heading straight for the group of villages!"

The only verbal response was a curse; but abruptly the full-wing leaped forward, driving hard toward the doomed aircraft. A laser flashed out, sweeping dizzyingly as the gunner tried to lock onto the missile.

But it was too far away. And it was too late. The two exhausts coalesced into one; and with a surprisingly small flash of blue-white fire the aircraft disintegrated.

I watched helplessly, hands clenched around the safety straps. The full-wing, down to treetop level now, was driving swiftly toward the impact point. I could see a reddish glow ahead, mixing with the dawn light.

And suddenly we were there, swinging around again and

sweeping over the area. I could see the string of villages now, with a scattering of burning debris from the aircraft strewn around and among the buildings.

But that wasn't where the red glow I'd seen was coming from. The main body of the aircraft had slammed into the cone of the nearest volcano, and just below the point of impact a new lava vent had opened up.

I reached for the intercom again, but Devaro beat me to it. "Markand, is that the volcano where they keep the calices?" he snapped.

"Yes," I confirmed. "That lava flow — it's headed toward Tawni's village —"

The intercom cut off. But I didn't need to hear Devaro's instructions to the captain to know what he was going to do next. The aircraft's crash had clearly shaken up the whole unstable region; plumes of smoke were beginning to appear from several of the other nearby volcanoes. If Devaro wanted the calices, he would have to get them now.

Even if it meant abandoning Tawni and her people to burn.

The full-wing was coming around back toward the volcano as I threw the bright red lever that opened the balcony's emergency drop-tube door. I dove inside, spun around and hit the "eject" plate. The door closed, the stasis webbing wrapped around me, and with a stomach-churning lurch I dropped free.

Ten seconds later I was down, the tube toppling delicately onto its side and popping open. I scrambled to my feet and looked around, trying to figure out where exactly I was. I couldn't see the light from the lava flow, but the wind was acrid with the smell of burning vegetation, so I knew it had to be somewhere close. A three-meter-high ridge of basalt cut across in front of me; unmindful of what the sharp rock might do to my hands, I slung the tube's survival pack over one shoulder and scrambled my way to the top.

There, no more than a hundred meters away, was the lava flow, making its slow but inexorable way down toward the sleeping villages below. At the top of the cone, its edges glowing a fiery red with reflected light, the full-wing was easing downward. Devaro, apparently unwilling to waste even a second, was taking the entire ship into the crater.

And then, even as I watched, a second source of light suddenly flickered from the full-wing's edges. A glow coming from inside the crater itself.

The volcano was getting ready to erupt.

"Get out of there," I whispered urgently to them, squeezing hard onto the basalt. Fumes were beginning to rise, and the glow was growing brighter. If they didn't leave right now . . .

But they didn't. The full-wing continued down, its dark shape disappearing below the rim of the crater. I held my breath, for some perverse reason counting the seconds.

And as I reached eleven, it happened. Abruptly, the crater belched out a huge plume of smoke and ash and red fire, lighting up the ground even as it darkened the sky. Three seconds later it was eclipsed by a second burst of flame, this one the clean and brilliant blue-white of the full-wing's missiles exploding.

My stomach wanted desperately to be sick. But there was no time for that now. That first lava flow was still headed toward Tawni's village, and they were going to need all the help they could get if they were to evacuate in time. Easing my legs over the ridge, I braced myself to jump.

And paused, as something near the leading edge of the lava flow caught my eye. Someone or something was moving down there among the burning vegetation. I squinted, fumbling in the survival pack for a set of binoculars —

And nearly fell off the ridge as the front of the lava flow erupted in a flash of green flame.

I fought for balance as a second flash followed the first, a fresh surge of horror stabbing into me. That was the flash of a Kailth hand weapon.

And there were only two reasons I could think of why anyone might be firing into the gloom down there. Either he was shooting at another survivor from the full-wing, or else he thought that was where I'd gone down.

My hand had been hunting in the survival pack for a set of binoculars. Now, it moved instead to the butt of a SkyForce-issue 12mm pistol. Gripping it tightly, I swung my legs back to the far side of the ridge again —

And found myself looking down into the face of a Kailth warrior.

If I'd taken even half a second to think about it I would have realized how stupidly suicidal the whole idea was. But I didn't take that half second. I hauled the 12mm out of the pack, flicked off the safety, and fired.

The weapon boomed, the recoil again nearly knocking me off the ridge. But the Kailth was no longer there. Without any preparatory movement whatsoever he had effortlessly leaped up to straddle the ridge beside me. Even as I tried desperately to swing the pistol around toward him, he reached across my chest and plucked it from my hand. "Human male," he said. "Come."

"Come where?" I asked, my voice trembling with reaction. "Why?"

145

The bumblebee face regarded me. "That you may understand."

There were two other Kailth warriors standing by the lava flow when we arrived. Two Kailth, and Tawni.

"Stane!" she burst out, running to my arms as soon as she saw me. "Oh, thank the God of Mercy — you are all right. You are all right."

I looked past her at the two Kailth, finally seeing what all the shooting was about. With those awesome handguns they were blasting a trench in the hard igneous rock of the volcano cone, diverting the slow-moving lava away from the villages below. "Yes, I'm safe," I murmured, holding Tawni close. "For now."

"For always," she insisted, drawing back to look into my face. "They have promised me your safety."

"Have they really." I looked at the warrior standing silently beside us and nodded toward the two Kailth digging the trench. "Is this what I need to understand?"

The Kailth stirred. "You must understand all that has happened."

I snorted. "Oh, I understand. All of it."

"Tell me," he challenged.

I glared at him, knowing that it was over. But at least before I died Tawni would get to see what her adored liberators really were. "You used me," I said. "You got Tawni to give me a calix to take back to the UnEthHu. Which you've now used to kill Convocant Devaro and everyone aboard that full-wing."

"We regret the loss of the other humans," the alien said. "As we also regret the loss of the Kailthaermil warriors aboard the flyers which were destroyed. But their deaths were of Convocant Devaro's devising, not ours."

"How can you say that?" I demanded. "If I hadn't taken that calix back with me, none of this would have happened."

There was a soft hissing sound. "You do not yet understand, Stane Markand," the Kailth said. "If not for the calix, it would indeed not have happened this way. But it would still have happened."

I shook my head, my brief flash of defiance draining away. "You're not making any sense," I said with a sigh. "It was the calix that brought Convocant Devaro here."

"No," the Kailth said firmly. "It was Convocant Devaro's desire for power over others that brought him. The calix did nothing but bring that desire into focus."

"You did not seek to use my gift for such purposes," Tawni added earnestly. "For you it was a joy, and a blessing. It was only Convocant Devaro who sought to use it for his own gain."

I gazed back at her face. "So you knew all along," I said. "From the beginning I was nothing but a pawn in this."

Her mouth twitched as if I'd raised a hand to her. But she held my gaze without flinching. "I gave you a gift from my heart," she said. "For friendship. It was not part of any plan."

"The Citizen-Three is correct," the warrior said. "Our plan was to begin there." He pointed up at the bubbling fire of the volcano. "Tawnikakalina's gift was indeed only a gift." He regarded me thoughtfully. "If you were no more than a pawn, we would not tell you this."

"So why *are* you telling me?" I countered. "What do you want from me?"

"I have said already," the Kailth said. "Understanding." He reached out an armored hand to touch Tawni's shoulder. "There is ambition that drives one to be the best one can be," he said. "That is the ambition Tawnikakalina has for her art. Perhaps you have such ambition as well."

He lowered his hand. "But there is also ambition that seeks power over others, and does not care what destruction is left in its wake. We have seen this cruel madness in the Phashiskar, and the Baal'ariai, and the Aoeemme. And we see it now in the humans.

"And when such ambition threatens the Kailthaermil, we must offer it the means to destroy itself."

I looked over at the other warriors still cutting their trench. "Convocant Devaro said war with you is inevitable. Is that what you mean?"

"No," the Kailth said. "We have no desire for war with the UnEthHu. You do not subjugate the other beings within your boundaries, but treat them with justice. Nor are there fundamental human interests or needs which demand conflict with the Kailthaermil. War will come only if individual humans choose to create it for their own purposes."

I glanced up at the volcano. "Men like Devaro."

Tawni's grip tightened on my arm. "I do not wish war with your people, Stane," she said quietly.

"I don't want it either, Tawni," I said, looking at the Kailth warrior again. "But it seems to me that the war may have already begun. Whether or not Devaro did this of his own free will, the fact remains that it was the Kailth who provided the calix that tempted him down that path."

"You are correct," the Kailth said. "The war has indeed begun."

Reaching into his armor, he pulled out the pistol he'd taken from me. I caught my breath, feeling Tawni shrink against my side. "But it is not a war against humans," the Kailth continued. "It is a war against meaningless and unnecessary war."

He held up the pistol. "This is such a war, Stane Markand, the war Convocant Devaro sought to create against the Kailthaermil Empire for his own purposes. It may be stopped thus —"

He grasped the barrel with his other hand, and with a sharp crack of broken gunplastic snapped the weapon in half. A squeeze with the armored hand, and the barrel shattered into splinters.

"Or it may be stopped thus." Reaching into the shattered frame with two fingers, he gave a sharp tug and pulled out the firing pin. "It is a war that must be fought, or many innocent lives will be lost," he said quietly, handing me the pin and what was left of the ruined gun. "Which way would you choose for us to fight it?"

I looked at Tawni. She was gazing back up at me, the skin of her face tight with quiet anxiety. Waiting to see how I would react to all this.

Perhaps waiting to see if she had lost a friend.

"What about Tawni's people?" I asked the Kailth. "Devaro gave his calices away to others. If any of them tries to use them the same way he wanted to, they may come here to get more."

"The Kailthaermil freed us when we had no hope," Tawni said quietly. "To help them free others, we willingly accept the danger."

"Perhaps," the Kailth said, "you can help make them safer."

I looked down the slope, toward the villages below. "Yes," I said. "Perhaps I can."

And with a lot of help, I did. Ten months later, in a precedent-shattering treaty, Quibsh became joint colonial territory of the Kailth and UnEthHu. Three years after that, convention was again shattered as the humans of Quibsh and Sagtt'a were granted full joint citizenship between the two races. Over those three years, six SkyForce officers and five more Convocants figured out Devaro's brainscan trick and attempted to use the calices to amass power. All of them either died in the attempt or were politically destroyed.

And in the midst of it all, in the greatest miracle of all, Tawni became my wife. And later, of course, your mother.

And so, as we stand here on the eve of the Fifth Joint Kailthaermil-UnEthHu Expedition into the unknown areas of the galaxy, I wanted you to know how my Year of YouthJourneying came out. It was the year I learned about politics and war, about ambition and selflessness, about art and death and love.

The year I grew up.

Our hopes and blessings go with you, my son, as you leave with the expedition tomorrow. May your nineteenth year be as blessed as mine.

With love, Dad.

The Play's the Thing

The whole trouble started when the Fuzhtian ambassador announced that he wanted to see a Broadway play.

Though I suppose you could equally well say the trouble started when those first silent Fuzhtian probes snuggled coyly up behind our geosynchronous TV satellites and began shipping the signals back home. You might even go back further and say that it all started when Marconi's first radio went on-line and began spewing electromagnetic radiation out into space for everyone to hear.

Oh, well, hell, let's be honest. All of it *really* started with whoever the bunch of trouble-making Sumerians were who sat around on a rainy Sunday afternoon and invented *entertainment*.

Because that's *really* what started the trouble: our vast entertainment industry, and the Fuzhties' maniacal love for it.

For a simple example — and this isn't supposed to be noised about — when the Fuzhtian ship landed outside the White House, the "Greetings and Joy to Humankind" line that will be going into the history books were actually his second words to the Secretary-General. His actual first words were an expression of disappointment from his government that Johnny Carson was no longer hosting the "Tonight Show." For those of you who'd always wondered why Carson suddenly came out of retirement right after that to do a one-month stint as guest-host, now you know.

I suppose it could have been worse. No, strike that — it

could have been a <u>lot</u> worse. You've heard all the similes: a walking barn door with gorilla arms, a four-hundred-pound bag of blubbery muscle with pinfeathers; a cross between a bull and Doberman on steroids. Even without the kind of technology we know they had, the Fuzhties could have stomped the planet flat as Florida if they'd taken a mind to do so.

Which is why everyone had been falling all over themselves trying to satisfy the ambassador's slightest whim. Partly it was residual fear that he might suddenly stop being congenial and start behaving the way any self-respecting B-movie creature his size ought to; but mainly it was because every national leader on the planet was visibly salivating over the prospect of getting their hands on Fuzhtian technology.

Anyway, at the time the ambassador made his Broadway request he'd been on Earth about six months, getting everything he wanted. And I mean *everything*. He had the top two floors of an exclusive Washington hotel, specially commissioned airplanes and cars, and three of the premier chefs in Europe. Along the way he'd also collected an astonishingly eclectic entourage, consisting of top US government officials, a smattering of foreign representatives whose countries had somehow caught his interest — we still don't know how or why he picked the ones he did — and a few oddballs like me. I'd been up on a ladder doing some woodwork repair in the White House when the ambassador apparently expressed some sort of vague approval of me. The next thing I knew I'd been hauled down, poured into a suit and handed a briefcase, and tossed in among the smiling State Department wonks whose job it was to dog the ambassador's size-28 footsteps.

Long afterward I learned that what had captured the ambassador's attention was not me but rather the hammer I'd been using. But by then I'd overheard enough under-the-breath comments about my relative usefulness to the group that sheer native orneriness required me to keep quiet about the error.

Besides, the briefcase they'd handed me that first day had contained a presidential plea for my cooperation and about two bucketfuls of money, both of which I was far too patriotic to walk away from.

But for whatever reason, I was in that elite group. And I'd been with them for about five weeks when, from out of the blue, the ambassador made his request.

We still don't know what prompted him to bring it up at that particular time. For that matter, we're not even sure how he knew about Broadway, unless he'd picked up a reference from one of those pirate transmissions their probes had been making. But however it happened, there it was, plain as day, that morning on the RebuScope:

"Are you *sure* that's what it means?" Dwight Fogerty, a senior State Department wonk and head of our little group, asked as he peered back and forth between the RebuScope and the tentative translation.

"I don't see what else it could be, sir," chief translator Angus MacLeod said. He'd been loaned to us by MI6 because he was both a whiz at cryptanalysis and a huge "Concentration" fan. Angus always called Fogerty "sir" because he was polite, not because Fogerty deserved it. "It's clearly 'eye w-ant two cee a br-rod-weigh' something. What else but play?"

"Well, who says that scale thing is 'weigh?' " Fogerty countered. "Maybe it's 'Broadscale' something."

"There's no such word as Broadscale," someone pointed out. "Or place, either."

"There's a Broad Sound, though," someone else said, punching keys on a laptop. "It's near Rockhampton in Australia, near the Great Barrier Reef. Maybe that's a radio or stereo speaker, not a scale."

"And what, that last picture is us and him throwing a beach ball back and forth?" Fogerty scoffed.

"Well, then, maybe it's supposed to be 'Broadsword,' " one of the other wonks said. "The damn RebuScope's screwed up before. Maybe he wants to see some sword demos from one of those Medieval-nutcake groups."

"It's 'I want to see a Broadway play,' " Angus said firmly. "I'm sure of it."

Fogerty muttered something vicious-sounding under his breath. Why the ambassador had chosen to use a gadget as ridiculously hard to understand as the RebuScope for his messages to us was a mystery, but most of us had gradually developed a sort of resigned acceptance for the procedure. Fogerty, who dealt with the gadget more than anyone except Angus, roundly hated the thing, and seemed to be running systematically through his vast repertoire of multilingual curses in regards to it. "All right, fine," he said. "We'll take him to a Broadway play. Smith, get on the horn and find out who the hell we talk to about doing that."

I cleared my throat. "You don't need to call the White House, Mr. Fogerty," I said. "I know some people on Broadway."

"We're not interested in pretzel venders, thank you," Fogerty said tartly, gesturing at Smith. "We need a producer or theater manager or —"

"I know all of them."

Fogerty stopped, his gesturing hand still poised in mid-air, and turned his head to look at me. "You what?" he asked.

"I know all of them," I repeated. "Up until a year ago I was working with one of the top set designers on Broadway."

It was, and I'll admit it, an immensely soul-satisfying moment. The whole bunch of them just stood there, professionals and wonks alike, staring at me like something that had just crawled out of the primordial ooze and asked whether the Metro Blue line stopped here. All except Angus, that is, who had a faint but knowing smile on his face. Obviously, he was the only one in the group who'd bothered to read the FBI's rundown on me after I was booted aboard.

Fogerty recovered first, in typical Fogerty fashion. "Well, don't just stand there, Lebowitz," he said, waving Smith forward with his phone. "Let's get to it."

The first step, I decided, would be to figure out which Broadway offering would be the best one to take the ambassador to see. I put in a call to Tony Capello, theater critic, and we spent fifteen minutes discussing the current crop of plays and musicals in town.

Actually, the first twelve of those minutes were spent talking over the old times when I was a lowly carpenter and Tony was chief gopher for a succession of minor choreographers. I would have cut off the reminiscences earlier, except that the delay so obviously irritated Fogerty. When I finally got Tony down to business, his advice was instant and unequivocal: "*And Whirred When It Stood Still,*" currently in previews at the St. James.

"So what's the play about?" Fogerty asked when I re-

155

layed the recommendation.

"According to Tony, it's pleasantly harmless froth," I assured him. "Nothing that'll confuse the ambassador or put human beings in a bad light. At least, not in any worse light than plays typically do."

"Assuming he understands it at all," Fogerty growled, gesturing to his overworked secretary. "Lee, better have someone vet it anyway, just to be on the safe side. All right, what about this St. James Theater? It's on Broadway?"

"Well, actually, it's on West 44th Street," I said. "But it's —"

"West 44th Street?" Fogerty echoed. "He wants a *Broadway* play."

"It *is* a Broadway play," I told him stiffly. "The St. James is in the theater district, half a block off Broadway itself. It counts. Trust me."

He glowered, but apparently decided he'd shown enough ignorance for one conversation. "Fine," he grunted. "Let's just hope it counts with the ambassador."

The manager at the St. James, Jerry Zachs, was less than enthusiastic about the whole thing. "You must be joking," he said, looking back and forth between Fogerty and me. "Bring that behemoth into my theater? Who's going to pay for the fifty seats it's going to cost me?"

"Oh, do try not to go off the deep end here, Mr. Zachs," Fogerty said, his voice hovering between imperious and condescending. "We won't have to remove more than nine seats at the most to fit him in."

"Sure — to fit *him* in," Jerry shot back. "What about these seats in front of him you want left empty?"

"That's only another twelve seats," Fogerty told him. "Four rows by three seats —"

"I can multiply, thank you," Jerry growled. "I can also multiply by ticket prices and see I'm already out about a grand and a half. *And* what about all the seats right behind him where no one's going to be able to see? Huh?"

Fogerty shrugged. "Fine. We'll put his entourage there."

"At full price?"

Fogerty lifted his eyebrows. "Don't be silly. They won't be able to see the show from there. How do you expect to charge full price?"

Jerry's complexion was edging into a soft pink, which from my experience with him was a dangerous sign. "I'm sure we can work something out," I jumped in before he could say anything. Fogerty had a virtually unlimited budget to work with, but he could go all chintzy at the oddest moments. "What's important is that the ambassador be treated like the VIP he is."

"That's right," Fogerty said, apparently believing I was on his side here. "The Fuzhties have a great deal to offer humanity, Mr. Zachs, and the more favors he owes us, the sooner he'll start coming across with some of this magic technology of theirs. This is just one of those favors."

" 'The play's the thing,' " I said in my best soliloquy voice, " 'Wherein I'll catch the conscience of the king.' "

Fogerty frowned at me. "What?"

"*Hamlet*," I said.

"Shakespeare," Jerry added acidly. "He's done some plays and poems and stuff."

"Thank you," Fogerty said, matching Jerry's acid pH for pH. "I *have* heard of the man. The point is that I can requisition your theater, no questions asked, like it or lump it. So you might as well like it. Anyway, you should be honored to have their first ambassador in your theater."

"Besides, think of the great publicity," I reminded him.

"You'll be able to use photos of the ambassador in all your future ads and —"

"Wait a minute," Fogerty cut me off, his face suddenly stricken. "He can't use the ambassador as a cheap come-on. This is a serious diplomatic mission."

"Oh, I don't know," Jerry mused, picking up the cue and running with it. "When the King of Sweden came here, he let us use his name in some of our promotionals. I don't see how this is any different."

"Of course it's different," Fogerty snapped. "And if you even *think* about trying to take advantage of him that way —"

"Taking advantage?" Jerry asked mildly. "You mean like a six-hundred pound government gorilla trying to gouge a poor innocent theater manager on ticket prices?"

Fogerty glared daggers at both of us. But he didn't have time for a fight, and we all knew it. "Fine," he bit out. "Full ticket prices for the whole entourage."

"And full payment for the crew handling the alterations?" Jerry asked.

"We'll be doing it all ourselves," Fogerty gritted. "My people are already downstairs, waiting for the green light."

"Well, then, I guess I'd better give it to them," Jerry said, reaching for his phone. "A pleasure doing business with you, Mr. Fogerty."

The alterations took only a few hours, about the same time it took to get the ambassador and the rest of the entourage up from Washington and settled into a hotel a couple of blocks from the St. James. We headed out that evening for the theater in the ambassador's special car, which would have been a major challenge to drive in midtown Manhattan if the police hadn't cordoned off the area for us. I'm sure that stunt made us lots of friends among the local drivers. Probably just as well we couldn't hear what the cabbies were saying.

The theater goers at the St. James, to my mild surprise, seemed to take the whole thing pretty much in stride. There'd been some hassles at Jerry's end, I knew, sorting out the people who'd already bought the seats Fogerty had appropriated, but they'd all been moved or paid off or otherwise placated, and by the time we walked in with the ambassador everyone was feeling cordial enough to give him a round of polite applause. I presume he understood — there'd certainly been enough applause on the TV programs the Fuzhties had pilfered — but if he was either pleased or annoyed he didn't show it. Fogerty showed him to his chair — which had indeed required the removal of a square block of nine seats — and the rest of us filled in behind him. The house lights dimmed, the curtain went up, and the play started. In the reflected light from the stage I saw Fogerty lean back in his seat and cross his legs, the tired but smug image of a man who has faced yet another political brush fire and successfully stomped it out.

He got to be smug for exactly three minutes.

I had given up trying to see anything around the ambassador's bulk when, without warning, he heaved himself to his feet. Someone behind me gasped — the Trinidadian representative, I think — and I remember having the fleeting, irrational thought that the ambassador had realized I couldn't see and was courteously getting out of my way. An instant after that I realized how absurd that thought was, and my second thought was that he must have to go to the bathroom or stretch his legs or something.

He didn't. With a roar that shook the spotlight battens, he climbed up on the empty seat backs in front of him and made a ponderous beeline for the stage.

The actors froze into statues, staring wide-eyed at this pinfeathered Goliath bearing down on them in slow motion. Making his way across the seats and the covered orchestra pit, he made a huge bound up onto the stage, landing with a thud that must have shaken the whole block. He turned around, filled his lungs, and bellowed.

You've never seen a theater clear out so fast. The orchestra and mezzanine both — it just emptied out like someone was giving away free beer outside. It was a miracle that no one was killed or seriously injured; even more of a miracle, in my book, that no one filed any lawsuits afterward for bruised shins or torn clothing. I guess the thought of facing a huge unpredictable alien in court made quiet discretion the smart move on everyone's part.

But at the time, I wasn't convinced any of us would be getting out of the St. James alive. With the ambassador's second bellow even the actors lost it, scurrying for the wings like they'd spotted a critic with an Uzi. I was cowering in my seat, trying desperately hard to be invisible, unwilling to move until I had a straight shot at an exit that wasn't already jammed with people. The ambassador, still bellowing, had begun pacing back and forth across the now empty stage when Angus grabbed my arm. "Look!" he shouted over the hysterical bedlam.

"I see him!" I shouted back, momentarily hating Angus for drawing unnecessary attention our direction. "Shut up before he —"

"No!" Angus snapped, jabbing a finger at the RebuScope monitor he was carrying. "He's not just roaring at nothing — he's *talking* to us!"

I looked at the RebuScope . . . and damned if he wasn't right.

"Fine," I shouted. "So what does it mean?"

"I don't know," Angus said. More pictures were starting to scroll along the screen; punching for a hard copy, he tore off the first part of the message and thrust it into my hands. "Here — see what you can figure out."

I shrank back into my seat, half my attention on the paper, the other half on the ambassador still pacing and roaring. *Th-hiss book hiss awl th-hat eye knee-d —*

None of this made any sense. It really didn't. In the five weeks I'd been with the ambassador he'd never so much as raised his voice.

Howl two howl two drink —

And anyway, what in the world could be important enough for him to interrupt a play for? A play he himself had asked to attend?

Drink? No, not drink. Straw? Howl two straw? No. Ah — suck. Howl two suck-see-d . . .

And then, with a sudden horrible jolt, I had it. I took another look at the rebus — glanced at the new pictures that Angus was getting —

"I've got it!" I yelled, grabbing Angus's arm and waving my paper in front of him. " 'This book is all that I need/ How to, How to Succeed.' "

He blinked at me. "What?"

"It's part of a song," I told him. "The opening song from

the classic musical 'How to Succeed in Business Without Really Trying.' "

Angus looked up at the ambassador, his mouth falling slightly open. "You mean — ?"

"You got it," I said. "The ambassador's not *talking* to us. He's *singing*."

It took till after midnight for Fogerty to get the preliminary damage control finished with the St. James management. An hour after that, he held a council of war in the hotel.

A very small council of war, consisting of Fogerty, Angus, and me. I'm still not exactly sure why I'd been included, unless that as our resident Broadway expert I was the one Fogerty was planning to pin the fiasco on.

Not that he wasn't willing to apportion everyone a share of the blame if he could manage it. Fogerty was generous that way. "All right, MacLeod, let's hear it," he said icily as he closed the door behind us. "What the bloody-red hell happened?"

"The same thing that's happened before, sir," Angus said calmly, letting Fogerty's glare bounce right off him. "The RebuScope made a mistake."

"Really," Fogerty said, turning the glare up another couple of notches. "The RebuScope. Convenient enough excuse."

"I don't think 'convenient' is exactly the word I would have chosen," Angus said. "But it is what happened."

He pressed keys on the RebuScope monitor, pulling up a copy of the ambassador's original Broadway request. "A very simple error, actually, compared with some we've seen. You see this letter C? It should have been a B."

A frown momentarily softened Fogerty's glare by a

couple of horsepower. "What?"

"The message wasn't 'I want to see a Broadway play,' "
Angus amplified. "It was 'I want to *be* a Broadway play.' "

For a long minute Fogerty just stood there, staring down
at the RebuScope, a look of disbelief on his face. "But
that's absurd," he said when he finally found his voice
again. " 'I want to be in a — ?' No. It's ridiculous."

"Nevertheless, sir, that's what he wants," Angus said.
"The question now is how you're going to get it for him."

Fogerty tried the glare again, but his heart was clearly no
longer in it. "Me?"

"You're the head of this operation," Angus reminded
him. "You're the one who talks to the White House, autho-
rizes the expenditures, and accepts the official plaudits. We
await your instructions. Sir."

For another minute Fogerty was silent, gazing at and
through Angus. Then, with obvious reluctance, he turned
to look at me. "I suppose you have the contacts for this one,
too?"

With anyone else who treated people the way Fogerty
did, I'd have been tempted to demand a little groveling before I gave in. But, down deep, I suspected that being polite
to underlings was as close as Fogerty ever got to a grovel. "I
know a few people," I said. "There may be a way to pull it
off."

"Seems to me there are at least two stage versions of
'Beauty and the Beast' out there, aren't there?" Angus suggested. "He'd be a natural."

"Wouldn't work," I said, shaking my head. "Too many
lines. Too much real acting."

"How about a non-speaking role, then?" Fogerty suggested. "Maybe a walk-on part?"

I snorted. "Would *you* travel a three hundred light-years for a walk-on part?"

A muscle in his jaw twitched. "No, I suppose not," he conceded. "I suppose that also lets out any chance of using him as part of the set decoration."

"It does," I agreed. "Which leaves only one approach, at least only one I can think of. We're going to have to have a play written especially for him."

Fogerty waved a hand. "Of course," he said, as if it had been obvious all along. "Well. The phone's over there — better get busy."

"What, you mean *now?*" I asked, looking at my watch. "It's after one in the morning."

"New York is the city that never sleeps, isn't it?" he countered, jabbing a finger at the phone. "Besides, we need to get this on track. Go on, start punching."

There were six New York playwrights with whom I had at least a passing acquaintance. The first five numbers I tried shunted me to answering machines or services. My sixth try, to Mark Skinner, actually went through.

"Mr. Skinner, this is Adam Lebowitz," I said. "I don't know if you remember me, but I was assistant set designer when your play *Catch the Rainbow* was at the Marquis. I'm the one —"

"Oh, sure," he interrupted. "You're the one who came up with that rotating chandelier/staircase gizmo, weren't you? That was a snazzy trick — tell you the truth, I was damned if I could see how that was going to work when I wrote it into the play. So what's up?"

"I'm currently attached to the State Department group in charge of escorting the Fuzhtian ambassador around," I said. "We're —"

"Oh, yeah, sure — Lebowitz. Yeah, I remember seeing you in the background in one of those TV shots. Couldn't place you at the time — that was you in the brown suit and Fedora sort of thing, right? Sure. So what's up?"

"The ambassador wants to be in a Broadway play," I told him. "We need you to write it for him."

There was a long silence. "You what?"

"We need you to write a play for him," I repeated.

"Ah," he said. "Uh . . . yeah. Well . . . can he act?"

"I don't know," I said. "Oh, and the only translator he brought with him prints everything he says in rebus pictures."

"Uh-*huh*. And you're sure he really wants to do this?"

"We think so. He climbed up on the stage at the St. James tonight and started singing from 'How to Succeed.' "

Mark digested that. "So you're wanting a musical?"

"I don't think it really matters," I said. "Fuzhtian singing voices seem to be the same as their speaking ones, except a lot louder. Might help with stage projection, but otherwise it's not going to make much difference."

"Yeah," Mark said. "And how loud can you make a rebus, anyway? Sure, I'll take a crack at it. How soon do you need this?"

I looked at Fogerty. "He says sure, and how soon."

"Tell him two days."

I goggled. "What?"

"Two days." Fogerty gestured impatiently at the phone. "Go on, tell him."

I swallowed. "Mr. Fogerty, the head of the delegation, says he needs it in two days."

I don't remember Mark's response to that exactly. I do know it lasted nearly five minutes, covered the complete emotional range from incredulity to outrage and back again, tore apart in minute detail Fogerty's heritage, breeding, intelligence, integrity, and habits, and never once used a single swear word. Playwrights can be truly awesome sometimes.

Finally, he ran down. "Two days, huh?" he said, sounding winded but much calmer. "Okay, fine, he's on. You want to tell him what it's going to cost?"

He quoted me a number that would have felt right at home in a discussion of the national debt. I relayed it to Fogerty and had the minor satisfaction of seeing him actually pale a little. For a second I thought he was going to abandon the whole idea, but he obviously realized he wouldn't do any better anywhere else. So with a pained look on his face he gave a single stiff nod. "He says OK," I told Mark.

"Fine," Mark said, all brisk business now. "I'll have it ready in forty-eight hours. Incidentally, I trust you realize how utterly insane this whole thing is."

Privately, I agreed with him. Publicly, though, I was a company man now. "The Fuzhties have a great deal to offer humanity," I told him.

"I hope you're right," he grunted. "So where do you want the play delivered?"

The next two days were an incredible haze of whirlwind chaos. While Fogerty and a skeleton crew escorted the ambassador on a tour of New York, the rest of us worked like maniacs to organize his theatrical debut. There was a theater to hire on a couple of days' notice — no mean feat on Broadway — a complete stage crew to assemble, a casting agent to retain for whatever other parts Mark wrote into this forty-eight-hour wonder, and a hundred other details that needed to get worked out.

To my quite honest astonishment, they all did. We got the Richard Rodgers theater hired for an off-hours matinee, the backstage personnel fell into line like I'd never seen happen, and Mark got his play delivered within two hours of his promised deadline.

The play was a masterpiece in its own unique way: an actual, coherent story completely cobbled together from famous scenes and lines from other plays and movies. Fogerty nearly had an apoplectic fit when he saw it, wondering at the top of his lungs why he should be expected to pay a small fortune for what was essentially a literary retread. I calmed him down by pointing out that (A) this would allow an obvious entertainment buff like the ambassador to learn his lines with a minimum of rehearsal time, which would get this whole thing over with more quickly and enable us to get out of our overpriced Manhattan hotel and back to the overpriced Washington hotel which the government already had a lease on; and (B) that Mark had even managed to choose scenes and lines that should translate reasonably well on the RebuScope, which would help make the show at least halfway intelligible for the audience. Eventually, Fogerty cooled down.

We met at nine sharp the next morning for the first rehearsal . . . and, as I should have expected, ran full-bore into our first roadblock.

"What's the problem now?" Fogerty demanded, hovering over Angus like a neurotic mother bird.

"I don't know," Angus replied. "It's the same message that started this whole thing: 'I want to be in a Broadway play.' "

"So he's in one," Fogerty bit out, throwing a glare up at the brightly lit stage. The ambassador was standing motionless in the center, repeating the same message over and over, while the other actors and crew stood nervously watching him, most of them from what they obviously hoped was a safe distance. News of the St. James incident had clearly gotten around.

"I know that, sir," Angus said calmly. "Perhaps he doesn't understand the concept of rehearsals."

Fogerty trotted out the next in line of his exotic curses, sharing this one between the RebuScope and the ambassador himself. "Then you'd better try to explain it to him, hadn't you?"

Angus stood up. "I'll try, sir."

"Wait a minute," I said suddenly, leaning over Angus's shoulder. "That doesn't say 'I want to be *in* a Broadway play.' It says 'I want to *be* a Broadway play.' "

"What?" Fogerty leaned over Angus's other shoulder.

"There's no 'in' in the message," I explained, pointing. "See? 'Eye w-ant to —' "

"I see what it says," Fogerty snapped. "So what the hell does it mean?"

Angus craned his head to look at me. "Are you suggesting . . . ?"

"I'm afraid so," I said, nodding soberly. "He wants to be a Broadway play. The *whole* Broadway play."

There was a moment of shocked silence in which the only sound was the ambassador's rumbling. "He must be joking," Fogerty choked out at last. "He can't do a one-man show."

"Would it be any more incomprehensible to an audience than what we've already got planned?" Angus pointed out heavily. "None of this really makes any sense in the first place."

Fogerty turned a glare on me. "I am not," he said, chewing out each word, "mortgaging the White House to pay for another play."

"The Fuzhties have a great deal to offer humanity," I reminded him. "If we don't keep him happy —"

"I am not," he repeated, gazing unblinkingly at me, "paying for another play."

I looked up at the stage, trying to think. A one-man play. . . . "Well, then, we'll just have to use this one," I said slowly. "The ambassador's already got the lion's share of the lines. If we just take the other actors off the stage . . ."

"Rear-project them, maybe?" Angus offered. "Like — like what?"

"Like they're all part of a dream," I said. "The whole thing can be done as a monologue: his reminiscences of life on the stage."

"You're both crazy," Fogerty said. But there was a thoughtful tone in his voice, the tone of someone who has exactly one straw to grasp at and is trying to figure out where to get the best grip on it. "You think you could do the rewrite, Lebowitz?"

I shrugged. "You'd do better to see if Mark would — but if you'd rather, I could probably handle it," I corrected hastily at the sudden glint in his eye. "But it would take some time."

"You've got three hours," he said, snapping his fingers and gesturing his secretary over to us. "Lee can handle the typing and other paperwork — you concentrate on being creative."

It turned out to be easier than I'd expected to convert the play down to a one-man format, and I still sometimes wonder if Mark deliberately designed it with that possibility lurking in the back of his coffee-soaked mind. Still, the whole job took nearly four hours, and Fogerty was about ready to climb the scrims by the time Lee and I emerged from the basement dressing room where we'd been working.

"Took your sweet time about it," he growled, snatching the sheaf of paper.

"You want it good or you want it fast?" I quoted the old line.

"I want it fast," he retorted, rifling through the pages. "Who's going to know from 'good' on this thing anyway? Come on."

He led the way onto the stage, where the ambassador was bellowing at the top of his lungs. Singing, Fuzhtie style. Vaguely, I wondered which musical he was doing this time. "While you two were twiddling your thumbs down there, we got a sort of rear projection system put together," Fogerty told us. "That'll take care of the other actors — excuse me; the *extras*. The bad news is that we've only got a couple of hours now before we have to clear out for today."

"That should be enough time for a run-through," I said. "And the ambassador seems to be a quick study. Let's try it."

We did, and he was. But even more than that: if Angus was interpreting the RebuScope messages correctly, he absolutely loved the play. We got all the way through it and were five pages into a second reading when the stage manager arrived to kick us out.

The ambassador didn't want to leave, of course, and seemed quite prepared to make a major diplomatic incident out of it. Fortunately, Fogerty had anticipated this one and had already arranged to rent one of our hotel's ballrooms so that we could continue the rehearsal over there. The ambassador acceded with what I thought was uncharacteristic good grace, and we all trooped back. For a long time after that, through the wee hours of the morning, you could hear his dulcet singing tones from everywhere near the ballroom, as well as from certain portions of two other floors. Rumors that he could also be heard in Brooklyn were apparently unfounded.

We had one more day of rehearsals, and then it was opening night. Opening afternoon. Whatever.

I'd been too busy the past few days to get around to wondering exactly what Fogerty was going to do about an audience. I suppose I was assuming he would simply round up the members of the local Federal employees' unions — and any other warm bodies he could find — and plop them down in theater seats, at direct gunpoint if necessary.

Nothing could have been farther from the truth. New York Mayor Grenoble and half the city council had turned out to see the play, along with several high-ranking members of the governor's office, and even the Vice President and a Secret Service contingent. The rest of the theater was packed with playwrights, actors, and your basic upper-crust New York intelligentsia. Somehow, Fogerty had managed to get this billed as The Event Of The Season, and no one who considered himself a theater aficionado was about to miss it. Under the circumstances, I wasn't surprised to learn Fogerty was also charging them $150 apiece.

They finished filing in, settled into their seats, and stopped rattling their programs. The house lights dimmed, the curtain went up, and the play started.

And to my utter surprise and endless relief, it was great.

I don't mean the ambassador was great as an actor. His Fuzhtian expressions and body language — if he had any — were completely opaque to the human audience. His singing voice as already noted was merely a much louder version of his speaking voice, and his speaking voice itself was no great shakes to begin with. Mark's play wasn't particularly impressive, either, though I have no doubt that it was the best Broadway play ever conceived and

171

written in under fifty hours.

Yet in some weird and inexplicable way, it all worked. What the ambassador lacked in acting ability he more than made up in sheer raw stage presence; his inability to sing his way out of a laundry sack created a strangely effective Yin/Yang with the rear-projected background singers; and over and through it all was woven the unceasing and surrealistic flow of pictures from the RebuScope.

And when it was over, they gave him a standing ovation.

"Well," Fogerty said, watching from the wings as the ambassador lumbered out for his fourth curtain call. "Thank God that's over."

"Yes," I agreed, watching the ambassador do the Fuzhtian version of a bow, which to me looked more like a seriously deformed curtsy. "It was fun while it lasted."

Fogerty gave me a look which would probably have been one of his famous glares if he'd had any emotional energy left to glare with. "You must be joking."

"No, really," I insisted. "It felt good to be on Broadway again. I hadn't realized how much I'd missed it."

"Missed the fawning and applause, you mean," he countered. Glares were out, but he could still handle snide. "Well, better tuck the greasepaint back in your suitcase. Time for you to go back to being anonymous again."

"I'm not so sure about that, Mr. Fogerty," Angus said, coming up to Fogerty's side and showing us his RebuScope monitor. "Here's what the ambassador said right after his second curtain call."

"At least it doesn't have the word 'Broadway' in it,"

Fogerty grunted. "You have a translation yet?"

"I'm not sure," Angus said. "It seems to be 'eye w-ant to go on street.' "

I sucked in my breath. "That's not *street*," I said carefully. "It's *road*."

Fogerty frowned at me. " 'Go on road'? What in hell does that — ?"

And then, suddenly, he got it. But to my amazement, his face actually brightened. "On the *road*," he said. "He wants to take the play *on the road*."

I threw Angus a look, saw my same surprise mirrored there. Fogerty, actually happy about this?

"No, I'm not having a breakdown," Fogerty assured us. "We'll take it on the road, all right. But this play is too good to waste on humans. We're going to take it to the *Fuzhtian* worlds."

He smiled with brittle slyness. "And along the way, I expect we'll finally get a look at some of this wonderful Fuzhtian technology we've been dying to see."

He gestured across the backstage to Lee. "Start getting everything organized," he called over the applause from out front. "We're taking this show on the road."

And we did. For three months we slogged across space in the ambassador's starship, stopping at star after star, planet after planet, theater after theater. Setting up, watching the ambassador play to packed houses, tearing down, and moving on again.

For the rest of the crew and me it was a lot of work, though fundamentally not a lot different than doing a tour back in the States. Fuzhtian worlds — and there were a *lot* of them — each had their own peculiar odors and sounds and colors and climates; but when you get right down to it roast *glimprik* and mixed *colfia* vegetables tasted about the same everywhere you go.

For Fogerty and the tech boys in the entourage, though, this tour was hog heaven. Every little gadget that fell into their hands, no matter how small or seemingly insignificant by Fuzhtian standards, had them salivating for hours as they carefully took it apart to see if they could figure out how it worked. In those three months they must have filled forty notebooks and at least that many multi-gigabyte CD-ROMs. Fogerty looked simultaneously more harried and more excited than I'd ever seen him, continually speculating about what we'd learn when we were able to get a look at their *really* interesting stuff. Unbelievable as it would have seemed to me when I first joined the group, the man was actually becoming a pleasure to be with.

And he was like that right up until the other shoe finally dropped.

I knew something was wrong the instant Angus sat down at my breakfast table and I got a look at his face. "What is it?" I asked, my *courf* melon cubes suddenly forgotten. "What's wrong?"

"Have you seen Mr. Fogerty?" he asked, his voice under rigid control.

"I don't think he's up yet — he and the tech boys were working late on that aroma-making gadget," I said. "What's wrong?"

Angus turned his head to gaze out the window at the Fuzhtian city stretching out beneath our hotel. "We were wrong, Mr. Lebowitz," he said quietly. "Our Broadway star here wasn't an ambassador at all. Not really. He was —" He waved a hand helplessly. "He was a penguin."

I set down my fork. "A penguin?" I asked carefully.

"Oh, not a real penguin, of course," he said. "That's just the image that jumped to mind." He sighed and looked back at me. "You've seen the nature specials. Seen all those penguins gathering at the edge of an ice floe in their little black and white tuxedos, flapping their flippers, all set to start hunting for breakfast. Do you remember why they don't all just jump in and get on with it?"

I glanced down at my own breakfast. "I must have missed that episode."

"It's because they're not the only ones on the hunt." Angus picked up my fork and began absently stirring the *courf* cubes in my dish. "There may be killer whales or other predators lurking under the surface, you see. So you know what the penguins do?"

"Tell me."

He stirred the cubes a little more vigorously. "They all keep jostling together on the edge until one of them gets jostled enough to fall into the water." He flicked the fork, and one of my cubes flipped up over the edge of the dish and landed on the table. "If nothing eats him," he said, gazing down at the cube, "the rest know it's safe to start going about the day's business."

I gazed at the piece of melon, watching the juice ooze onto the table. "All right," I said slowly. "So the ambassador was pushed into the water. But I'd have thought that we've treated him pretty well. Certainly no one's tried to eat him."

Angus snorted. "Oh, we treated him well, all right. We treated him too damn well. He's done it, he's lived through it . . . and now they all want to do it, too."

"Do what?" I asked, frowning. "Come to Earth?"

He looked up at me with a haunted expression. "No," he said. "Star in a Broadway play."

I felt my jaw fall open. "*All* of them?"

He nodded. "*All* of them."

175

We're on the last leg of the ambassador's tour now — two more planets, fifteen more shows, and then our ship will be heading back to Earth. Our ship, and two hundred more following right behind us. Packed to the gills with eager, star-struck Fuzhties.

I don't know what the White House and UN officials said to Fogerty when he broke the news to them. I know that when he came out of the ambassador's communication room he had the grim look of a man who's just watched his career crash in ruins, in glorious full-color slow motion.

Still, he may yet be able to pull this off. Assuming the officials accepted our suggestions, there should be hordes of workmen at this very moment scurrying around the Gobi, the Sahara, the Australian Outback, and a dozen other of the remotest places on earth. Building a hundred exact movie-lot-style replicas of Broadway for the Fuzhties to perform on. With luck, they'll all be ready by the time we get back. If not, the real Broadway will never be the same again.

They say the Fuzhties have a great deal to offer humanity. They had better be right.

Star Song

The woman was somewhere in her mid-fifties, I estimated, wearing a lower-middle-class blue-green jacket suit and a professional scarf of a style I didn't recognize. In one hand she held a boarding ticket; with the other she balanced the inexpensive and slightly scuffed carrybag slung over her shoulder. Her hair was dark, her features unreadable, and her stride, as she toiled up the steep gangplank toward me, stiffly no-nonsense with an edge of disdain.

In short, she looked like any of the thousands of business types I'd seen in hundreds of spaceports across the Expansion. She certainly didn't look like trouble.

But that's always the way with life, isn't it? It's right when everything's going along nice and smooth and you're all relaxed and bored that you suddenly discover that you're in fact eighty degrees off course with a dead stick, straked engines, and a comatose musicmaster.

And everything right then was indeed going along nice and smooth. The flight deck had been showing flat green when I'd left three minutes earlier, Rhonda had the engines running at peak efficiency — or at least what passed for peak efficiency with those rusty superannuates — and Jimmy, while his usual annoying self, was very much awake.

And yet, if I'd been paying better attention, I might have wondered a little as I watched the woman approaching me. Might have seen that her completely ordinary exterior wasn't quite matched by the way she walked.

The way she walked and, as I quickly found out, the way

she talked. "I'm Andrula Kulasawa," she announced to me in a no-nonsense voice that matched the stride. It was a voice that sounded very much like it was accustomed to being listened to. "I'm booked on your transport; here's my ticket."

"Yes, Angorki Tower just informed me," I said, popping the plastic card into my reader and glancing at it. "I'm Jake Smith, Ms. Kulasawa, captain of the *Sergei Rock*. Welcome aboard."

A flicker of something touched her face — amusement, perhaps, at the pilot of a humble Class 8 star transport calling himself a captain. "Captain," she said, nodding her head microscopically as a hooked finger pulled the scarf away from her throat. "And it's *Scholar* Kulasawa."

"My apologies," I said, hearing my voice suddenly go rigid as I stared at the neckpiece that had been concealed behind the nondescript scarf.

And if the walk and voice hadn't made me wonder, that should have. Scholars were one of the most elite of the upper/professional classes, and I'd never seen one yet who wouldn't freeze his or her throat in winter rather than wear something that would cover up that glittering professional badge. "The, uh, the Tower didn't —"

"Apology accepted," she said, her tone somehow managing to carry the message that it was her graciousness, not my worthiness, that was letting me off the hook for my unintended social gaffe. "Has my equipment been loaded aboard yet?"

"Equipment?" I asked, throwing a glance down the gangplank behind her. There was no other luggage there that I could see.

"It's not back there," she said, an edge of strained patience in her voice now. "I have two Size Triple-F

Monshten crates back at the loading ramp. Research equipment for my work on Parex. It's on the ticket."

I looked at my reader again. It was there, all right. "I didn't know, but I'll see to it right away," I promised, stepping back and gesturing her through the hatchway. "In the meantime, may I help you get settled?"

"I'll manage," she said, twitching the carrybag away as I reached for it. "Where is my seat?"

"The passenger cabin is aft — back that way," I told her. "First hatchway on the left."

"I *do* know what 'aft' means, thank you," she said shortly, brushing past me and disappearing down the passageway.

I heard her carrybag scraping against the wall as she maneuvered her way down the narrow corridor. But she didn't call for assistance, so I just sealed the outer hatchway and headed straight up to the flight deck.

The cramped room was empty when I arrived, but a glance at the status board showed the cargo hatch was still open. That would be where my copilot would be. Dropping into the pilot's seat, I keyed the intercom for the cargo bay. "Yo, Bilko," I called. "How's it going?"

"Coming along nicely," First Officer Will Hobson's voice replied. "Got all the power lifters aboard, and it looks like we'll have room for most of that gourmet food, too."

"Well, don't start figuring the profit per cubic meter yet," I warned. "Our passenger has a couple of Triple-F Monshtens on the way."

"She has *what?*" he demanded, and I could picture his jaw dropping. "What is she, a rock sculptor?"

"Close," I said. "She's a scholar."

"So what, she's shipping her lecture hall to Parex?"

"I haven't the foggiest what she's shipping," I told him.

179

"You're welcome to ask her if you want."

He snorted, a noise that sounded like a bad connection somewhere in the circuit. "No, thanks," he said. "I had my fill of the scholar class on Barsimeon."

"Let me guess. Card tournament?"

"Dice, actually. And man, those scholars are real poor losers. Wait a minute — here come her Monshtens now. Triple-F's, all right. Let's see . . . code imprint says it's Class-I electronics. Your basic off-the-shelf consumer stuff."

That did seem odd. "Maybe she's running a holotape business on the side," I suggested.

Bilko snorted again. "Or else she's bringing a podium sound system she could lecture in the Grand Canyon with," he said.

Days afterward, I would remember that line. Right then, though, it just sounded like Bilko's usual brand of smart-mouthing. "What she's got in her luggage is none of our business," I reminded him. "Just get it aboard and secured, all right?"

"If you insist," he said with a theatrical sigh.

"I insist," I said, keying off. Bilko, I had long ago concluded, was privately convinced he'd been switched at birth with some famous stage actor, and he seldom if ever passed up a chance to get in some practice in his might-have-been profession. Personally, I'd always considered those attempts to be a continual reminder of the great contribution the hypothetical baby-switcher's action had made to live theater.

I keyed the intercom to the engine room. "Rhonda?"

"Right here," Engineer Rhonda Blankenship's voice came. "We in pre-flight yet?"

"Just started," I told her. "Engines up and running?"

"Ticking like a fine Swiss clock," she reported. "Or like

180

a mad Bolshevik's bomb. Take your pick."

"You're such a joy and comfort to have around," I growled. She'd been after me for years to get new engines or at least have the old ones extensively overhauled. "You might be interested to know we have a professional passenger aboard. A scholar."

"You're kidding," she said. "What in space is a scholar doing here?"

"Probably a study on the struggles of lower/working-class star transports," I told her. "No, actually, it's probably out of necessity. The Tower said she needed to get to Parex right away, and we were the only scheduled transport for the next nine days."

"What, all the liners running full today?"

"The liners don't take Monshten Triple-Fs as check-on luggage," I said. "And don't ask me what's in them, because I don't know."

"I wasn't going to," she assured me. "If they look at all interesting, Bilko will figure out a way into them."

"He'd better not even think it," I warned. As far as I knew, Bilko had never actually stolen anything from any of our cargoes, but one of these days that insatiable curiosity of his was going to skate him over the edge.

"If he asks, I'll tell him you said so," Rhonda promised.

"If he asks, it'll be a first," I growled. "You just concentrate on getting us into space without popping any more preburn sparkles than you have to, OK? Sending a middle-aged scholar screaming to the lifepods wouldn't be good for business."

"At our end of the food chain, I doubt anyone would even notice," she said dryly. "But if you insist, OK."

I keyed off, and spent the next few minutes running various pre-flight checks. And finding ways to stall off the inevitable moment when I'd have to head back and talk to our musicmaster, Jimmy Chamala, about the details of our jump to Parex.

It wasn't that I didn't like the kid. Not really. It was just that he *was* a kid, barely past his nineteenth birthday, and as such was inevitably full of the half-brained ideas and underbaked worldly wisdom that had irritated me even when I was a teenager myself. Add to that the fact that the musicmaster was the single most indispensable person aboard the *Sergei Rock* — and we all knew it — and you had a recipe for cocky arrogance that would practically find its own way to the oven.

To be fair, Jimmy tried. And to be even more fair, I probably didn't try hard enough. But even with him trying not to spout nonsense, and me trying not to point out what nonsense it was, we still had a knack for rubbing each other the wrong way.

Fortunately, by the time I finished the pre-flight — thereby running out of delaying tactics — Bilko called to say that the cargo was aboard and the hold secured. I called the Tower, found that our efficiency had gotten us bumped to three-down in the lift list, and gave the general strap-in order. Once we were in space, there would be plenty of time to go see Jimmy.

We lifted to orbit — without popping even a single preburn sparkle, amazingly enough — dropped the booster for the port tuggers to retrieve, and headed for deep space.

And now, unfortunately, it *was* time to go see Jimmy.

"Double-check that we're on the Parex vector," I told Bilko, maneuvering carefully past the banks of controls and status lights in the slightly disorienting effect of the false-grav. The fancier freighters with their variable-volume speakers and delimitation plates could handle some limited post-wrap steering, but we had to be already running in the direction we wanted to go. "I'll see if Jimmy's ready yet."

"Right-o," Bilko said, already busy at his board. "Be sure to remind him we're running heavy today. Probably need at least a Green, maybe even a Blue."

"Right."

I headed down the corridor past the passenger cabin, noting the closed hatchway and wondering if our esteemed scholar might be having a touch of *mal de faux-g*. I could almost hope she was; in a Universe of oppressively strict class distinctions, nausea remained as one of the great social levelers.

Still, if she missed the bag, I was the one who'd have to clean it up. All things considered, I decided to hope she wasn't sick. Passing her hatchway, I continued another five meters aft and turned into the musicmaster's cabin.

I've already mentioned that Jimmy was a kid of nineteen. What I haven't mentioned was all the irritating peripherals that went along with that. His hair, for one thing, which hadn't been cut for at least five planets, and the mostly random tufts of scraggly facial fuzz he referred to in all seriousness as a beard. In a profession that seemed to take a perverse pride in its lack of a dress code, his wardrobe was probably still a standout of strange taste, consisting today of a flaming pais-plaid shirt that had been out of style for at least ten years and a pair of faded jeans that looked like they'd started their fade ten years before that. His official musicmaster scarf clashed violently with the shirt, and was sloppily knotted besides. His shoes, propped up on the corner of his desk, were indescribable.

As usual, he twitched sharply as I swung around the hatchway into view. Rhonda had mostly convinced me it was nothing more than the fact that he was always too pre-occupied to hear me coming, but I couldn't completely shake the feeling that the twitch was based on guilt. Though what specifically he might feel guilty about I didn't know. "Captain," he said, the word coming out halfway between a startled statement and a startled gasp. "I was just working up the program."

"Yeah," I said, throwing a look at the shoes propped up on the desk and then deliberately looking away. He knew I didn't like him doing that, but since it was his desk and there were no specific regulations against it he'd long since decided to make it a point of defiance. I'd always suspected Bilko of egging him on in that, but had never uncovered any actual proof of it. "Did First Officer Hobson send you the mass numbers?"

"Yes, sir," Jimmy said. "I was thinking we ought to go with a Blue, just to be on the safe side."

"Sounds good," I grunted, carefully not mentioning that a Blue meant Romantic Era or folk music, both of which I preferred to the Baroque or Classical Era that we would need to attract a Green. It wouldn't do for Jimmy to think he was doing me a favor; he'd just want something in return somewhere down the line. "What have you got planned?"

"I thought we'd start with the Brahms Double Concerto," he said, raising his reader from his lap and peering at his list. "That's thirty-two point seven eight minutes. Dvorak's Carnival Overture will add another nine point five two, the Saint-Saens Organ Symphony will clock in at thirty-two point six seven, and the Berlioz Requiem will add seventy-six minutes even. Then we'll go to Grieg's Peer Gynt at forty-eight point three, the Mendelssohn Violin Concerto at twenty-four point two four, and Massenet's Scenes Alsaciennes at twenty-two point eight two."

He probably thought that throwing the numbers at me rapid-fire like that would have me completely lost. If so, he was in for a disappointment. "I read that as four hours six point three three minutes," I said. "You're six minutes overdue for a break."

"Oh, come on," he said scornfully. "I can handle an extra six minutes."

"The rules say four hours, max, and then a half-hour break," I countered. "You know that."

"The rules were invented by senile old conservatory professors who could barely stay *awake* for four hours," he shot back. "I did eight hours straight once back at OSU — I can sure do four hours six."

"I'm sure you can," I said. "But not on *my* transport. Change the program."

"Look, *Captain* —"

"Change the program," I cut him off. Spinning around, I strode out the hatchway and headed back down the corridor, seething silently to myself. Now he was going to have to find something else to fill in the last part of the program; and knowing Jimmy, he'd try to run it right up to the four-hour limit. Finding the right piece of music would take time; and in this business, time was most definitely money.

I was still seething when I reached the flight deck. "How's the vector?" I demanded, squeezing past Bilko to my seat.

"Looks clean," he said, throwing me a sideways look as I sat down. "Trouble with Jimmy?"

"No more than usual," I growled, jabbing my main display for a status review. "How close to time margin are we running?"

He shrugged. "Not too bad —"

"Bilko?" Jimmy's voice came over the intercom. "I'm ready to go."

Bilko looked at me, raised his eyebrows. I waved disgustedly at the intercom — I sure didn't want to talk to him. "OK, Jimmy," Bilko told him. "Go ahead."

"Right. Here we go."

The intercom keyed off. "What was that about the time margin?" Bilko asked.

"Never mind," I gritted. The damn kid must have had an alternative program figured out and ready to go before I even got there. Which meant the whole argument had been nothing more than him pushing me on the time rule, just to see if I'd bend. No absolutes; no rules; do whatever works or whatever you can get away with. Typical underbaked juvenile nonsense.

A deep C-sharp note sounded, and I felt my chair shaking slightly as the hull vibrated with the pre-music call. I shifted my attention to the forward viewport, staring unblinkingly out at the distant stars, and waited. Ten seconds later the C-sharp was replaced by the opening notes of the Brahms Double Concerto —

And with breathtaking suddenness the stars vanished.

I looked back down at my control board, disappointment mixing into my already irritated mood. Only once had I ever actually seen a flapblack as it came in, and I'd been trying ever since to repeat the experience. Not this time.

"We've got a good wrap," Bilko reported, peering at his displays. "Inertial confirms four point six one light-years per hour."

"Definitely a Blue, then."

"Or a real slow Green," Bilko said. "Computer's still running the spectrum."

I nodded, listening to the music and gazing out at the nothingness outside. And marveling as always at this strange symbiosis that humanity had found.

They were called flapblacks. Not a very imaginative name, and one which subsequent study had shown to be inaccurate anyway, but it had stuck now for five decades and there was no reason to assume it would ever get changed to something better. The first crew to run into one of the things had overscrubbed their meager sensor data until the creature had looked like a giant pancake shape wrapping itself around their ship and blocking off the starlight.

At which point, to their stunned amazement, it had picked up their ship and moved it.

As far as I knew, we still didn't have the faintest idea how the flapblacks did what they did. The idea that an essentially insubstantial being that apparently lived its entire life in deep space could physically carry multiple tons of star transport across multiple light-years at rates of up to five light-years per hour was utterly absurd. We didn't know what they were made of, how they lived, what they ate, what else they did, how they reproduced, or how many of them per cubic light-year there were. In fact, when you boiled it down, there was virtually only one thing we *did* know about them.

And that was that they loved music. All kinds of music: modern, classical, folk melodies, Gregorian chants — you name it, some flapblack out there loved it. Play a clean musical tone through your hull and within seconds you'd have flapblacks crowding around like seagulls at a fish market. Start the music itself, and one of them would instantly wrap itself around the transport, and you'd be off for the stars.

"Spectrum's coming up," Bilko reported. "Yep — definitely a Blue."

I nodded again in acknowledgment. The flapblacks themselves showed little internal structure, and of course no actual color at all. But it hadn't taken long for someone to notice that, just as the transport was being wrapped, the incoming starlight experienced a brief moment of interference. Subsequent study had shown that the interference pattern looked and behaved like an absorption spectrum, with the lines from any given flapblack grouped together in a particular color of the spectrum.

That had been the key that had turned the original musical-shotgun approach into something more scientific. Flapblacks whose lines were in the red part of the spectrum were fairly slow, were apparently not strong enough to wrap transports above a certain mass, and came when you played musicals or opera. Orange flapblacks were faster and stronger and liked modern music — any kind — and Gregorian chants. I'd yet to figure that one out. Yellows were faster and stronger yet and liked jazz and classical rock/roll. Greens were still stronger, but now a little slower, and liked Baroque and Mozartian classical. Blues were the strongest of all, though slower than any of the others except Reds, and liked 19th century romantic and any kind of folk melody.

It was the flapblacks and their love of our music which had finally freed humanity from Sol and allowed us to stretch out to the stars. More personally, of course, space travel was what provided me with my job, for which I was mostly grateful.

The catch was that it wasn't just the music they needed. Or rather, it wasn't the music alone. Which was, unfortunately, where musicmasters like Jimmy came in.

You see, you couldn't just play the music straight for them. That would have been too easy. What you had to have was someone aboard the transport listening to the music as you pumped it out through the hull.

And not just listening; I mean *listening*. He had to sit

there doing nothing the whole time, following every note and rest and crescendo, letting his emotions swell and ebb with the flow. Basically, just really getting into the music.

The experts called it *psycho-stereo*, which like most fancy words was probably created to cover up the fact that they didn't know any more about this than they did anything else about the flapblacks. Best guess — heavy emphasis on *guess* — was that what the flapblacks actually liked was getting the music straight while at the same time hearing it filtered through a human mind. They almost certainly were getting the pre-music call telepathically — until they wrapped, there was no other way for them to pick up the sound in the vacuum of space.

However it worked, the bottom line was that I couldn't handle the job. Neither could Bilko or Rhonda. Sure, we all liked music, but we also all had other duties and responsibilities to attend to during the flight. Even if we hadn't, I doubt any of us had the kind of single-track mind that would let us do something that rigid for hours at a time. And you *had* to keep it up — one slip and your flapblack would be long gone and you'd have to stop and pull in another one.

That wasn't a problem in itself, of course; there were always flapblacks hanging around waiting to be entertained. The problem came in not knowing to the microsecond exactly how long you'd been traveling. At flapblack speeds, a second's worth of error translated into a lot of undershoot or overshoot on your target planet.

And even apart from all that, I personally still wouldn't have wanted the job. I've always considered my emotions to be my own business, and the thought of letting some alien will-o'-the-wisp listen in was right next to chewing sand on my list of things I didn't like to think about.

Enter Jimmy and the rest of the musicmaster corps. *They* were the ones who actually made star travel possible. People like Bilko, Rhonda, and me were just here to keep them alive along the way, and to handle the paperwork at the end of the trip.

It was a train of thought I'd been running along quite a lot lately, more or less beginning with our previous musicmaster's departure two months ago and Jimmy's arrival. My digestion was definitely the worse for it.

"Looks like everything's smooth here," Bilko commented, pulling his lucky deck of cards from his shirt pocket. "Quick game?"

"No, thanks," I said, looking at the cards with distaste. Considering that it purported to be a lucky deck, those cards had gotten Bilko into more trouble over the years. I'd lost track of how many times I'd had to pacify some pick-up game partner who refused to believe that Bilko's winnings were due solely to skill.

"Okay," he said equably, fanning the deck. "Want to draw cards for first turn in the dayroom, then?"

Mentally, I shook my head. For all his angling, Bilko could be so transparent sometimes. "No, you go ahead," I told him, keying in the autosystem and giving the status lights a final check. The dayroom, situated across the main corridor from the passenger cabin, was our off-duty spot. On the bigger long-range transports dayroom facilities were pretty extensive; all ours offered was stale snacks, marginal holotape entertainment, and legroom.

"Okay," he said, unstrapping. "I'll be back in an hour."

"Just be sure you spend that hour in the dayroom," I added. "Not poking around Scholar Kulasawa's luggage."

His face fell, just a bit. Just enough to show me I'd hit the target dead center. "What makes you think — ?"

The intercom beeped. "Captain Smith?" a female voice asked.

I grimaced, tapping the key. "This is Smith, Scholar Kulasawa," I said.

"I'd like to see you," she said. "At your earliest convenience, of course."

A nice, polite, upper-class phrase. Completely meaningless here, of course; what she meant was *now*. "Certainly," I said. "I'll be right there."

I keyed off the intercom and looked at Bilko. "You see?" I told him. "She read your mind. The upper classes can do that."

"I wouldn't put it past them," he grumbled, strapping himself back down. "I hope your bowing and cringing is up to par."

"I guess I'll find out," I said, getting up. "If I'm not back in twenty minutes, dream up a crisis or something, will you?"

"I thought you said she could read minds."

"I'll risk it."

Scholar Kulasawa was waiting when I arrived in our nine-person passenger cabin, sitting in the center seat in a stiff posture that reminded me somehow of old portraits of European royalty. "Thank you for being so prompt, Captain," she said as I stepped inside. "Please sit down."

"Thank you," I said automatically, as if being allowed to sit in my own transport was something I needed her permission to do. Swiveling one of the other seats around to face her, I sat down. "What can I do for you?"

"How much is your current cargo worth?" she asked.

I blinked. "What?"

"You heard me," she said. "I want to know the full value of your cargo. And add in all the shipping fees and any nondelivery penalties."

What I should have done — what my first impulse was to do — was find a properly respectful way to say it was none of her business and get back to the flight deck. But the sheer unexpectedness of the question froze me to my seat. "Can you tell me why that information should be any of your business?" I asked instead.

"I want to buy out this trip," she said calmly. "I'll pay all associated costs, including penalties, add in your standard fee for the side trip I want to make, and throw in a little something extra as a bonus."

I shook my head. "I'm sorry to disappoint you, Scholar," I said, "but this run is already spoken for. If you want to charter a special trip at Parex, I'm sure you'll be able to find a transport willing to take you."

She favored me with a smile that didn't have a single calorie of warmth anywhere in it. "Meaning you wouldn't take me?"

"Meaning if you wish to discuss it after we've offloaded at Parex I'll be willing to listen," I said, standing up. I had it now: her scholarhood was in psychology, and this was all part of some stupid study on bribery and ethics. "But thank you for the offer —"

"I'll pay you three hundred thousand neumarks," she said, the smile gone now. "Cash."

I stared at her. The power lifters and gourmet food we were carrying were worth maybe two hundred thousand, max, with everything else adding no more than another thirty. Which left the little bonus she'd mentioned at somewhere around seventy thousand neumarks.

Seventy thousand neumarks . . .

"You don't think I'm serious," she went on into my sudden silence, reaching into her jacket and pulling out what looked like a pre-paid money card. "Go on," she invited, holding it out toward me. "Check it."

Carefully, suspiciously, I reached out and took the card. Pulling out my reader, I slid it in.

As the owner of a transport plying some of the admittedly less-than-plum lanes, I had long ago decided that buying cut-rate document software would ultimately cost me more than it would save. Consequently, I'd made sure that the *Sergei Rock*'s legal and financial authenticators were the best that money could buy.

Scholar Kulasawa's money card was completely legitimate. And it did indeed have three hundred thousand neumarks on it.

"You must be crazy to carry this around," I told her, pulling the card out of my reader as if it was made of thousand-year-old crystal. "Where in the worlds did you get this kind of money, anyway?"

"From my university, of course. No — keep it," she added, waving the card back as I held it out to her. "I prefer payment in advance."

With a sigh, I stood up and set the card down on the seat next to her. Seventy thousand neumarks . . . "I already told you this trip's been contracted for," I said. "Talk to me when we reach Parex." I turned to go —

"Wait."

I turned back. For a moment she studied my face, with something that might have been grudging admiration in her expression. "I misjudged you," she said. "My apologies. Allow me to try a different approach."

I shook my head. "I already said —"

"Would you accept my offer," she cut me off, "if it would also mean helping people desperately in need of our assistance?"

I shook my head. "The Patrol's got an office on Parex," I

said. "You want help, talk to them."

"I can't." Her carefully jeweled lip twisted, just slightly. "For one thing, they have no one equipped to deal with the situation. For another, if I called them in they'd take it over and shut me out completely."

"Shut you out of what?"

"The credit, of course," she said, her lip twisting again. "That's what drives the academic world, Captain: the politely savage competition for credit and glory and peer recognition." She eyed me again. "It would be so much easier if would trust me. Safer, too, from my point of view. If this should get out . . ." She took a deep breath, still watching me, and let it out in a rush. "But if it's the only way to get your cooperation, then I suppose that's what I have to do. Tell me, have you ever heard of the *Freedom's Peace?*"

"Sounds vaguely familiar," I said, searching my memory. "Is it a star transport?"

She snorted gently. "You might say it was the ultimate star transport," she said dryly. "The *Freedom's Peace* was one of the five Giant Leap ark ships that headed out from the Jovian colonies 130 years ago."

"Oh — right," I said, feeling my face warming. Nothing like forgetting one of the biggest and most spectacular failures in the history of human exploration. The United Jovian Habitats, full of the arrogance of wealth and autonomy, had hollowed out five fair-sized asteroids, stocked them with colonists, pre-assembled ecosystems, and heavy-duty ion-capture fusion drives, and sent them blazing out of the solar system as humanity's gift to the stars.

The planetoids had stayed in contact with the home system for a while, their transmissions growing steadily weaker as the distances increased and there was more and more interstellar dust for their transmission lasers to have to punch through. Eventually, they faded out, with the last of the five going silent barely six years after their departure. The telescopes had been able to follow them for another five years or so, but eventually their drives had faded into the general starscape background.

And then had come the War of Reclamation, ruthlessly bringing the Habitats back under Earth dominion and in the process wiping out virtually all records of the Giant Leap project. By the time humanity started riding flapblacks and were finally able to go out looking for them, they had completely vanished. "Okay — the *Freedom's Peace*. What about it?"

"I've found it," she said simply.

I stared at her. "Where?"

"Out in space, of course," she said tartly. "You don't expect me to give you its exact location until you've agreed to take me there, do you?"

"But it's somewhere near Parex?" I prompted.

She eyed me closely. "It's accessible from Parex," she said. "That's all I'll say."

I pursed my lips, trying to think, listening with half an ear to the Brahms playing in the background. At least now I understood why there was so much money involved. Never mind the academic community; a historical find like this would rock the whole Expansion, from the Outer March colonies straight up to Earth and the Ten Families. Not to mention putting the discoverers permanently into the history books themselves.

Which did, however, bring up an entirely new question. "So why me?" I asked. "Your university could hire a much better transport than the *Sergei Rock* with the money you're willing to spend."

Her thin lips compressed momentarily. "There are —

competitors, shall we say — who want to reach the *Freedom's Peace* first. I know of at least one group that has been watching me."

"You're sure they don't know the location themselves?"

"I'm sure *this* group doesn't," she retorted. "But there are others, and some of them may be getting close." She waved a hand at the cabin around her. "I had to grab the first transport that was heading anywhere near it."

"But you *are* authorized to use that money card?" I asked.

She smiled coldly. "Trust me, Captain: if I succeed here, the university will gladly authorize ten times what's on that card. The historical significance of the furnishings alone will send shock waves through the Expansion. Let alone all the rest of it."

"All the rest of what?" I asked, frowning. I'd have thought the historical artifacts they would find aboard would be all there was.

"I thought I mentioned that," she said with a sort of malicious innocence. "When I asked about people needing assistance, remember? The *Freedom's Peace* isn't just drifting dead in space — it's still underway.

"Obviously, someone is still aboard."

The same rule book that said the musicmaster had to take a thirty-minute break every four hours also said that the crew was never to all be away from their posts at the same time, while in flight, except under extraordinary circumstances. I decided this qualified; and the minute Jimmy went on break, I hauled the three of them into the dayroom.

"I don't know," Bilko mused when I'd outlined Scholar Kulasawa's proposition. "The whole thing smells a little fishy."

"Which parts?" I asked.

"All parts," he said. "For one thing, I find it hard to believe this race is so tight she had to settle for a transport like the *Sergei Rock.*"

"What's wrong with the *Sergei Rock*?" I demanded, trying not to take it personally and not entirely succeeding. "We may not be fancy, but we've got a good clean record."

"And don't forget those boxes of hers," Jimmy put in. I didn't have to ask how he was leaning — he was practically bouncing in his seat with excitement over the whole thing. "She needed a transport that could carry them."

"Yes — let's not forget those boxes," Bilko countered. "Did our esteemed scholar happen to tell you what was in them?"

"She said it was her research equipment," I told him.

"That's one hell of a lot of research equipment."

"Historians and archaeologists don't make do with a magnifying glass and tweezers anymore," I said stiffly.

"Why are we all arguing here?" Jimmy put in earnestly. "I mean, if there are people out there who are lost, we need to help them."

"I don't think Scholar Kulasawa cares two sparkles about whoever's aboard," Bilko growled. "It's Columbus Syndrome — she just wants the credit for discovering the New World."

"Shouldn't it be the Old World?" Jimmy suggested.

Bilko threw him a glare. "Fine. Whatever."

I looked at Rhonda. "You've been pretty quiet," I said. "What do you think?"

"I don't think it matters what I think," she said quietly. "You're the owner and captain, and you've already made up your mind. Haven't you?"

"I suppose I have, really," I conceded. "But I don't want

to steamroll the rest of you, either. If anyone has a solid reason why we should turn her down, I want to hear it."

"I'm with you," Jimmy piped up.

"Thank you," I said patiently. "But I was asking for dissenting opinions. Bilko?"

"Just the smell of it," he said sourly. "I might have something solid if you'd let me look into those crates of hers."

I grimaced. "Compromise," I said. "You can do a materials scan and sonic deep-probe if you want. Just bear in mind that Angorki customs would have done all that and more, and apparently passed everything through without a whisper. Other thoughts?"

I looked at Rhonda, then at Bilko, then back at Rhonda. Neither looked particularly happy, but neither said anything either. Probably had decided that arguing further would be a waste of breath. "All right, then," I said after a minute. "I'll go tell Scholar Kulasawa that we're in and get the coordinates from her. Bilko and I will figure out our vector and then you, Jimmy, will work out a program. Got it? Good. Everyone back to your posts."

Kulasawa accepted the news with the air of someone who would have found it astonishing if we *hadn't* fallen properly into line behind her. The location she gave me would have been a ten-hour trip from Parex, but as it happened was only about six hours from our current position. I couldn't tell whether she was genuinely pleased by that or simply considered it another example of the Universe's moral obligation to reconfigure itself in accordance to her plans and whims.

Regardless, the distance was reasonable and the course trivial to calculate. By the time Bilko and I had the vector worked out, Jimmy was ready with several alternative programs. I got him started on a four-hour program — he argued briefly for doing the entire six hours in one gulp, but I'd already stretched the rules enough for one trip — and had him get us underway.

And then, when everything was quiet again, I headed back to the engine room to see Rhonda.

Most of the engineer's job involved the lift and landing procedures, leaving little if anything for her to do while we were in deep space. Despite that, we almost never saw Rhonda in the dayroom. She preferred to stay at her post, watching her engines, listening to Jimmy's concert in solitude, and creating the little beadwork jewelry that was her hobby.

She was working on the latter as I came in. "Thought I'd check and see how you were doing back here," I greeted her as I stepped in through the hatchway.

"Everything's fine," she assured me, looking up from her beads.

"Good," I said, stepping behind her and peering over her shoulder. The piece was only half finished, but already it looked nice. "Interesting pattern," I told her. "Good color scheme, too. What's it going to be?"

"A decorated comb," she said. "It holds your hair in place in back." She twisted her head to look thoughtfully up at me. "For those of us who have enough hair to need holding, of course."

"Funny." I came around to the front of the board and pulled down a jumpseat. "I wanted to talk to you about this little side trip we're making. You really don't like it, do you?"

"No, I don't," she said. "I have no quarrel with locating the *Freedom's Peace* or even going there, though reneging on a contract is going to damage that clean record you mentioned in the dayroom."

"I know, but we'll make it right," I promised. "Kulasawa's given us more than enough money to cover that."

"I know," Rhonda said sourly. "And that's what's really bothering me: your motivation for all of this. Altruistic noises aside, are you sure it's not just the money?"

"If you'll recall, I turned down the money when she first offered it," I reminded her.

"But was it the money or the fact you didn't know anything about the job?" she countered.

"Some of both," I had to concede. "But now that we know what we're doing —"

"Do we?" she cut me off. "Do we really? Has Scholar Kulasawa thought through — I mean *really* thought through — what she intends to do once we get there? Is she going to volunteer the *Sergei Rock* passenger cabin to take them all back to Earth? Make grandiose promises of land on Brunswick or Camaraderie or somewhere that she has no authority to make?"

She waved a hand in the general direction of the passenger cabin. "Or maybe she doesn't intend to bring them home at all. She could be planning to leave them out there like some lost rain-forest culture for her academic friends to study. Or maybe she'll organize weekly tour-groups for the public and sell tickets."

"Now you're being silly," I grumbled.

"Am I?" she countered. "Just because she's a scholar and has money doesn't mean she's got any brains, you know." She cocked her head slightly to the side. "Just how much above our expenses *is* she offering you?"

I shrugged as casually as I could. "Seventy thousand neumarks."

Her eyes widened. "Seventy *thousand?* And you *still* don't see anything wrong with this?"

"There's prestige involved here, Rhonda," I reminded her. "Prestige and academic glory. That's worth a lot more to any scholar than mere money. Remember, we know next to nothing about the Great Leap colonies — all that stuff went up in dust when the Ganymede domes were hit late in the war. We don't know what kind of astrogation system they had, how you create a stable ecosystem that compact, or even how you set about hollowing out eighteen kilometers' worth of asteroid in the first place. Scholars go nuts over that sort of thing."

"Yes, but three hundred thousand neumarks worth?"

I shrugged again. "It's the bottom line of being the ones who go down in history," I reminded her. "And remember, the Tower's own records showed that we were the only transport headed for Parex for over a week. If her competitors have their own ship, then we're her only chance to get there first."

Rhonda shook her head. "I'm sorry, but I find that utterly incomprehensible."

"Frankly, so do I," I readily admitted. "That's probably why we're not scholars."

She smiled lopsidedly. "Besides being from the wrong end of the social spectrum?"

I shrugged. "Besides that. So I guess we'll just have to concentrate on the fact we're going to be helping to rescue some people who've been marooned in space for the past century and a third."

"And hope Kulasawa isn't planning to renege on her deal if we lose the race," Rhonda warned. "I don't suppose that topic happened to come up in conversation, did it?"

"As a matter of fact, it didn't," I said slowly, feeling my forehead wrinkling. "Maybe I'd better introduce it."

"You can do that when you ask about her cargo," Rhonda suggested helpfully. "Incidentally, assuming we get it, I trust you'll be spreading that seventy-thousand bonus around equally?"

"Don't worry," I assured her, standing up and stepping to the hatchway. "What I've got in mind will benefit all of us."

"New engines, maybe?" she asked hopefully, her eyebrows lifting.

I gave her an enigmatic smile and left.

Bilko's materials scan on Kulasawa's crates was quick and not terribly informative. It revealed the presence of electronics components, some pretty hefty internal power supplies, magnetic materials, and some stretches of rather esoteric synthetic membranes. The sonic deep-probe was more interesting; from two directions on each of the crates the probe signals got bounced straight back as if from solid plates of conditioned ceramic.

Kulasawa's explanation, once I asked her, cleared up the confusion. The crates, she informed me, contained a set of industrial-quality sonic deep-probes. Though tradition said that each of the Great Leap Colonies had consisted mainly of a single large chamber hollowed out of the center of the asteroid, there was no solid evidence to back up that assumption; and if the *Freedom's Peace* proved instead to be a vast honeycomb of rooms and passages, it wouldn't be smart for us to start exploring it without first mapping out the entire network.

The first four-hour program ended, Jimmy chafed and groused his way through his regulation-stipulated break, and then we were off again. The transit time to the spot Bilko and I had calculated came out to be a shade over one hour forty-eight minutes, and Jimmy had worked up a program that nailed us there dead center on the nose.

The music stopped, the flapblack unwrapped itself, and Bilko and I gazed out the forward viewport.

At exactly nothing.

"Where is it?" Kulasawa demanded, leaning over our shoulders to look. "You said we were here."

"We're where your data took us," I said, resisting the urge to lean away from her in the cramped space. Her breath was unpleasantly warm on my cheek, and her lip perfume had clearly been applied with a larger room in mind. "We're running a check now, but —"

"My data was accurate," she snapped. From the suddenly increased heat on my cheek, I guessed she had turned a glare my direction. Fortunately, I was too busy with my board to turn and look. "If we're in the wrong place, you're the ones to blame."

"We're working on it, Scholar," Bilko soothed in the same tone of voice I'd heard him use on card partners suddenly suspicious by how deep in the hole they'd gotten themselves. "In any astrogate calculation there's a certain margin of error —"

"I don't want excuses," Kulasawa cut him off, the temperature of her voice dropping into the single digits. "I want results."

"We understand," Bilko said, unfazed. "But those results may take time." He threw her a sideways glance. "And we do need room to work."

Kulasawa was still radiating frustration, but fortunately common sense prevailed. "I'll be in the passenger cabin," she said between clenched teeth, and stalked out.

The flight deck door slid shut behind her, and Bilko and I looked across at each other. "The lady's deadly serious about this, isn't she?" Bilko commented. "I'll bet you could bargain us up a little on the deal."

"I'd say she's at least two stages past deadly," I countered. "And I think trying to shake her down for more money would be an extremely poor idea right now. Rhonda, are you listening?"

"I'm right here," Rhonda's voice came over the intercom. "I presume you've both figured out the problem, too?"

"I think so," Bilko said.

"It's obvious in hindsight," I agreed. "Her location was based on raw observational data from Zhavoronok and Meena, both of which are ten light-years away from here."

"Right," Bilko added. "Obviously, she fed us the location directly without realizing that she was looking at where the colony was ten years ago."

"You got it," I said. "Hard to believe a scholar would make such a simple error, though."

"Unless she didn't realize they were still moving," Rhonda offered.

"No, she told me they were still underway," I said. "That's how she knew there was still someone aboard, remember?"

"She's a historian," Bilko said, waving a hand in dismissal. "Or maybe an archaeologist. Probably doesn't even know what a light-year is — you know how rampant upper-class specialization is."

"And someday all of us in the tech classes will take over," Rhonda echoed the populist slogan. "Dream on. Okay, we know the problem. What's the solution?"

"Seems straightforward enough," Bilko said. "We know they were headed away from Sol system, so we figure out how much farther they could have gone in ten years and go that far along that vector."

"And how do we figure out what speed they were making?" I asked him.

"From the redshift in their drive spectrum, of course," he said. "Assuming, of course, that Kulasawa was smart enough to bring some of the actual telescopic photos with her." He smiled at me. "You can be the one to go ask for them."

I grimaced. "Thanks. Heaps."

"Don't go into grovel mode quite yet," Rhonda warned. "Even if she has photos they won't do us any good, because we don't know what the at-rest spectrum for their drive was."

"Why not?" Bilko asked, frowning at the intercom speaker. "I thought it was just a standard ion-capture drive."

"There was nothing standard about it," Rhonda told him. "You can't just scale up an ion-capture drive that way — the magnetic field instabilities will tear it apart. Even now our biggest long-range freighters are running right up to the wire. God only knows what trick the Jovians pulled to make theirs work."

"If you say so," Bilko said. "Engines aren't really my field of expertise."

"Of course." I cocked an eyebrow at him. "What was that again about rampant specialization?"

He smiled lopsidedly. "Touché," he said. "So let's hear *your* idea."

I gazed out the viewport. "We start with a focused search along the vector from Sol system," I said slowly. "Even if we don't know what the spectrum looks like, we know they can't have gotten too far away from here yet. That means the drive glow will be reasonably bright, and our astrogator ought to be able to pick up on a major star that's not supposed to be there. Right?"

"Sorry," Rhonda said. "Astrogation's not my field of expertise."

"Give it a rest, Blankenship," Bilko growled. "Assuming it's still firing hot enough to look like a major star, yes, it'll work. Then what?"

"Then we head at right angles to that direction for a small but specified distance," I said. "Say, a few A.U. Then we come back out, find the drive trail again, and get the location by straight triangulation."

"Can we do a program that short?" Rhonda asked. "Even at Blue speeds an A.U. must go by pretty fast."

"A shade under six hundredths of a second, actually," Bilko said. "And no, we can't do that directly."

"What we *can* do is run a few minutes out and almost the same number of minutes back," I added. "Some of the bigger freighters do that all the time to fine-tune their arrival position. Jimmy should have what he needs to work up that kind of program."

"We assume so, anyway," Bilko added. "But of course musicmastery isn't our field of expertise."

"Look, Bilko —"

"Play nicely, children," I said. "Bilko, get the sensors going, will you?"

The *Sergei Rock*'s sensors weren't quite up to the same ultra-high standard of quality as our legal and financial software was. But they were certainly nothing to sneer at, either — the myriad of transport regulators that swarmed like locusts across the Expansion made sure of that. And so it came as something of a surprise when, thirty minutes later, the result of our search turned up negative.

"Great," Bilko said, tapping his fingers restlessly on the

edge of his board. "Just great. *Now* what?"

"They must have turned off their drive," I said, looking over the astrogate computer's report again. "That, or else it's failed. Rhonda?"

"Seems odd that they would turn it off," Rhonda said doubtfully. "Certainly not in the middle of nowhere like this. And for it to have run 130 years and just happened to fail now would be pretty ironic."

"Yeah, but about par for the way my luck's been going," Bilko said sourly. "That last game I had on Angorki —"

"The Universe does not have it in for you personally, Bilko," Rhonda interrupted him. "Much as you'd like to think so. Jake, I'd guess it's more likely they simply changed course. If they shifted their vector even a few degrees their drive wouldn't be pointed directly at us anymore."

Abruptly, Bilko snapped his fingers. "No," he said, turning a tight grin on me. "They didn't change course. Not from *here*."

"Of course not," I said as it hit me as well. "All we need is to reprogram the searcher —"

"I'm on it," Bilko said, hands already skating across the computer board.

"Any time you two want to let me in on this, go ahead," Rhonda invited.

"We've assumed they hit this point on the way from Sol," I explained, watching over Bilko's shoulder. "But maybe they didn't. Maybe they headed out on a slightly different vector, paused to take a look at some promising system along the way, then changed course and headed out again."

"Passing through this point on an entirely different vector than the direct line from Sol," Bilko added. "OK, here it comes . . . computer says the only real possibility is Lalande 21185. That would put the vector . . . right. OK, let's try that focused search again. And keep your fingers crossed."

We didn't have to keep them crossed for very long. Three minutes later, the computer had found it.

"No doubt about it," Bilko decided. "We are definitely genius-class material."

"Don't start making laurel-leaf soup too fast," Rhonda warned. "Now, I take it, comes the tricky part?"

"You take it correctly," I said, unstrapping. "I'll go tell Kulasawa we've found her floating museum. And then go have a chat with Jimmy."

Kulasawa was elated in a grim, upper-class sort of way, managing to simultaneously imply that I should keep her better informed and that I also shouldn't waste time with useless mid-course reports. I escaped to Jimmy's cabin, wondering if maybe Bilko's suggestion of upping our price would really be unethical after all.

As Rhonda had suggested, the tricky part now began. Two successive performances of Schubert's "Erlkönig," the versions differing by exactly point five seven second gave us our triangulation point. Another reading on the *Freedom's Peace*'s drive glow, and we had them nailed at just over fifty A.U. away.

"Not exactly hauling Yellows, are they?" Bilko commented. "I mean, fifty A.U.s in ten years?"

"The engines were probably scaled for low but constant acceleration," Rhonda said. "They would have lost a lot of their velocity when they stopped to check out the Lalande system."

"Just as well for us they did," I pointed out. "If they'd been pulling a straight acceleration for the past 130 years we wouldn't have a hope in hell of matching speeds with them."

"Good point," Rhonda agreed. "Any idea what speed they *are* making?"

"As a matter of fact, I do," I said smugly, keying for the calculation I'd requested. "I took a spectrum of their drive at both our triangulation points. Because we were seeing the red-shifted light from two different angles — well, I won't bore you with the math. Suffice it to say the *Freedom's Peace* is smoking along at just under thirty kilometers a second."

"About three times Earth escape velocity," Bilko murmured. "Can the engines handle that, Rhonda?"

"No problem," she assured him. "We'll probably pop a few preburn sparkles, though. So what's the plan?"

"We'll set up a program that'll put us just a little ways ahead of them," I told her. "That way, we'll get to watch them go past us and can get exact numbers on their speed and vector."

"Provided they don't run us down," Rhonda murmured.

"They're not hardly going fast enough for that," Bilko scoffed. "Fifty A.U.s means another forward-back program, of course."

"Right," I said, nodding. "You work out the course while I go help Jimmy set it up."

"Right," he said, turning to his board. "You going to give our scholar the good news on the way to Jimmy's?"

"Let's let it be a surprise."

Fifteen minutes later we were ready to go. "Okay, Jimmy, this is it," I called toward the intercom. "Let's do it."

"Okay," he said. "Here goes Operation Reverse Columbus."

I flicked off the intercom. "Operation Reverse Columbus?" Bilko asked, cocking an eyebrow.

I shook my head as the pre-music C-sharp vibrated through the hull. "He thinks he's being cute," I said. "Just ignore him." The pre-tone ended; and as the strains of Schumann's Manfred Overture began the stars vanished, and I settled in for the short ride ahead.

A ride which turned out to be a lot shorter than I'd expected. Barely two notes into the piece, with the music still going, the stars abruptly reappeared.

"Jimmy!" I snarled his name like a curse as I grabbed for my restraints. Of all times to break his concentration and lose our flapblack —

And then my eyes flicked to the viewport . . . and my hands froze on the release.

Flashing past from just beneath us, no more than twenty kilometers away, was the *Freedom's Peace*.

And it was definitely cooking along. Even as I caught my breath it shot away from us toward the stars, its circle of six drive nozzles blazing furiously from the stern and dimming with distance —

And then, without warning, it suddenly flared into a brilliant blaze of light.

My first, horrified thought was that the colony had exploded right in front of us. My second, confused thought was that an explosion normally didn't have six neatly arranged nexus points . . . and as the six blazing circles receded in the direction the *Freedom's Peace* had been going, I finally realized what had happened. Not the how or the why, but at least the what.

On that, at least, I was ahead of Bilko. "What the hell?" he gasped.

"The music's still going," I snapped, belatedly hitting my restraint release and scrambling to my feet. "As soon as it got far enough ahead of us, we got wrapped again and caught up with it."

"We *what?* But — ?"

"But why are we unwrapping when we get close?" I ducked my head and peered out the viewport, just in time to see us do our strange little microjump and catch up with the asteroid again. "Good question. Let me get Jimmy shut down and we'll try to figure it out."

I sprinted back to his cabin, cursing the unknown bureaucrat or planning commission hotshot who'd come up with the idea of locking out the musicmaster's intercom whenever the music was playing. If these insane little wrap/unwraps were damaging my transport —

I reached the cabin and threw myself inside. Leaning back on his couch with his eyes closed and the massive headphones engulfing his head, Jimmy probably never realized anything was wrong until I slapped the cutoff switch.

At which point his reaction more than made up for it. He jolted upright like someone had applied electrodes to selected parts of his body, his eyes snapping wide open. "What — ?" he gasped, ripping off his headphones.

"We've got trouble," I told him briefly, jabbing the intercom switch. "Rhonda?"

"Here," she said. "Why have we stopped?"

"It wasn't our idea," I said. "We lost our flapblack."

"About six times in a row," Bilko put in tensely from the flight deck. "As soon as we get close enough to the *Freedom's Peace*, we lose them."

"What's going on?" a voice demanded from behind me.

I turned around. Kulasawa was standing in the open doorway, her gaze hard on me. "You heard everything we know so far," I told her. "We've lost our flapblack wrap six times now trying to get close to the *Freedom's Peace*."

Her gaze shifted to Jimmy, hardening to the consistency

211

of reinforced concrete. "It wasn't me," he protested quickly. "I didn't do anything."

"You're the musicmaster, aren't you?" she demanded.

"It's not Jimmy's fault," I put in. "It's something having to do with the *Freedom's Peace* itself."

The glare turned back to me. "Such as?"

"Maybe it's the mass," Jimmy spoke up, apparently still too young and inexperienced to know when to keep his mouth shut and pretend to be furniture. "That's why flapblacks can't get too close in to planets —"

"This is an asteroid, musicmaster," Kulasawa cut him off icily. "Not a planet."

"Yes, but —"

"It's not the mass," Kulasawa said, dismissing the suggestion with a curl of her lip. "What else?"

"It could be their drive," Rhonda suggested over the intercom. "Maybe the radiation from an ion-capture drive that big is scaring them away."

"Or else killing them," Bilko said quietly.

It was a strange, even eerie thought, but one which I think had already occurred to all of us. We knew nothing about how flapblacks lived or died, or even whether they died at all. What we *did* know is that we traveled with them, and the thought that we might have been even indirectly responsible for killing a half dozen of them was an unpleasant one for all of us.

Or at least, most of us. "Regardless of the reason, we know the result," Kulasawa said briskly. "How do we proceed, Captain?"

"Actually, the situation isn't much different from what we were expecting anyway," I said, trying to push the image of dying flapblacks from my mind. "Except that it's going to be easier than we thought to get close to the *Freedom's*

Peace. We should have gotten a good reading on their vector while we were tailgating them that way, so all we have to do now is boost our speed to match them and then get a flapblack to wrap us and get us close again."

"Even if it means killing another one of them?" Jimmy asked.

"What if it does?" Kulasawa said impatiently. "The Universe is full of the things."

"Besides which, we don't *know* it's hurting them," I added.

And immediately wished I hadn't. The expression on Jimmy's face was already somewhere between stricken and loathing; the look he now shot toward me was the sort you might give someone who'd just announced he enjoyed ripping the heads off small birds.

"Then let's get to it," Kulasawa said into the suddenly awkward silence. "We've wasted enough time out here already. You in the engine room: how long to bring us up to speed?"

"Depends on how much acceleration you want to put up with," Rhonda said, her tone a little chilly. Apparently, she wasn't happy with my comment, either. "At one *g*, we're talking an hour or so."

"You ran two *gs* lifting off Angorki," Kulasawa said.

"That was for ten minutes," I reminded her. "Not thirty."

"You're all young and healthy," she countered. "If I can handle it, so can you. Two *gs*, Captain. Get us moving."

It took Rhonda ten minutes to bring the engines up from standby, roughly the same amount of time it took Bilko and me to double-check the *Freedom's Peace*'s vector and make sure the *Sergei Rock* was configured for high acceleration.

After that came our half hour of two *gs,* unpleasant but certainly nothing any of us couldn't take.

More unpleasant was the subtle but definite chill I could feel all around me. Orders were scrupulously obeyed and reports properly given, but all of it in crisp, formal tones and without the casual give-and-take that was the normal order of the day. I was used to frosty air between Jimmy and me, but for Rhonda and Bilko to have joined in struck me as totally unfair.

And yes, I blamed all of them. Maybe my comment had sounded insensitive; but damn it all, we *didn't* have any evidence that were killing or even hurting the flapblacks by pushing them close to the *Freedom's Peace.* My personal theory was that there was something about the asteroid that was simply distracting them enough to lose their wrap, and I tried to tell the others that.

But it didn't seem to make any difference. In their minds, I'd sold out to Kulasawa, and I'd now shown that nothing was going to keep me from getting hold of that money. Not even if it meant slaughtering flapblacks right and left.

The acceleration process seemed to take forever, but at last we had the *Sergei Rock* up to speed and it was time to go.

Theoretically, we didn't need to use the flapblacks at all, since the *Freedom's Peace* was close enough that boosting our speed a little more would enable us to catch up with it. But that would have meant more acceleration, more delay, and pushing the engines more than we already had, so I told Jimmy to set us up with another program. He wasn't at all happy about it, but I was long past caring about Jimmy's happiness. If Bilko and Rhonda had opinions on the subject, they were smart enough to keep quiet about them.

The music started, sparking a wrap/unwrap that was again too fast for human eyes to see, and once again we were flying above and behind the *Freedom's Peace*.

Even twenty kilometers away and only glimpsed for an instant, the colony had looked impressive. Now, with us steadily approaching it, the thing was flat-out awesome. It was one thing to read the numbers; it was something else entirely to actually *see* a huge asteroid driving its way through deep space.

It looked just like the handful of publicity shots that had survived the War of Reclamation: a craggy-surfaced, vaguely ovoid asteroid, roughly eighteen kilometers long and maybe twelve across at its widest point, lit only by the faint sheen of reflected starlight. The glare from the drive washed out any details of the engines themselves, but it was obvious that they were massive. Slightly brighter spots here and there across the surface indicated the presence of antenna or sensor arrays and a couple of rectangles that looked like access hatchways.

"It's rotating," Bilko breathed from beside me. Apparently, he was so dazzled by the view that he'd forgotten we weren't on speaking terms. "Look — you can see that drive nozzle array turning around."

"Using rotation to create artificial gravity," I agreed. "They didn't have false-grav back then."

"I'm going to take a spectrum off the hull," he decided, keying his board and swiveling around his viewer. "A Doppler will give us better numbers on the rotation than — yow!"

I jerked against my restraints. "What?" I snapped.

"Something just flicked across the stars," he said tightly, punching keys on the spectrometer.

"Relax," Rhonda's voice came over the intercom. "It

was probably a flapblack."

"Yeah, but it didn't wrap," Bilko said. "I've never heard of a flapblack coming in but not wrapping."

"Maybe they can't wrap this close to the *Freedom's Peace*," I said. "Like I suggested earlier —"

I broke off at the look on Bilko's face. "What is it?"

"It reads like a flapblack, all right," he said, his voice low and rigidly under control. "Only it's not a kind we've ever seen before. This one's spectrum was in the infrared."

I stared at him. "You're joking."

"Check it yourself," he said, keying the analysis over to my display. "The spectrum's definitely below the standard flapblack red — let's call it an InRed."

I looked at the numbers, and damned if he wasn't right. "OK," I said. "So we've found a new breed. So we get into the history books."

"You're missing the point," he said grimly. "We have a new breed of flapblacks, all right: a breed *that chases other flapblacks away*."

There was a soft whistle from the intercom. "I don't like the sound of that," Rhonda said.

"Me, neither," Bilko said. "Maybe we ought to forget the whole thing and get out of here."

I gazed out the viewport at the rapidly approaching asteroid below. "But it doesn't make sense," I told them. "For starters, if it's a predator or whatever —"

"If *they're* predators, plural," Bilko interrupted me. "Another InRed just went past."

"Fine; if *they're* predators," I amended, "then why haven't we seen them before? More to the point, what are they doing hanging around the *Freedom's Peace* in the middle of nowhere?"

If Bilko had an answer, he never got to give it. Without

warning, there was the faint flicker of a laser from the asteroid and our comm speaker crackled. "Approaching transport, this is the *Freedom's Peace*," a female voice said. "Please identify yourself."

Bilko and I exchanged startled glances. Then I dove for the comm switch. "This, uh, is Captain Jake Smith of the star transport *Sergei Rock*. We, uh . . . who is this?"

"My name is Suzenne Enderly," the woman said. "Are you in need of assistance?"

"We were just about to ask you that question," Kulasawa said, stepping through the hatchway behind me onto the flight deck. "This is Scholar Andrula Kulasawa, in charge of this mission."

"And what mission would that be?"

"The mission to see you, of course," Kulasawa said. "We would like permission to come aboard."

"We appreciate your concern," Enderly said. "But I can assure you that we're doing fine and have no need of assistance."

"I'm very glad to hear that," Kulasawa said. "But I would still like to come aboard."

"To study us, I presume?"

I looked up at Kulasawa in time to catch her cold smile. "And to allow you to study us, as well," she said. "I'm sure each of us can learn a great deal from the other."

There was a brief silence. "Perhaps," Enderly said. "Very well."

And on the dark mass below a grid of running lights suddenly appeared. "Follow the lights to the colony's bow," Enderly continued. "There's a docking bay there. We'll use our comm lasers to guide you in."

"Thank you," I said. "We'll look forward to meeting you."

The laser winked out, and I keyed off the comm. "Well?" I asked Kulasawa.

"Well, what?" she countered. "You have your docking instructions. Follow them."

I had envisioned some kind of makeshift docking umbilical stuck perhaps to one of the hatchways we'd spotted on our approach. To my relieved surprise, the docking bay proved to be a real bay: a wide cylindrical opening leading back into the asteroid proper, fully equipped with guide lights and beacons. And, at the far end, a set of ancient but functional-looking capture claws that smoothly caught the *Sergei Rock* and eased it into one of the half dozen slots set around the inside of the open space.

"What now?" Kulasawa asked as we touched gently onto the bare rock floor and the overhead panel slid closed.

"We wait," I said, switching off the false-grav and fighting against the momentary disorientation as the asteroid's rotational pseudogravity took over.

"Wait for what?" Kulasawa demanded. This close to the asteroid's axis the pseudogravity was pretty small, but if she was suffering from free-fall sickness she was hiding it well.

"For them," Bilko told her, pointing out the viewport.

From a door in the far wall three people wearing milky-white isolation suits and gripping carrybag-sized metal cases had appeared and were making their slightly bouncing way toward us. "Off-hand," he added, "I'd say it's a medical team."

He was right. We opened the hatchway at their knock, and after some stiffly formal introductions we spent the next hour having our bodies and the transport itself run through the microbiological soup-strainer. Their borderline paranoia was hardly unreasonable; with 130 years of bacteriological divergence to contend with, something as harmless to us as a flu virus could rage through the colony like the Black Death through Europe.

In fact, it was something of a mild surprise to me when, after all the data had been collected and analyzed, we were pronounced safe to enter. The team gave each of us a broad-spectrum immunization shot to hopefully protect us from their own assortment of diseases, and a few minutes later we were all finally riding down an elevator toward the colony proper.

The ride was longer than I'd expected it to be, and it wasn't until we were well into it that I realized the elevator had been made deliberately slow in order to minimize the slightly disconcerting mixture of increasing weight and Coriolis forces as we headed "down" toward the rim of the asteroid. Personally, I didn't have any trouble with it, but it appeared this was finally the combination that had gotten to Kulasawa's heretofore iron stomach. Her eyes gazed straight ahead as we descended, the expression on her face one of tight-lipped grimness. I watched her surreptitiously, trying not to enjoy it too much.

Considering the historic significance of our arrival, I would have expected a good-sized delegation to have been on hand. But apparently this wasn't a society that went in heavily for brass bands. Only three people were waiting for us as the elevator doors opened: two stolid-looking uniformed men, and a slender woman about Kulasawa's age standing between them.

"Welcome to the *Freedom's Peace*," the woman said, taking a step forward as we stepped out. "I'm Suzenne Enderly; call me Suzenne."

"Thank you," I said, glancing around. We were in a long room with an arched ceiling and no decoration to speak of. Set into the wall behind our hosts was a pair of heavy-looking doors. "I'm Captain Jake Smith," I continued, re-turning my attention to the woman. "This is my first of-ficer, Will Hobson; my engineer, Rhonda Blankenship; my musicmaster, Jimmy Chamala. That one's a little hard to explain —"

"That's all right," the woman assured me, her eyes on Kulasawa. "And you must be Scholar Andrula Kulasawa."

"Yes, I am," Kulasawa said. "May I ask your title?"

Suzenne tilted her head slightly to the side. "What makes you think I have one?"

"I recognize the presence of authority," Kulasawa said. "Authority always implies a title."

Suzenne smiled. "Titles aren't nearly as important to us as they obviously are to you," she said. "But if you insist, I'm a Special Assistant to King Peter."

I felt a stir go through us over that one. The traditional concept of hereditary royalty had long since vanished from the Expansion's political scene, though it was often argued that that same role was now being more unofficially filled by the Ten Families. Still, the idea of a real, working king sounded strange and anachronistic.

For some of us, though, it apparently went beyond merely strange. "A king, you say," Kulasawa said, her voice heavy with disapproval.

Suzenne heard it, too. "You disapprove?"

For a moment the two women locked gazes, and I prayed silently that Kulasawa would have the sense not to launch into a political argument here and now. Suzenne's two guards looked more than capable of taking exception if they chose, and getting thrown into the dungeon or what-ever they had here was not the way I had hoped to end what had become a long and tiring day.

Fortunately, she did. "I'm just a scholar," she told

Suzenne, her voice going neutral again. "I observe and study. I don't pass judgment."

"Of course." Suzenne smiled around at the rest of us. "But I'm forgetting my manners, and I'm sure you're all anxious to see our world. This way, please."

She turned and walked back toward the door, the two guards stepping courteously aside to let our group pass and then closing ranks behind us. "Incidentally, the study team tells me you have several large crates aboard," Suzenne added over her shoulder. "May I ask what's in them?"

"Two of them contain my personal research equipment," Kulasawa said before I could answer. "The others contain food and some power lifters which we brought as gifts for you."

Out of the corner of my eye, I saw Rhonda start. "Gifts?" she echoed. "But that's our cargo."

"Which if you'll recall I purchased from you," Kulasawa said, throwing a sharp look at her. "They're mine to do with as I choose."

Rhonda turned to me. "Jake?"

"That *was* part of the deal," I reminded her.

"Yes, but —" She broke off, an oddly betrayed look on her face.

"You're most generous," Suzenne said, pulling out a plastic card and holding it up to a panel beside the doors. "But I'm afraid we can't accept gifts. One of our techs will evaluate the items and issue you credit slips." The doors slid open, and we stepped out onto a wide, railed balcony —

And I felt my mouth drop open. Stretching out before us, exactly as Enderly had said, was an entire world.

It was like looking at a giant diorama designed to show young schoolchildren all the various types of terrain and landscape one might come across. Far below us, extending for at least a few kilometers, was what seemed to be a mixture of farmland and forest, marked by gentle hills of various heights and dotted with occasional clusters of houses. Numerous ponds were scattered around, glistening in the sunlight, and there was at least one river wending its way across the ground. Farther away, I could see what looked like a small town, then more greenery — grassland or more farms, I couldn't tell which — then more trees and buildings and finally the tall spires of an actual city.

"Look at that," I heard Jimmy murmur. "The edges — they turn up."

I looked to the side. In the distance, I could indeed see the edges of the landscape rising up toward the sky.

And in that moment, at least for me, the illusion abruptly collapsed. I was no longer gazing out over some nice planetside rural area. I was inside an asteroid, billions of kilometers from anywhere, driving hard through the blackness of space.

"I suppose it does take some getting used to," Suzenne said quietly from beside me. "I grew up with it, of course, so to me it seems perfectly natural."

"I guess it would," I said, following the curve upward with my eyes. It was mostly more of the same, though the pattern of farm and forest had been varied and there was what looked like a large lake visible part way up. I tried to follow the curve all the way up, but began to lose it in the glare of the sun.

The sun? "I see you have the ultimate light fixture," I commented, pointing. "I hope that's not a real fusion generator."

"It's not," Suzenne assured me. "We don't have any problem with generating heat inside the colony — it's dumping the excess we sometimes find troublesome, particularly during the winter season. No, our sun is just a very bright light source, running along inside a tunnel through the rotational axis. It fades in at this end of the chamber in the morning, crosses slowly to the other end throughout the day, and then is faded out to give us some twilight. Then it's sent back across during the night and prepped for the new day. It's not the same as living on a planet, I suppose, but it's the closest arrangement the designers could come up with and it's probably pretty accurate."

I squinted up at it. The light was bright enough, but not the blinding intensity of a real G-type sun. "Looks like it's getting toward evening."

"About another hour to sunset," she said. "And yes, we do call it sunset. I'm afraid that's not going to leave you much time to look around tonight."

"Don't worry about it," I assured her. "We're not very far off your schedule ourselves, and I for one could do with an early night."

"That will work best for us, too," she said. "I'll arrange for rooms for all of you, and you can look around and meet King Peter in the morning."

"Sounds good." I looked up again as another thought struck me. "You don't have any stars, of course."

"Not real ones," she said. "But the various city lights look a little like them from the opposite side. And there are observation rooms at the bow for anyone who wants to see the stars for real."

"The landscape looks pretty real, too," I commented. "But you seem to have forgotten about mountains."

She smiled. "Not really. You're standing on one. If you'll excuse me, I have to see to our transportation."

She walked away. Grimacing slightly, I crossed to the far

edge of the balcony. Making sure I had a solid grip on the railing, I looked down.

And found myself gazing down the slope of a rocky cliff at a pasture a kilometer or more below.

"Do you believe this?" Bilko commented, coming up beside me and glancing casually down. "Mountain climbing the easy way — you can start at the top if you want to."

"You really think people climb this?" I asked, taking a long step back from the edge.

"Oh, sure," Bilko said. "Probably designed that way on purpose. In fact, if you look around, you can see different-grade slopes all around this end of the chamber. I'll bet they ice some of them up in the winter so that the really committed nutcases can ski, too."

I grunted. "They're welcome to it."

"Personally, I'd rather have a good game of skill myself." Leaning an elbow on the railing, he nodded casually off to the side. "Speaking of nutcases, did you happen to notice the crowd of cardsharps over there?"

Frowning, I turned to look. *Cardsharps* was the current cutesy slang term for *cops* among Bilko's gambling buddies; but all I could see over there was Suzenne and a half dozen men in coveralls maneuvering a compact multi-passenger helicopter out of a hangar carved out of the rock. Between us and them, the two uniformed men she'd had up above were standing their stolid guard. "Since when do two men constitute a crowd?" I asked.

"Oh, come on, Jake, use your eyes," Bilko chided. "Those aren't techs rolling out that helicopter. They're cops, every one of them."

I threw him a look, turned back to the techs. "Sorry, but I still don't see it."

"It's your innate honesty," Bilko said. "Take my

word for it, they're cops."

"Fine," I said, stomach tightening briefly with old memories. "So they're a little nervous and want to keep an eye on us. So what? Don't forget, we're the first outside contact they've had in 130 years."

"I suppose," Bilko said reluctantly. "It's just that a mix of uniformed and non-uniformed always makes me nervous. Like they're trying to con us."

Suzenne turned and beckoned us toward her. "Which qualifies as working your side of the street, no doubt," I commented as Bilko and I headed across the balcony toward her.

"Hey, I play a clean game," he protested. "You know that."

"Sure," I said. "Just do me a favor and don't try to draw cards with the pilot until we've actually landed, all right?"

Rhonda and Jimmy, who'd been admiring the view from a different part of the balcony, reached the helicopter the same time we did. Kulasawa, who'd wandered off on her own, arrived maybe ten seconds behind us. "We're ready to go," Suzenne said. "Rooms are being prepared for you in the guest house across from the Royal Palace. It's not nearly as grand as the name might imply," she added, looking at Kulasawa. "As I said, titles really aren't that important here."

"Of course," Kulasawa said. "Should we have brought some food from the transport?"

"A meal will be awaiting you," Suzenne promised. "Nothing fancy, I'm afraid, but it should tide you over until the more formal welcoming dinner tomorrow."

"And my research equipment?"

"It will be brought to the guest house tonight," Suzenne said. "Along with the rest of the cargo." She looked around the group. "Are there any other questions before we go?"

"I have one," Jimmy said hesitantly, looking warily at the twin helicopter blades hanging over our heads. "You're sure it's safe to fly in here?"

"We do it all the time," Suzenne assured him with a smile. "Bear in mind that the chamber is over thirteen kilometers long and that it's five kilometers from the ground to the sun tunnel. There really is plenty of room."

"And now," she continued, looking around again, "if there are no other questions, please go ahead and find a seat inside. It's time for us to go."

The Royal Palace was indeed not nearly as fancy as its name had implied. Situated near the center of the city I'd seen from the balcony, it much more resembled an extra-nice government building than it did a medieval castle or even your basic Presidential mansion.

But it had a helipad on the roof, and the guest house Suzenne had mentioned was right across the street, and for me that was what counted. What with the long flight and strain of finding and getting to the *Freedom's Peace* — plus the two short nights that had gone before — I discovered midway through the helicopter ride that I was unutterably tired.

The meal Suzenne had promised, consisting of a buffet of cold meats, cheeses, fish, bread, and fruit, had been laid out in the common area of the suite we'd been booked into. I wolfed down just enough to quiet the rumblings in my stomach and then went in search of my bed. My room was quiet and dark, the bed large and comfortably firm, and I was asleep almost before the blankets settled down around me.

★ ★ ★ ★ ★

I awoke to sunlight streaming in through a gap in the curtains and a smell of roast chicken in the air that reminded my stomach that the previous night's meal hadn't been much more than a gastronomic promissory note. Throwing on yesterday's clothes, I made a quick trip to the attached bathroom and headed out into the common area.

The remains of another buffet were on the side board where the evening meal had been laid out, with a short stack of used plates on a tray near the door. Over at the window, sitting across from each other at the long dining table, were Rhonda and Suzenne. A sampling of Rhonda's beadwork was spread out on the table between them.

"About time," Rhonda commented as I stepped into the room. "The rest of us have been up for a couple of hours now."

"I had more sleep to catch up on than the rest of you," I reminded her as I snagged a clean plate and started stacking it with food. "I was the one who spent most of the past two nights sitting up with sick paperwork, remember?"

"Sick paperwork?" Suzenne asked, frowning.

"We had some strange problems at the Angorki spaceport," Rhonda explained. "Lost or fouled-up permits and such. It took a couple of days to get it all straightened out."

"Just as well it did, I suppose," I commented, picking up a set of flatware and taking my breakfast over to the table. "If we hadn't been delayed, Scholar Kulasawa would have had to find some other transport." I gestured out the window. "And then we'd have missed seeing all this."

"Yes," Suzenne murmured, dropping her eyes to the beadwork.

I nodded toward the beads. "Working on a new customer, I see."

"I beg your pardon," Rhonda said, mock-annoyed. "I am not working a new customer; I'm participating in a cultural exchange."

"We don't have these here," Suzenne said, fingering one of the earrings. "I've never even seen anything like it, even in our archives."

"I'm sure it's there," Rhonda said. "It's a pretty ancient art form, but its popularity does rise and fall."

"Whatever its heritage, it's beautiful," Suzenne said. "I'm sure you'll be able to sell a lot of these pieces here if you want to. You could probably teach classes, too."

"I doubt we'll be here long enough for that," I warned. "Where's everybody else, by the way?"

"They're all outside looking around," Rhonda said. "Jimmy went to find where the music was coming from —"

"Music?" I echoed, frowning.

She nodded. "You can't hear it very well in here, but it's quite audible if you step outside. Beautiful, but very alien."

"We write most of our own music here," Suzenne said. "We play it as a service to —" Her lips compressed briefly. "Well, we can talk about that later."

"Bilko's out, too," Rhonda continued. "He said he was going to hunt down a card game."

I made a face. "Well, good luck to him," I said. "I'll bet the *Sergei Rock* to his lucky deck he won't find a game that'll take Expansion neumarks."

"No, we're still using the First Citizens' supply of Jovian dollars," Suzenne said. "But he took one of the credit slips with him, and he'll be able to exchange that for the coins."

I felt my jaw drop a few millimeters. "One of the credit slips for our cargo?" I demanded, looking at Rhonda. "And you *let* him?"

She returned my glare evenly. "It was his share of the

money," she pointed out. "Besides, he usually makes a profit on these games of his."

"Usually antagonizing the local populace in the process," I pointed out darkly. "And this is one place you do *not* want to get run out of town."

"I'm sure he'll be fine," Suzenne soothed me. "And just for the record, we don't run troublemakers out of town. We have a proper prison, though it's fortunately not used very much."

"I see," I said, peering past her out the window. The room faced east, toward the end we'd come in from; and blamed if it *didn't* look like real mountains over there. "You know, this chamber looks pretty big, but if I remember the numbers you gave us there's still a lot of the asteroid unaccounted for. What do you do with the rest of it?"

"All around the main chamber, beneath our feet, is the bulk of our recycling equipment," Suzenne said. "Of course, that takes up only a fraction of the kilometer or so of stone between us and the outside, so there's still plenty of structural strength and radiation protection. At the aft end of the asteroid are the fusion generators and ion-capture engines, along with the hydrogen-scooping equipment to fuel them. The designers also left a fair amount of space completely untouched for our future needs. We've dug into some of that to get materials for new buildings and to replace the inevitable losses in the recycling system."

She smiled. "And since we had to dig anyway, we went ahead and fashioned the resulting holes into a series of caves. It provides a little recreation for our resident spelunkers."

"You think of everything, don't you?" I said, shaking my head in admiration. "I wish the leaders of the Expansion were this competent."

Suzenne shrugged. "We're flattered, of course, but you have to realize it's not a fair comparison. With a population still under half a million people, we're more like a small city than we are a nation, let alone an entire world. Government on this scale is nearly always more efficient."

"You haven't asked about Kulasawa," Rhonda spoke up.

I hadn't asked about Kulasawa because I frankly didn't care where she was. But there was something in Rhonda's expression . . . "Okay, I'll bite," I said. "What about Kulasawa?"

Rhonda gestured to Suzenne. "Why don't you tell him?" she invited.

"It's not all that mysterious," Suzenne shrugged. "She was up early asking permission to set up her recorders around the colony, that's all."

I frowned. "Recorders?"

"Those large flat panels," Suzenne amplified. "They were stacked together inside two of the crates we brought over from your transport."

The equipment Kulasawa had told *me* was a set of sonic deep-probes. "Ah," I said. "And what did you tell her?"

"Actually, we thought it was a good idea," Suzenne said. "We have a lot of unified records from the first few years of the voyage, but nothing very organized after that. She agreed to give us copies we could edit into a true-time documentary, and so we let her go."

"They also lent her a driver and a couple of helpers," Rhonda put in. "She's been gone — how long?"

"Not quite three hours," Suzenne said, consulting her watch. "I'm hoping she'll be done before your meeting with King Peter."

"And when is that exactly?" I asked, suddenly aware of my grubby and unshowered state.

"I've set it up for two hours from now," Suzenne said. "Will that give you enough time to prepare?"

"Oh, sure," I said, digging an oddly shaped fork into a sculpted piece of melon. "I wonder if you could get my carrybag in from the *Sergei Rock*, though — this uniform is getting a little rank."

"Our luggage has already been delivered," Rhonda told me. That odd look, I noted uneasily, was still on her face. "They're in the closet over there."

"And I'd better get out of your way," Suzenne added, pushing her chair back and standing up. "If there's anything else you need, there's a phone on the table over there. Just punch the call button and give my name — Suzenne Enderly — and they'll connect us."

"Thank you," I said.

"I'll be back in a little under two hours to escort you to the Palace," she said, walking toward the door. "Until then, if you get ready early, feel free to look around the city. Just be sure to take the phone with you."

She left, closing the door behind her. "An audience with a real king," I commented, stuffing a bite of chicken in my mouth. "Something I've wanted to do since I was a kid. Too bad his name couldn't have been Arthur."

"Too bad," Rhonda agreed, her voice neutral, her expression gone from odd to flat-out accusing as she stared hard at me. "All right, Jake, let's hear it."

"Let's hear what?"

"The reason you didn't tell her that Kulasawa's gadgets aren't recorders," she said. "Or had you forgotten she told *us* they were sonic deep-probes?"

"Who says they're not recorders, too?" I asked. "They could be both probes *and* recorders."

"Or they could be something else entirely," she countered. "The point is that she's either lying to Suzenne or else she lied to us. And you didn't blow the whistle on her."

"Neither did you," I shot back. "If you're so worried about it, why didn't *you* say something?"

"Because I was waiting for your lead," she said. "And because I wanted to see just how strong a hold Kulasawa has on you."

I jabbed my fork viciously into my fruit cup, splattering a few drops of juice onto the plate. "She hasn't got any hold on me," I insisted.

"My mistake," Rhonda said. "It's not her, it's the seventy thousand neumarks."

I glared at her, my hand squeezing the fork hard, wanting to tell her it was none of her damn business.

But I couldn't. And she obviously could read that in my face. "This is me you're talking to, Jake," she said quietly. "We've been flying together for over three years now. If something's wrong, isn't it time you told me what it was?"

I closed my eyes, exhaling my anger with a chest-aching sigh. "I'm in something of an awkward situation," I said, the words feeling like ground glass in my mouth. "Five years ago . . . well, let's just say it: I stole some money from the TransShipMint Corporation."

Her eyes widened, just enough to make the admission hurt that much more. *"You?"* she asked disbelievingly.

"Yes, me," I growled. "Why, is that so hard to believe?"

"Frankly, yes," she said. "You're the one who's always so brass-butted about following the rules." She waved a hand as if to erase that. "Sorry — I didn't mean it that way."

"Yes, you did," I said. "I don't suppose it ever occurred to you that there might be a reason why I was always so strict? Like a metric ton of guilt, maybe?"

She grimaced. "I guess that never occurred to me," she conceded. "So what happened?"

I shrugged uncomfortably. "Like I said, I stole some money. Oh, I rationalized it — told myself I need some new equipment for my transport, that if I invested it in this sure-fire deal I was being offered I could get what I wanted and still pay the company back out of my profits. But the bottom line is, I stole it."

"How much?"

"A lot," I told her. "Two hundred thousand neumarks."

Her eyes went even wider this time. "Oh, *Jake*."

"Oh Jake and a half," I agreed ruefully. "You can guess the rest: the sure-fire deal went sour and I lost the whole wad."

She winced. "What did they do to you?"

"Strangely enough, they didn't seem to notice the loss," I said. "Or maybe they did but couldn't figure out where it had gone. I thought maybe I'd gotten away with it, at least from a legal standpoint, though I knew I was going to have to pay them back."

"All two hundred thousand?"

"Every last pfennig," I said. "Why do you think you haven't gotten me to spring for new engines yet? Every half-neumark of profit I've made for the past five years has gone into a special account I've got stashed away on Earth. I figured I'd wait until the statute of limitations was up, just in case, and then send them the money along with an explanation and confession. Anonymous, of course."

"So what went wrong?"

I looked out the window at the distant pseudo-mountains. "About a month ago a TransShipMint agent contacted me," I said. "He said they'd figured it out, and were going to press charges unless I could pay back all the money by the end of the month."

"My God," she breathed. "What did you do?"

"Begged and pleaded another month out of them." I shook my head. "But everything else I've tried has come up dry."

Rhonda sighed softly. "And then Scholar Kulasawa showed up on our gangplank and offered you seventy thousand neumarks."

"I've got a hundred thirty already banked away," I said. "Kulasawa's seventy thousand would just cover it."

"Yes, it would." Rhonda paused. "You told me earlier you were going to use the money in a way that would benefit all of us. You were planning to sell the *Sergei Rock*, weren't you?"

"There was no other way," I said. "It would have cost all of you your jobs, but there was no other way. Until Kulasawa came along."

I looked back at Rhonda. "But if you're right, and she's pulling some kind of scam on the people here —"

"Wait a minute — I didn't say she was pulling any scams," she said quickly, holding up a hand.

"But you implied it."

"I implied she was stretching the truth," she insisted. "That's not the same."

I folded my arms across my chest. "Look, Rhonda, I appreciate your attempts to salve my conscience. But I'm not going to trade one load of guilt for another."

"And I'm not going to let you sacrifice your transport over my vague and unfounded suspicions," she countered. "Not to mention all our jobs."

"You and Bilko won't have any problem finding new jobs," I told her. "And Jimmy'll be snapped up so quick it'll make your head spin."

"Then let me put it another way," she said quietly. "I don't want to see the team broken up."

I forced a smile. "Got seventy thousand neumarks on you?"

Reaching across the table, she squeezed my hand reassuringly. "We'll figure something out," she said. "Thanks for telling me."

She stood up. "I'd better get to the shower and then practice my curtsies. I'll see you later." Collecting her carrybag from the closet, she returned to her room.

I turned back to my breakfast. On one level, it was something of a relief to have the dark secret out in the open at last, to have someone whose opinions I cared about still accept me despite it all.

But neither the soul-cleansing nor Rhonda's compassion in any way changed the basic situation. And the food, delicious barely five minutes ago, now tasted like sand.

The arched doorway facing us was far more impressive than the actual exterior of the Palace. And for a good reason: it was the entrance to King Peter's royal reception room, the place where he held public audiences and from which he did his broadcasts to the entire colony when such was deemed necessary.

All this came from Suzenne, who had also assured us that the two uniformed guards flanking the archway would momentarily be getting the word from inside that the king was ready. At which point they would pull open the heavy wooden doors and admit us.

Us consisting of Rhonda, Suzenne, and me.

"Stop fidgeting," Rhonda murmured in my ear.

"I am *not* fidgeting," I insisted, rubbing my fingertips restlessly against my leg and throwing baleful glances at the door we'd entered the anteroom though. Kulasawa was supposedly on her way; but Jimmy and Bilko had both disappeared somewhere into the city and no one knew where to find them. When this was all over, assuming King Peter didn't throw me in the dungeon for the impertinence of wasting his time with only half a crew, I was going to strangle both of them.

"Scholar Kulasawa's just coming into the Palace," Suzenne said softly, her phone to her ear. "Oh, and we've found Jimmy — he was with one of our musicians. They're bringing him straight over."

Which still left Bilko unaccounted for. Predictably. "Any chance Jimmy will actually be here before those doors open?"

"Probably not," Suzenne said, smiling as she consulted her watch. "But don't worry about it. This is just an informal introductory meeting — anything formal we decide to do will happen this evening or tomorrow. He isn't going to be upset if you're not all here."

She drifted away, turning her back to us as she spoke quietly into the phone. "Then why are you trying so hard to find him?" I muttered under my breath. I turned to Rhonda to detail what I intended to do to Bilko when he finally surfaced —

And paused. Rhonda was staring at Suzenne's back, a suddenly tight look on her face. "Relax," I told her. "I'm the nervous one in this group, remember?"

"Something's wrong here, Jake," she said slowly, her voice barely audible. "Something having to do with Jimmy."

I felt my heart seize up. Jimmy was our musicmaster, a vital ingredient for getting the *Sergei Rock* back home. "You think he's in danger?"

"I don't know," she said, her eyes focused on infinity. "It's something that's been nagging at me ever since last night."

I looked over at the guards flanking the doorway. The way their uniforms were cut, I couldn't tell whether they were armed or not. "What time last night? After we got to the city?"

"No, before that," Rhonda said, her forehead creasing a little harder. "It was on the flight over here; but it started before that . . ."

Abruptly, she looked up at me. "It was when we first met Suzenne," she hissed. "When you introduced Jimmy as our musicmaster. *She never asked what a musicmaster was.*"

I played the whole scene back in my mind. Rhonda was right. "Could she have asked someone during the flight?"

"No," Rhonda said, shaking her head microscopically. "I was sitting next to her, remember? Jake, they didn't have musicmasters until fifty years ago."

"I know," I said, a sudden tightness in my stomach. "I think I even mentioned to Suzenne that it was hard to explain."

"So why didn't she ask about it?" Rhonda persisted. "Either she's not very curious . . . or else she already knew."

I looked over at Suzenne, still on the phone. "But that's impossible," I murmured. "If someone else had found the *Freedom's Peace*, we'd have heard about it."

Rhonda shivered. "Only," she said, "if they made it home again."

I swallowed hard. "That new species of flapblacks Bilko spotted hanging around the asteroid. The InReds."

"I was just wondering that," Rhonda murmured. "Suzenne and the others might not even realize the previous transport or transports hadn't made it back alive."

"Maybe it's time for a few direct questions," I suggested.

"You sure you want to hear the answers?"

"No," I admitted. "But I'd better ask them anyway." Squaring my shoulders, I took a step toward Suzenne —

And at that moment, the two guards suddenly came to life. Stepping to the center of the double doors, they each took one of the handles and pulled.

Suzenne was beside us before the doors even started to open. "All right, here we go," she said. "Remember, don't be nervous. Ah — Scholar. Good; you made it."

I turned my head to see Kulasawa step into line between Suzenne and Rhonda. Her outfit was a surprise: a flowing-line jacket-blouse of a rich-looking brocade over a contrasting flare skirt. It made our transport-crew uniforms look positively shabby, I thought with vague resentment, and I wondered briefly why in the worlds a scholar would bring such an outfit on a trip between Angorki and Parex. But then, unlike the rest of us, she'd known what the *Sergei Rock*'s true destination was. "Where are the others?" she muttered to Suzenne.

"Not here," Suzenne said. "Don't worry about it. Everyone; here we go."

We walked forward in unison, crossing the rest of the foyer and stepping between the open doors.

My first impression of the room was that its tone fit the outer building much more than it did the ornate doorway leading into it. More like an expansive office than the way I would have envisioned a throne room, it was dominated by a large desk near the back wall. A few meters to our right, a semicircular couch that could comfortably seat eight people was positioned around a low circular table on which was a carafe and several glasses. Scattered around the room were a few free-standing lamps and sculptures on pedestals; on the walls were some paintings and textureds, tastefully arranged and spaced. Off to the left, almost looking like an afterthought, was a high-backed throne that had apparently been carved out of a single block of pale, blue-green stone.

And seated there waiting for us was King Peter.

He was a bit older than I'd expected — somewhere in his eighties, I guessed — clean shaven instead of with the bushy beard I'd sort of expected every self-respecting monarch automatically came equipped with. His clothing was also something of a disappointment: no crown and royal robes, but merely a subdued white suit with gold buttons and trim. Kulasawa's outfit, I thought uneasily, was going to make him look a little shabby, too.

"Welcome to the *Freedom's Peace*," he said, rising to his feet as we turned to face him. "I'm King Peter, titular ruler of this world. I trust you've been properly looked after?"

"Yes, sir, we have," I said, suddenly realizing to my chagrin that Suzenne hadn't given us any pointers in protocol. "I mean, Your Highness —"

" 'Sir' will suffice, Captain Smith," he assured me, stepping up and offering me his hand. "I'm pleased to meet you."

"Thank you, sir," I managed, shaking his hand. "I'm pleased to meet you, too."

He smiled. "Actually, a simple 'Peter' will do, if you're so inclined," he said in a conspiratorial tone. "The citizens here like the idea of having a monarch, but we all have too much common sense to take the idea too seriously."

He took a step to the side and offered his hand to Rhonda. "Engineer Blankenship," he nodded, shaking her hand. "Welcome."

"Thank you sir," she said. "You have a beautiful world."

"We like it," he said, moving to Kulasawa. "And Scholar

Kulasawa. What do you think of the *Freedom's Peace*, Scholar?"

"It's more than merely beautiful," she said. "I'm looking forward to examining it in much more detail."

"You'll be given that chance," Peter promised gravely, waving toward the wraparound couch. "But please; let's be comfortable."

We crossed to the couch and sat down, Peter and Suzenne taking one end as the rest of us spread out around the curve, Kulasawa taking the far end. "I'm sure you have many questions about our world," Peter said as Suzenne began pouring drinks from the carafe. "If there's anything you'd like to know right now, I'll do my best to answer."

I took a deep breath. So he wanted questions. So OK, here it came. "I have one," I said. "Are we the first visitors you've had in the past fifty years?"

Peter and Suzenne exchanged glances. "An interesting question," Peter murmured. "A very interesting question, indeed."

"I thought so," I said, forcing my voice to stay steady. Whatever was going on here, that single glance had been all I needed to know I'd hit the target dead center. Whatever the hell the target was. "I'd like an answer, if I may."

A muscle in Peter's jaw tightened briefly. "As it happens, you're the fourth Expansion transport to find us," he said.

I felt Rhonda stir beside me. "And what happened to the other three?" I asked carefully.

"The crews are still here," Peter said, his gaze steady on me. "Most of them. There were two . . . fatalities."

"What kind of fatalities?" Kulasawa asked.

"They were killed trying to escape," Suzenne said. "I'm sorry."

"What do you mean, escape?" I asked.

"What she means is that you can't leave, my friends," Peter said quietly. "I'm afraid you're going to have to stay with us for the rest of your lives."

A lot of different thoughts go shooting through your mind when you hear something like that. My first thought was that this was some kind of strange joke Peter and Suzenne liked to play on visitors, that any second now they would smile and say, no, they were just kidding. My second thought was that the TransShipMint Corporation was going to be seriously unhappy if I disappeared without paying back their two hundred thousand. My third was that *I* wasn't going to be very happy either if I wasn't allowed to make that debt right.

And the fourth, which overrode them all, was that I was damned if I would walk meekly into this cage they were casually telling me to step into.

I kept my eyes on Peter, trying hard to think. Were the guards outside monitoring us? Probably not. Could Rhonda and I take out Peter and Suzenne? Probably. But that wouldn't get us across the colony and back to the *Sergei Rock*.

And even if we got there, would it do any good? There were still those InReds hanging around out there. We knew they scared away normal flapblacks — were they waiting like ghostly sharks to grab us and haul us to oblivion?

Rhonda was the first to break the silence. "I don't understand," she said. "You can't just order us to stay here."

"I'm afraid we have to," Peter said. "You see, if you leave you'll bring others back here. That's something we can't allow to happen. I'm sorry."

"Why not?" Kulasawa asked.

Frowning, I turned to look at her. My ears hadn't deceived me: her face was as calm and controlled as her voice.

Peter must have noticed it, too. "If you're expecting to be rescued, Scholar, I can assure you that the chances of that are vanishingly small. None of the other transports who came here ever had anyone come looking for them."

"And you think that means no one will come looking for us?" Kulasawa asked.

"Did you tell anyone else where you were going?" Suzenne countered. "Or where you would be looking for us?"

Kulasawa shrugged fractionally. "That's irrelevant."

"Not really," Suzenne said. "You see, we've learned from the other fortune-hunters that a prize like the *Freedom's Peace* tends to inspire great secrecy on the part of the searchers. All any of you want is to make sure you get all the profit or glory —"

"That's enough, Suzenne," Peter murmured. "Let me hasten to assure you that you'll all be treated well, with homes and jobs found for you —"

"Suppose we don't choose to roll over and show our throats," Kulasawa interrupted. "Suppose we decide we're not going to feed your megalomania."

Peter's eyebrows lifted, just a bit. "This has nothing to do with megalomania," he said. "Or with me."

"Then what *does* it have to do with?" Rhonda asked quietly.

"The fact that if the Expansion learns where we are, they'll want to bring us back," Peter said. "We don't want that."

Kulasawa frowned. "You must be joking," she said. "You'd kidnap us for *that?* Do you seriously think anyone in the Expansion cares a pfennig's worth for any of you?"

"If you think that, why are you here?" Peter asked, regarding her thoughtfully. "And please don't try to tell me it was in the pure pursuit of knowledge," he added as she began to speak. "The more I study you, the more I'm convinced you're not actually a scholar at all."

Kulasawa favored him with a thin smile. "One for two, Your Highness," she said. "You're right, I'm not a scholar."

I looked at Rhonda, saw my own surprise mirrored in her face. "Then who are you?" I demanded.

"But on the other point, you're dead wrong," Kulasawa continued, ignoring my question. "Pure knowledge is exactly the reason I'm here."

"I see," Peter said. "Any bit of knowledge in particular you're interested in?"

"Of course," Kulasawa said. "You don't really think I care about your little world and your quaint little backwater duck-pond monarchy, do you?"

"Yet you were willing to pay three hundred thousand neumarks to come here," Rhonda pointed out.

"Don't worry, I intend to get full value for my money," Kulasawa assured her coldly. "By the time I'm finished here, I'll have completely changed the shape of Expansion space travel."

There was a sort of strangled-off gasp from the other end of the couch. I turned that direction just in time to see Peter put a restraining hand on Suzenne's arm. "What do you mean by that?" the king asked, his voice steady.

"It should be obvious, even to you," Kulasawa said, regarding both of them with narrowed eyes. Clearly, she'd caught the reaction, too. "I want those ion-capture engines of yours."

"Of course," I murmured under my breath. It *was* obvious, at least in retrospect. The current limit on spaceship size was due solely to the limits in the power and size of their drives; and those limits were there solely because the Jovians' unique engineering genius had died with their bid for independence from Earth. Examination of the *Freedom's Peace*'s drive would indeed revolutionize Expansion space travel.

As I said, obvious. And yet, at the same time I felt obscurely disappointed. After all of Kulasawa's lies and manipulation, it seemed like such a petty thing to have invaded an entire world for.

But if Peter was feeling similarly, he wasn't showing it. In fact, I could swear that some of the tension had actually left his face. "I presume you weren't planning to disassemble them for shipment aboard your transport," he said. "Or did you think we would have the plans lying conveniently around for you to steal?"

"Actually, I was hoping to persuade you to come back with me," Kulasawa said. "Though the engines are my primary interest, I'm sure there are other bits of technological magic the Jovian engineers incorporated into the design of this place that would be worth digging out."

"I'm sure there are," Peter agreed. "But you already have our answer to that."

"But why *don't* you want to come back with us?" Rhonda asked. "We have true interstellar travel now — there's no need or reason for you to stay out here this way."

"She's right," I put in. "If you want your own world, I'm sure the Expansion could provide you with something."

"We already have our own world," Suzenne pointed out.

"I meant a real world," I said.

"So did I," Suzenne said. "You think of a world as a physical planet orbiting a physical sun; no more, no less. I think of a world as a group of people living together. I think of the society and culture and quality of life."

"Our ancestors left Sol for reasons involving all of those," Peter added. "Don't forget, we've had three other visitors from the Expansion, from which we've learned a great deal about your current society. Frankly, there are things happening there we'd just as soon not involve ourselves with."

"Typical provincial thinking," Kulasawa said contemptuously. "Fear of the unknown, and a ruthless suppression of anything that might rock the boat of the people in power. And I presume that if I wanted to put my proposal to the whole colony you'd refuse to let me?"

"There would be no need for that," Peter said. "The decision has already been made."

"Of course," Kulasawa sniffed. "The glories of absolute monarchy. *Dieu et mon droit, ex cathedra,* and all that. The king speaks, and the people submit."

"The Citizens' Council agreed with the decision," Suzenne told her. "All the citizens understand our reasoning."

Kulasawa shrugged. "Fine," she said. "As I said, I'd hoped to persuade you. But if you won't come willingly, you'll just have to do so unwillingly."

Peter's forehead furrowed slightly. "An interesting threat. May I ask how you intend to carry it out?"

"As I said, I could start by addressing the people," Kulasawa said. "Give them a taste of real democracy for a change."

Peter shook his head. "I already said you wouldn't persuade them."

"Then why are you afraid to let me try?" Kulasawa countered. "Still, there's no reason to upset your well-trained sheep out there. All I really need to do is explain to you why you can't make me disappear as conveniently as you have all the others. Why there *will* be people who'll come looking for me."

I frowned at her, a sudden hope stirring within me. Up until that moment, it hadn't really sunk in on an emotional level that what we were discussing here was a permanent — and I mean *permanent* — exile to this place. If Kulasawa had some kind of trick up her sleeve that could get us home . . .

"By all means," Suzenne invited. "Tell us what sort of clues or hints you left behind."

"No clues or hints," Kulasawa said loftily. "Merely a simple matter of who I am."

"And who are you?" Suzenne asked.

And at that moment, the double doors behind Peter swung open again. I looked that direction to see Jimmy come into the room, his hair looking even more unkempt than usual. He must have missed seeing Peter and Suzenne, with their backs mostly to him; but he spotted me instantly. "Captain!" he said, bounding toward us as the doors closed again behind him.

I hissed under my breath, trying to gesture his attention to Peter without being obvious about it. Talk about your oblivious bull in a china shop —

But he was bubbling too hard to even notice. "Guess what?" he called, a huge grin plastered across his face as he came around the end of the couch. "These people can *talk* to the flapblacks!"

I froze, my gesturing hand still in midair. "What?"

"Yeah, they can talk to —" He broke step, suddenly flustered as he abruptly seemed to focus on the rest of the people seated in front of him on the couch. "Oh. Uh . . . I'm sorry . . ."

"No, that's all right," I said, throwing a hard glance at

Peter. But his face was unreadable. "Tell us more."

Jimmy's eyes darted around, his throat working uncertainly. "Uh . . . well, I was talking to one of their musicians," he said hesitantly. "And he said . . ."

His voice trailed away. "He said we can communicate mentally with the beings you call flapblacks," Peter said. His voice was calm again, and with a flash of insight I realized that this was the secret he'd thought Kulasawa had stumbled on earlier when she'd spoken of revolutionizing space travel. "We would have told you about it eventually."

"Of course," I said. "How about telling us about it now?"

He held his hands out, palm upward. "There's not much to tell," he said. "Our first hint was a few years out, when we began to realize that the supposedly imaginary friends our first-born children were telling their parents about were not, in fact, imaginary at all. It took awhile longer to realize who and what the beings were they were in contact with."

"And Jimmy said you *talked* to them?"

"A figure of speech," Peter said. "It's actually a direct mental contact, a wordless communication."

"Why didn't you tell the Habitats?" Kulasawa put it. "You must have still been in contact with Jupiter at that point."

"We were already beginning to fade," Suzenne said. "By the time we'd figured it all out, it would have been problematic whether we could have gotten enough of the message through."

"And besides, you thought it might be a useful secret to keep to yourselves?" Kulasawa suggested, smiling thinly.

Peter shook his head. "You don't understand," he said. "In the first place, it's hardly a marketable secret — any child who's conceived and brought to term away from large planetary masses will have the ability. Everyone aboard has it now, except of course for the handful of recent visitors like yourselves."

"That doesn't change the fact that it's an enormously useful talent," Kulasawa said. "You people don't need a musicmaster to get where you're going, do you? You just order the flapblack to take you where you want to go, and that's it."

"It's not like that at all," Suzenne protested. "They're not servants or slaves we can order to do anything. It's more like . . ." She floundered.

"I sometimes think of it as similar to those dolphin and whale shows they have on Earth," Peter said. "You train them by giving them a reward when they do something you want, but you aren't really *communicating* with them. In this case, you provide the reward — the music — concurrently with the action, but you have no real understanding as to who and what you're dealing with —"

"Let's put the philosophy aside for a minute," Kulasawa cut in brusquely. "Bottom line: you can tell them were to go and they take you there. Yes or no?"

Peter pursed his lips. "For the most part, yes."

He looked back at me. "You see now why we can't let even a hint of this get back to the rest of the Expansion. If they knew we could move their transports between the stars without the uncertainties and complications of the music technique, they would carry every one of us away into slavery."

Kulasawa snorted. "Give the melodramatics a rest, Your Highness. What you mean is that you've got a platinum opportunity here and you're just afraid to grab it."

"Believe whatever you wish," Peter said. "For you, perhaps, it would be an opportunity. For us, it would be slavery."

"You really think they would just take you away like that?" Rhonda asked. "I can't believe our leaders would allow that."

"Of course they would," Peter said, gesturing toward Jimmy. "Just look at your own musicmaster. The music-master on the first transport to find us was a forty-six-year-old former professor of composition. How old is Mr. Chamala?"

"Nineteen," I said, looking at Jimmy. "He has the right kind of mind, and they hustled him straight through school."

"Did he have a choice?"

I grimaced. "As I understand it, there's a great deal of subtle pressure brought to bear on potential musicmasters."

"Do you think it would be any different with us?" Peter asked quietly. "There's a virtual explosion in the volume of interstellar travel and colonization — just comparing the *Sergei Rock*'s planetary charts with those of our earlier visitors makes that abundantly clear. If they knew we could feed that appetite, do you really think they would hesitate to press us into service?"

"And do you have any idea what prices you could command for such service?" Kulasawa demanded. "That's what Smith's 'subtle pressure' mostly consists of: huge piles of neumarks. Play your cards right and your world could be one of the richest in the Expansion."

"And who would be left to live there?" Suzenne countered. "Children under five and elders over ninety? They'd take everyone else."

"Now you're being ridiculous," Kulasawa growled.

"I don't think so," Suzenne said. "But whether I am or

not is irrelevant. The decision has been made, and we're not going to change it."

"Fine," Kulasawa said. "If you won't bring freedom to your people, Jimmy and I will have to do it for you."

Jimmy, who'd been largely frozen in place ever since planting himself near Peter's end of the couch, came unstuck in a rush. "Who — me?" he gulped, his eyes turning into dinner plates.

"You're the only one who can help them, Jimmy," Kulasawa said, her voice abruptly soft and earnest. "The only one who can free them from the prison King Peter and his power elite have locked them into."

"Wait just a second," I protested. "If the people have decided —"

"The people haven't decided, Smith," Kulasawa cut me off scornfully. "Or haven't you been paying attention? What proportion of the people here, do you think, would jump at the chance to get out of this flying coffin and see the Universe?"

"We can't let even one of our people leave here," Suzenne said. "If there was so much as a single slip on anyone's part, the entire colony would be doomed to slavery."

"There's that slavery buzz-word again," Kulasawa scoffed. "Do you feel like a slave, Jimmy? Well, do you?"

Beneath that mop of hair Jimmy's face looked like that of a cornered animal, his eyes darting around as if seeking help or a way to escape. "But if they don't want to do it —"

"Do you feel like a slave?" Kulasawa repeated sharply. "Yes or no?"

"Well . . . no . . ."

"In fact, you're extremely well paid for what you do, aren't you?" Kulasawa persisted. "And with opportunities and privileges most teens your age would give their left arm to have." She stabbed an accusing finger at Peter and Suzenne. "And *that's* what these people are afraid of. They've been the big ducks in the small pond all their lives. And they know the only way to hold onto that power is to keep their people ignorant."

Her lip twisted. "Slavery, you said, *King* Peter? *You're* the real slavemaster here."

"But what can I do?" Jimmy asked plaintively, his expression still looking hunted. "If they won't let us leave —"

"You can save them, that's what," Kulasawa told him. "You see, those plates I had aboard the *Sergei Rock* aren't deep-probe sonics. They're actually highly sophisticated monodirectional resonance self-tuning loudspeakers. Loudspeakers which are at this moment scattered at strategic points all around this asteroid."

She reached her left hand beneath her brocaded jacket-blouse and pulled out a small flat box. "And *this* is a wireless player interface to them."

"You can't be serious," Rhonda said, a sandbagged look on her face. "You want to take the whole colony back?"

"Can you think of a simpler way to solve the problem?" Kulasawa asked. "The choices will be presented to the citizens, and they'll be allowed to decide for themselves what they want to do. Those who want to enter the musicmaster profession — I suppose we'll have to come up with a new name for them — can do so. Those who don't can go on to new homes or the world of their choice."

Rhonda glanced at Peter and Suzenne, looked back at Kulasawa. "And the *Freedom's Peace*?"

"As I said, there are technological secrets here that will benefit the whole Expansion," she said. "The colonists will be properly compensated, of course."

"And what makes you think our people will just sit by

and let you do this?" Peter asked.

"The fact that we can do it without leaving this room," Kulasawa said, her right hand dipping beneath her jacket-blouse. "And the fact that I have this."

I looked at the tiny gun in Kulasawa's hand, a sudden hollow sensation in the pit of my stomach. "It's called a Karka nerve pistol," Kulasawa continued, her tone almost off-handed. "It fires needles that dissolve instantly in blood, disrupting neural chemistry and totally incapacitating the target. Usually nonfatal, though an allergic reaction to the drug will kill you pretty quick."

There was a soft click as she moved her thumb against the side of the gun. "There's also a three-needle burst set-ting," she added. "That one *is* fatal."

She clicked back to the one-needle setting. "We can all hope that won't be necessary. All right, Jimmy, come over here and take the interface. Be sure to stay out of my line of fire."

Jimmy didn't move. His eyes darted around the couch one last time —

And stopped on me. "Captain?" he whispered.

"You don't need to ask him," Kulasawa said. "*You're* the one who holds the key to these people's freedom, not him."

"It's not our decision to make, Jimmy," I said quietly, knowing even as I said it how futile my words were. If there was one button guaranteed to start Jimmy's juices running it was the whole question of personal freedom versus au-thority. Stupid rules, restrictive rules, unnecessary imposi-tions of power — I seemed to go around that track with him at least once per trip. Kulasawa couldn't have come up with a better way to trip him to her side if she'd tried.

And then, to my eternal amazement, Jimmy squared his shoulders, turned to face her, and shook his head. "No," he said. "I can't do it."

From the look on her face, Kulasawa was as stunned by his answer as I was. "What did you say?" she demanded.

"I said no," Jimmy said. His voice quavered slightly under the blazing heat of her glare, but his words were as solid as a sealant weld. "Captain Smith says it's wrong."

"And *I* say it's right," Kulasawa snapped. "Why listen to him instead of me?"

"Because he's my boss." Jimmy looked at me. "And because I trust him."

He turned back to Kulasawa. "And because he's never needed a gun to tell me what to do."

Kulasawa's face darkened like an approaching storm. "Why, you stupid little —"

"Leave him alone," Rhonda cut her off. "Face it: you've lost."

"Sit down, Chamala," Kulasawa growled, gesturing Jimmy toward the couch. "And if I were you, Blankenship, I'd keep my mouth shut," she added to Rhonda, all her heat turned to crushed ice now. "Of all the people in this room, you're the one I need the least."

She looked back at Peter, her face under control again. "Fine; so our lapdog of a musicmaster is afraid to make decisions like a man. I'm sure one of your musicians out there will see things differently. Where's the room's public-address system?"

Peter shook his head. "No," he said.

Kulasawa shifted her gun slightly to point at Suzenne. "I don't need her, either," she said.

Peter's lips compressed briefly. "In the throne. Controls are along the side of the left armrest."

"Thank you." Standing up, Kulasawa started to circle around the table.

I cleared my throat. "Excuse me, but there's just one little thing you seem to have forgotten."

Kulasawa stopped, her gun settling in to point at my chest. "And that is?"

"One of their musicians might be able to whistle up some flapblacks for you," I said. "But none of them can tell you how to get back to the Expansion."

The gun lifted a little. "I'm disappointed, Smith — I would have thought you could come up with something better. I've got the *Freedom's Peace*'s coordinates, remember? All I have to do is work backward from those and we'll wind up back at Angorki."

"We would," I agreed, "*if* we were anywhere near your coordinates. But we're not."

Her eyes narrowed. "Explain."

"Your coordinates didn't take into account the time-delay for the light," I explained. "Or the fact that the *Freedom's Peace* is no longer on a Sol-direct vector. You try a straight backtrack and you'll miss Angorki by about sixty A.U. That's about twice the distance from Earth to Neptune, in case you need help with the numbers."

For a long moment she studied my face. Then, her lips tilted in a slight smile. "And of course you're the only one who knows how to plot a course back, right?"

"Right," I said, folding my arms across my chest. "And I'm not going to."

"I suggest you reconsider," she said. "There's a little matter of two hundred thousand neumarks you owe the TransShipMint corporation."

The bottom seemed to fall out of my stomach. "How do you know about that?"

She snorted. "Oh, come now — you didn't really think I pulled your name out of a lotto ball, did you? You were one of a dozen transports I knew I could bring enough pressure on to get what I wanted. You just happened to be in the right place and the right time when the data finally came through."

I shrugged as casually as I could. "So fine. Renege on the seventy thousand if you want. What do I care — Peter says we're staying here anyway."

"Wrong," Kulasawa bit out. "One way or another, we're getting back." She arched her eyebrows. "And when we do, you're going to prison . . . because you don't owe just seventy thousand any more. You owe the full two hundred."

I stared at her. "What are you talking about?"

"I'm talking about the hundred thirty thousand you thought you had stashed away in the Star Meridian Bank," she said, openly gloating now. "The hundred thirty thousand that isn't there any more."

"You're bluffing," Rhonda said sharply. "How could you possibly get that kind of access to Jake's account?"

"For the same reason these people can't keep me here for long." Kulasawa straightened up slightly and looked around —

And as she did so, her face and posture and entire demeanor abruptly changed. Suddenly the upper-class scholar was gone; and in its place was someone or something that seemed far more regal even than the king seated at the end of the couch. "My name isn't Andrula Kulasawa," she said her voice rich and commanding. "It's Andrula Chen."

She turned hard, arrogant eyes on me. "Second cousin of the Chen-Mellis family."

I stared at her, my blood seeming to freeze in my heart. "Oh, my God," I whispered.

"Captain Smith?" Peter asked, his voice low. "What does she mean?"

With an effort, I turned away from her gaze. "Chen-Mellis is one of the Ten Families," I said, the words coming out with difficulty. "The people who effectively rule Earth and most of the Expansion."

"I prefer to think of it as one of the Six Families, actually," Kulasawa — Chen, rather — put in. "The other four survive solely at our pleasure."

"You told us there were other groups looking for the *Freedom's Peace*," Rhonda said, her voice low. "The other families?"

"You don't think I would have picked the *Sergei Rock* to hide from some bumbling academics, do you?" Chen retorted. "Members of the Hauptmann and Gates-Verazzano families have been sniffing along my trail for the past two months."

She gave Peter a brittle smile. "They want your engines, too," she added. "And I can assure you that Chen-Mellis will cut you a better deal than they will."

Peter shook his head. "We will deal with none of you."

"I'd love to see you try to persuade the Hauptmann family of that." Chen looked back at me. "Well, Smith? Co-operation and a share of the profits, or lofty ideals and a few years of your life in prison?"

"So now it's a share of the profits, too?" Suzenne murmured.

"Shut up, or I'll add your lives on the downside of the ledger," Chen snarled. "Well, Smith, what's it to be? Shall we say your freedom and, say, five million neumarks?"

I should have been tempted. After five years of scrimping every pfennig I got to put toward my debt, I should *really* have been tempted. But to my own amazement, I discovered that I wasn't. Maybe it was the condescension inherent in the offer, the casual assumption that I had my price just like everyone else she'd ever met. Or maybe it was the presence of Jimmy, sitting on Rhonda's other side now, who'd already resisted the pressure and made the right decision.

Or maybe it was the fact that I'd suddenly had an idea of how we might be able to get out of this. If I played my cards right . . .

I looked Chen straight in the eye. "Forget it," I told her. "And if you're thinking about upping the ante, save your breath. You're on your own here, lady. None of us are going to help you."

Her face had frosted over again at my refusal. Now, though, the ice cracked into a small but malicious smile. "Perhaps none of you three will," she said. "But you're not the only one who knows how to get us back to civilization. And I suspect First Officer Hobson will be more easily convinced of the realities of this situation."

Keeping her eyes on us, she began backing toward the throne and King Peter's public address system. Mentally, I crossed my fingers . . .

And then, abruptly, she stopped. "No," she said. "No, I see your game, Smith. You're hoping that anyone using the PA system except His Royal Highness will make the local secret police suspicious." She waved the gun toward the throne. "On the other hand, you're his captain, aren't you? What could be more natural than for you to call him to the Palace?"

I didn't move. "And how much were you planning to offer me for this service?"

"I wouldn't dream of insulting you that way again," she assured me, her voice not quite covering up the soft click as she shifted her gun to its three-needle setting. "So let's make it simple. You call Hobson, and Blankenship gets to live."

I felt my throat tighten. "You wouldn't dare."

"I've already said I don't need either her or Ms. Enderly," Chen reminded me. "In a pinch, I could probably do without the king, too."

I took a deep breath, exhaled it noisily, and got to my feet. "Don't do it, Jake," Rhonda pleaded. "She's bluffing — even the Chen-Mellis family couldn't get her off a murder charge."

"The Chen-Mellis family can do anything when the rewards are big enough," Chen said shortly.

"It's not worth the risk," I told Rhonda, reaching down to briefly squeeze her hand. "Besides, even if I don't, Bilko will be here eventually anyway."

The throne was more comfortable than it looked, with silky-soft cushions fitted to the stone. The controls on the left armrest were simple and straightforward: one basic on/off switch, one that determined whether or not the audio was accompanied by a visual, and five switches determining which section or sections of the colony would receive the broadcast. I set the latter group for full coverage, set the mode for audio only — this at Chen's insistence — and we were ready. "No tricks," she warned, stepping back well out of range of any desperate flying leaps I might have been contemplating. "Bear in mind this gun has a clip of just over two hundred fifty needles, and that I don't mind spending a few of them if I have to."

I cleared my throat and touched the "on" switch. "Attention; attention," I called. "First Officer Will Hobson of the *Sergei Rock*, this is your captain speaking. We're having a little party over here at the Palace you seem to have forgotten about. Greet the other cardsharps for me and hustle it over here, all right? Thank you; that is all."

I switched off the PA and stepped down from the throne.

"Happy?" I asked Chen sourly.

"What was that nonsense about a party and cardsharps?" she demanded, her face dark with suspicion.

"It's a private joke," I said briefly, striding past her and dropping onto the couch next to Rhonda.

"Make it a public joke," Chen ordered.

I could feel Rhonda's eyes on me, and could only hope she wasn't frowning too hard at this private joke she'd never heard of. "It goes back to a time on Bandolera when I got him into some trouble," I said. "I called him while he was in the middle of a game and told him to get back to the transport. He was winning big, and said he wouldn't be back until he'd finished the round. He turned off his phone; so I tracked down the numbers of the other players and started calling them and telling them to please send Bilko home."

"I imagine he was immensely pleased by that," Chen said.

"I don't think he ever lived it down," I said. "At least, not with that bunch. The point is the reference means he's to get his rear over here *now*, and not just whenever he finishes the current round or has won enough money or whenever."

Chen lifted the gun warningly. "He'd better."

"He will," I sighed, mentally crossing my fingers a little harder.

Peter cleared his throat. "I'm curious, Miss Chen," he said. "When you spoke earlier of changing the shape of Expansion space travel with our engine design, I naturally assumed a certain degree of exaggeration. Now that we know your true affiliation, do I now assume you were speaking literally?"

"Quite literally, Your Highness," Chen told him. "In ten

years, the Chen-Mellis family is going to completely domi-
nate intrasystem space travel. We're going to create super
tankers, mining ships like no one's seen since the Jovian
Habitats went down, passenger liners ten times bigger than
the *Swan of Tuonela* —"

"And warships?" Rhonda asked quietly.

Chen didn't even flinch. "Of course we're going to need
to defend our interests," she said. "I don't anticipate any
actual warfare, though."

"Of course not," I said sarcastically. "Subtle threats and
economic pressure bring the same results without making
so much of a mess, don't they?"

Chen shrugged. "You learn slow, Smith. But you do
learn."

"Possibly faster than you do," I said. "Has it occurred to
you that there may be a limit to how big a ship the
flapblacks are going to be able to carry?"

"Of course it has," she said. "That's another reason why
I want to try to bring the colony back with me. If they can
carry the *Freedom's Peace*, then the sky is very literally the
limit."

From across the room came the whisper of air that sig-
naled the opening of the double doors. Chen spun around
to face that direction, dropping her arm to her side to conceal the gun against the back of her right thigh. I felt my
muscles tense, reflexively estimating the distance to her gun
and the chances I could get there before she could aim and
fire . . .

Obviously not as subtly as I'd thought. "Don't, Jake,"
Rhonda hissed into my ear, gripping my arm. "It's still set
on three-needle."

"Hello, everyone," Bilko said, wandering almost casually
into the room. Wandering in alone; and even as I tried to

catch a glimpse of anyone else who might be out in the foyer the doors swung shut again. "Sorry to be late, Jake — my game went a little longer than I'd expecte —"

He broke off as his eyes landed on the gun Chen had brought back into view again. "Relax, Hobson, it's not what it seems," she assured him. "My name is Andrula Chen; second cousin of the Chen-Mellis family, with the mission of bringing this colony back to the Expansion. Unfortunately, the power structure here is resisting me, and I'm going to need your assistance."

"Well . . . sure," he said, throwing a puzzled look at the rest of us on the couch. "Jake?"

"Captain Smith wanted more than his assistance was worth," Chen said. "He demanded ten million neumarks; I could only offer five."

She looked at me as if daring me to contradict her. But though her eyes were on me, her gun was pointed at Rhonda. I held her gaze, and kept my mouth shut.

Bilko snorted derisively. "Five million neumarks not good enough, huh? Well, that's management for you. OK, Ms. Chen, you've got yourself a deal. What do you need me to do?"

"I need you to plot us a course from here back to Angorki," she said. "Can you do it?"

"Sure — no sweat," he said, glancing around and starting toward the desk. "I just need a computer — there must be one back here somewhere."

And across at Peter's end of the couch, Suzenne suddenly inhaled sharply.

Chen heard her, too. "Just a minute," she snapped, throwing a suspicious glare at Suzenne. "What was that all about?"

Suzenne seemed to shrink back into the cushions. "What was what?"

"What's over there at the desk?" Chen demanded.

"Nothing," Suzenne said guardedly. "What could be there?"

"Yeah, what could be there?" Bilko agreed, taking another step toward the desk. "Computer's probably in one of these drawers, right?"

"Get away from there," Chen said sharply, spinning back to face him. "I said *get away*."

"Sure, OK," Bilko said, taking a hasty step back and holding up both hands. "What's the problem?"

"Maybe you're a little too cooperative." Chen threw me a hard look. "And maybe there was more to Smith's private joke than he let on. Move away — *I'll* find the computer."

"Whatever you say," Bilko shrugged, taking another step back. Chen circled around behind the desk, clearly trying to watch all of us at once. She pulled the desk chair out and half stooped to pull open one of the drawers —

The thick glass panels were so perfectly transparent and moved so fast that they were almost impossible to see. But there was no missing the sudden thundercrack as they slammed out of disguised cracks in the floor and thudded solidly against the ceiling, sealing the desk and the area around it into its own isolated space.

Chen's curse — I assume she cursed — was lost in the echo of that boom, as was the sound of her shot. She ducked reflexively back as the needles ricocheted from the barrier; and then the guard who'd come through the doorway that had magically appeared in the wall behind the desk was on her, the momentum of his diving tackle slamming her hard against the glass. By the time the second and third guards made it through the door, she had run out of fight.

"Don't hurt her," Peter called. We were all on our feet

now, though I personally couldn't recall having stood up. "Take her to a holding cell."

"Make sure you search her first," Suzenne added. "Thoroughly."

They hustled her out through the hidden door, and Peter turned back to me. "Thank you," he said quietly. "However you did it, we're in your debt."

"No problem," Bilko assured him, coming up to join us. "When Jake says to whistle up the cops, I whistle up the cops." He looked back toward the desk, watching as the glass panels receded back into the floor. "Now that it's over, can someone tell me what I just blew five million neumarks over?"

"The biggest attempted hijacking in history," I said, looking at Peter. "And unfortunately, it's not over yet."

"You really think her people will be coming to look for her?" Suzenne asked.

"It's worse than that," I said grimly. "The implication she's out here alone is nonsense — no Chen-Mellis second cousin would be stupid or reckless enough to come out here without backup already on its way. My guess is we've got maybe two or three days before they get here. Maybe less."

"Wait a minute, wait a minute," Bilko cut in. "If they're that close, why didn't she just wait for them in the first place? Why bother coming in with us?"

"Because there are other people looking for the *Freedom's Peace*," I told him. "And the first one to get here is going to be the one with salvage rights claim. Odds are that those loudspeakers she scattered around the colony really are also recorders, just like she said, so that she'll have a record of her presence here."

"But then why didn't she wait for her people to arrive before revealing herself to us?" Peter asked, clearly confused. "Why risk tipping us off the way she did?"

"Pure arrogance," Rhonda suggested. "She wanted to deliver you personally to the backup team."

"Or else she wanted to be the one who got the flapblacks to get you moving," Bilko put in. "Maybe there's even some rivalry between her and the backup team — the Ten Families are supposed to be riddled with upper-level infighting. If she got the *Freedom's Peace* back to Angorki on her own, she'd look that much better."

"The reasons and motivations don't matter," I interrupted the budding debate. "The bottom line is that we've got trouble on the way."

"I can't allow my people to be forced into servitude, Captain," Peter said softly, the lines in his face deepening. "If it comes to that choice, we will fight."

"Let's see if we can't find a third choice," I said. "Tell me about those flapblacks that surround the colony, the ones who chase away the others. What are they, predators of some kind?"

Peter smiled sadly. "Hardly. They're merely the eldest of the Star Spirits. The ones marking their last few weeks as they wait for death."

An unpleasant shiver ran up my back. I knew all creatures died, of course, and in fact we'd had that argument on the way in over whether our wrapping flapblacks were getting eaten. But somehow the thought of a group of aging flapblacks hovering together waiting quietly to die was more disturbing than I would have expected it to be. Perhaps it took some of the magic away, or perhaps it felt too much like the death of a favorite pet.

"Like all Star Spirits, they enjoy music," Peter continued quietly. "But of a particular kind, the kind only we apparently know how to write for them. That's what the music in the colony is for."

Abruptly, Suzenne looked at me and smiled. "One of them remembers you, Captain. He says he carried you once a long time ago."

A second chill ran through me. "They get into our minds?" I asked carefully. "Not just the musicmaster's, I mean, but all the rest of us, too?"

"No, they can't read minds, Captain," Peter assured me. "Not even ours, and we're as attuned to them as any humans have ever been. No, they simply recognize you by the shape of your minds, just as you recognize them by the spectra of their passing."

"I see," I murmured. Like a favorite pet, I'd just thought. Only which of us was the pet? "So why do they drive the other flapblacks away?"

"They don't," Suzenne said. "The others stay away out of respect for the dying."

I scratched my cheek. Bits and pieces of a nebulous plan were starting to swirl together in my brain. "Does that mean that if you asked them to move aside for awhile and let the younger ones in, they would do it?"

Peter shook his head. "I know what you're thinking, my friend. But it won't work."

"Well, *I* don't know what he's thinking," Jimmy spoke up.

"It's simple, Jimmy," I told him. "Cousin Chen went to a lot of trouble to scatter all those loudspeakers around the colony. I think it would be a shame to waste all that effort."

"But it won't work," Peter repeated. "We've talked with the Star Spirits about this. They simply aren't strong enough to carry the *Freedom's Peace*."

"Maybe," I said. "Maybe not. You say you've talked to them; but you didn't say you've played music for them."

"Are you suggesting we *force* them to carry us?" Suzenne demanded, an ominous glint in her eye.

"It's not a matter of forcing," I said. "They enjoy the music — you know that as well as we do. I think it acts like a stimulant to them."

"So now you're suggesting we effectively drug them —"

"Excuse me," Rhonda put in gently. "Your Highness, how long have you been providing music for the dying flapblacks to listen to?"

"Quite a few years," Peter said, frowning. "All of my lifetime, certainly."

"And how often during those years have you had a younger flapblack carry any of you anywhere?"

He shrugged. "Three or four times, perhaps. But those were only our small scout ships. Not nearly as big even as your transport."

"Then perhaps that's the real problem," Rhonda said. "You can talk to the flapblacks, but your perception of them has been skewed by the fact that most of the time you're talking to the old and dying, not the young and healthy."

"You talked about whale and dolphins earlier," I put in. "I suggest a better analogy might be dogs."

"Dogs?" Peter asked.

"Yes." I waved a hand around. "You've been surrounded for decades by aging, crippled Chihuahuas. That's not what most of the flapblacks are like."

"And what are they like?"

"Big, exuberant malamutes," I told him. "And with all due respect, your people may understand them, but we know how to make them run."

For a moment there was silence. Then, with a sigh, Peter nodded. "I'm still not convinced," he said. "But you're right, it has to be tried."

"Thank you." I turned to Jimmy. "Go take a look at that player interface of Chen's and see what kind of music she's got programmed onto it. Then get in touch with that musician you were visiting this morning and have him whistle up the colony's whole music contingent.

"We're going to have ourselves a concert."

The Grand Center of the Arts was considerably smaller than I would have expected for a place with such an impressive title, though considering the colony's limited populace I suppose its size made sense. The main auditorium was compact but with a feeling of spaciousness to it and a main floor that would supposedly seat two thousand people.

We were only going to need a fraction of that capacity tonight. Gathered together by the front of the stage were Jimmy and the sixty-eight colonists he'd been able to sift through his impromptu musicmaster screening test in the past six hours. Above them in the balcony, I waited with Peter and eighty hand-picked colonists who were considered especially in tune with the flapblacks. Star Spirits. Whatever.

A motion down at the stage caught my eye: Jimmy, his final instructions completed, was giving me the high sign. I waved acknowledgement and keyed the radio link Suzenne had set up to the *Sergei Rock* in its hangar slot. "Bilko? Looks like we're about ready here. You all set?"

"Roger that," he confirmed. "Inertial's all calibrated and warmed up. If you get this chunk of rock moving, we'll know it."

"Okay," I said. "Stand ready."

I stepped over to Peter, standing alone at the balcony rail gazing down at the musicians gathered below. "We're all ready, sir," I said. "You can give the order any time."

He smiled faintly, a smile that didn't touch his eyes. "You give the order, Captain. It's your show."

I shook my head. "It may be my show. But it's your world."

His smile became something almost sad as he turned to face the others on the balcony. "Your attention, please," he said. "We're ready. Tell the Ancients it's time, and ask them to move away from the colony."

For a long moment there was silence. Then Peter turned back to me and nodded. "It's all clear," he said. "They may begin."

I looked down at Jimmy and raised my hand. He nodded and fiddled with something on Chen's player interface; and faintly from the tiles beneath my feet I heard the drone of the C-sharp pre-music call. A few seconds later the tone was replaced by the opening brass fanfare of the first movement of Tchaikovsky's Fourth Symphony.

I waited a few bars, then keyed my radio link. "Bilko?"

"Yeah, I can hear the music," he said. "I had a flapblack shoot past, I think, but so far — wait a second. I thought the inertial . . . yeah. Yeah, we're off. Moving in fits and starts, but we *are* moving."

"What do you mean, fits and starts?" I asked frowning. "Aren't they getting a good wrap?"

"When they've *got* the wrap, they seem to have it pretty solid," Bilko said. "They just keep losing it, that's all. Either they keep unwrapping because Jimmy's people aren't very good at this, or else we're just too big to lug very far at a time."

"I can understand that," I said. "I've done my share of helping friends move across town."

"Yeah, me too," Bilko said. "And you have to admit this

place *is* the ultimate five-section couch."

"True," I said. "But we're putting some distance between us and Chen's coordinates, and that's the important thing."

"Right," Bilko agreed. "We can sort out the details later. How long are you planning to run?"

I looked down at Jimmy's people, hunkered down and visibly concentrating on the music. "Just the first movement, I think," I told him. "Eighteen and a half minutes should be plenty for this first test."

"Sounds good. Let me know when to shut down the recorders."

"Sure."

I keyed off and looked around for Peter. He had moved off to an unoccupied part of the balcony while I was talking to Bilko and was again standing alone gazing down at Jimmy's people. Avoiding the small clumps of quietly conversing colonists that had formed around us, I crossed to his side. "It seems to be working, Your Highness," I told him. "A little slow, but we're making progress."

"I'm glad to hear it," he murmured, his eyes still on the musicians. "I wish I could say I was grateful for your help, Captain. Unfortunately, I can't."

I nodded. "I understand."

He gave me an odd look. "Do you? Do you really?"

"I think so," I said. "Up until a few minutes ago you had no decisions to make about the life of your people. You were sealed inside the *Freedom's Peace*, stuck in the empty space between stars, with nowhere else to go even if you'd wanted to."

I turned away from his eyes to look down at Jimmy. "But all that's changed now. Suddenly the whole galaxy is open to you . . . and you're going to have to decide whether you're willing to take the risks and challenges of finding and colonizing a new world for yourselves as your designers intended, or stay all nice and comfortable in here."

"We've always known that decision would eventually have to be made," Peter said quietly. "But until that first transport arrived it was something we expected the people ten generations down the line to have to deal with. I'm not at all sure my people are ready for this. Not sure *I'm* ready for it."

"I doubt King Peter the Tenth would have felt any more ready than you do," I said. "For whatever that's worth."

"To be honest, not very much," Peter conceded. "I'm very much afraid the colony is going to split, and split violently, over the decision."

He straightened up. "Still, humanity has been dealing with violent disagreements for a very long time now, and we've certainly had our fair share of lesser controversies aboard the *Freedom's Peace*. Hopefully, we'll find our way through this one, too."

"And remember that it'll be you who make the decision, not someone from the Chen-Mellis family," I reminded him. "That's worth something right there."

"Yes." He eyed me. "Which brings up the question of what we do with her."

"You can't keep her here," I said. "Not unless you keep us here with her. She's sure to have left a complete data trail for her backup and the rest of the family to follow, including her plan to come aboard the *Sergei Rock*. If we show up anywhere in the Expansion without her, our necks will be for the high wire."

"The problem is that you're not going to do much better if you do show up with her," Peter pointed out darkly. "She's a highly vindictive person, my friend, and you've not only robbed her of a great prize but humiliated her in front of other people. At the very least, she'll make sure you go to prison; at the worst, she might conceivably have you murdered."

I shook my head. "She won't have any of us murdered," I told him. "If she'd brought back the *Freedom's Peace* I have no doubt the Chen-Mellis family would have given her cover for any illegal act she'd done along the way. But she has no prize now, and none of the Ten Families support unnecessary and unprofitable violence by one of its members. Aside from the bad publicity involved, it leaves them wide open to blackmail from the other families."

"Perhaps," Peter said, not sounding convinced. "You know Expansion politics better than I do. Might she still do something against you on her own, though, without family support or knowledge?"

"That's possible," I said. "The trick is going to be to persuade her that she personally will suffer greatly if she tries anything."

Peter shook his head. "I don't know. I've met people like Miss Chen, and I suspect her pride would outweigh even threats against her life."

"Probably," I said. "But I think there are things a person like Chen would value more even than her life."

Peter regarded me thoughtfully. "That sounds like you have an idea."

I shrugged. "An idea, yes. But the execution of it is going to depend solely on you and your powers of persuasion."

Peter lifted his eyebrows. "I doubt seriously my powers are strong enough to persuade Miss Chen of anything."

"Actually, that's not who you have to persuade," I told him. "Here's what I have in mind . . ."

* * * * *

We convened in Peter's office in front of the throne — a more impressive locale, Peter had decided, from which to deliver his pronouncements than anywhere else in the colony.

If either of us was expecting Chen to have been subdued by her two days of confinement, we were disappointed. She stood stiff and erect in the drab prison clothing they'd given her, her head held high and her eyes smoldering with hidden fire. Proud, confident, and defiant; and if this didn't work, I was definitely going to be in for some big trouble down the line.

"So you've come to your senses after all," she said to Peter. "A wise move. My people will be coming back here regardless, of course; but if they'd had to come for the purpose of rescuing a kidnapped family member there would have been far less of this place left afterward for you to bargain with."

"I'm afraid you misunderstand, Miss Chen," Peter said. "You're not being released because I'm worried about reprisals from your family. You're being released because you and your family are no longer a threat to us."

Chen smiled cynically. "No, of course not. That's all right — you go ahead and tell your people whatever you have to."

"You're no longer a threat," Peter went on, "because we are no longer where you can find us."

The smile remained, but Chen's eyes narrowed. "And what's that supposed to mean?"

"It means that your idea of using speakers and music to call the Star Spirits worked quite well," he told her. "We've had four sessions in the past two days, and are now a considerable distance from the spot you first directed Captain Smith to."

Chen threw me a dagger-edged glance. "And you think that's all it takes to hide from the Chen-Mellis family?" she bit out. "You have no concept whatsoever of the scope of our resources."

"None of your resources will do you any good," Peter said. "Not only do you not know where to look for us, you also don't have anything to look for. Those wonderful ion-capture engines you covet so much have been shut down."

A muscle in Chen's cheek twitched. "You can't keep them off forever," she pointed out. "Not if you ever want to get anywhere. You'll have to decelerate sometime."

"True," Peter said with a shrug. "But we're in no particular hurry. Besides, by the time we begin our deceleration, you won't have even the faintest idea where to look for us."

"Perhaps," Chen said, her voice calmer than I would have expected under the circumstances. "But I'd warn you against the mistake of underestimating us."

"You're welcome to try," Peter said. "Still, I'd warn *you* against making any promises to your cousins just yet. Captain Smith tells me the Chen-Mellis family has a reputation for vindictiveness when they don't get what they've been promised."

Chen looked at me again. "Captain Smith will soon be a position to find out about that first hand."

"I don't think so," Peter said, shaking his head. "There is one final condition for your release: that you leave Captain Smith, his transport, and his crew strictly alone. No reprisals, no revenge, nothing."

Chen cocked her head. "An interesting demand. And if I decide to ignore it, what do you intend to do? Smother me with moral outrage?"

"Actually, we have a somewhat more effective demonstration prepared," Peter told her. "I'm told you were on your way to Parex when you diverted the *Sergei Rock* to come here. Do you know anything about that world?"

"It's the dregs of the backwater," Chen said, not bothering to conceal her contempt. "One city, a few small towns, and the rest just farms and useless alien wilderness."

"I doubt that it's quite that bad," Peter said. "It surely must have its own unique charms. Regardless, you'll have plenty of time to find out."

"Meaning?"

"Meaning that once you reach Parex, you won't be allowed to leave for a few weeks," Peter said quietly. "Or had you forgotten we're able to talk to the Star Spirits?"

Chen had her expression under good control, but there was no way for her to stop the blood from draining from her face. "You're bluffing," she said.

"It's already done," Peter told her gravely. "Once you reach Parex, the Star Spirits will refuse to wrap any transport that you're aboard."

Her eyes darted to me, as if seeking evidence that this was some elaborate trick. "I don't believe you," she snarled defiantly. "You can't have talked to that many flapblacks. Besides, they're aliens — they can't possibly recognize individual human beings."

"I don't expect you to take my word for it," Peter said. "By all means, try it for yourself."

His forehead darkened. "And as you do, I suggest you consider all of the implications of this demonstration. The Star Spirits see everything that happens in deep space; and we of the *Freedom's Peace* are in continual contact with them. Just because we're multiple light-years away doesn't mean we're out of touch, or that we can't call further retribution down on you. On you, or on the entire Chen-Mellis family."

For a long moment, Chen held that gaze unflinchingly. Then, almost reluctantly, she dropped her eyes. "Fine," she growled. "I'll play your game." She turned a glare on me. "Besides, I don't have to lift a finger to drop Smith down the sewer. The TransShipMint Corporation will be handing out all the revenge I could ever want."

I swallowed hard, trying not to let it show. I still had the money card she'd given me; but after paying off all the cargo and penalty clauses from this trip, I'd be lucky to clear the seventy thousand neumarks she'd originally promised me. Unless I could track down that hundred thirty thousand she'd ghosted out of my account —

"And if I were you I wouldn't count on digging up your bankroll in time," Chen said, reading my face despite my best efforts. "I'm the only one who can retrieve it . . . and according to His Highness here, I'm going to be stuck on Parex for a few weeks."

She looked at Peter. "Unless, of course, you want to call off your little demonstration. If not, he's going to prison."

Peter looked at me. "Captain?"

I shook my head. It was, we all knew, her one last chance to manipulate me, and I wasn't in any mood to be manipulated. "I appreciate the offer, Ms. Chen," I said. "But I think you need King Peter's object lesson. I'll take my chances with TransShipMint."

The cheek muscle twitched again. "Fine," she said. "I'll do my few weeks on Parex; you can do your ten years in prison. We'll see which of us gets the last laugh."

She waved a hand impatiently. "If you're finished with your threats, I'd like to get going. I have a life back in the Expansion, Smith here has charges of embezzlement to face; and you of course have some serious cowering to do."

"We are indeed finished," Peter confirmed with a nod. "Farewell, Miss Chen."

The ten-hour trip back to Parex was very quiet. Chen stayed in the passenger cabin with the hatchway sealed the whole time, while Jimmy, Rhonda, and I spent most of our time at our respective stations. Only Bilko took any advantage at all of the dayroom. He reported it as being pretty lonely in there.

The intended recipients of the cargo we'd left behind on the *Freedom's Peace* were not at all happy with the *Sergei Rock*'s empty cargo hold. I think Chen was hoping they would press charges, but application of the assets on her cash card — along with a little smooth talking on Bilko's part — got them sufficiently calmed down. It did, however, leave us with only sixty thousand neumarks, a far cry from the two hundred thousand TransShipMint was going to want in the next couple of weeks.

We were on Parex for about twenty hours, catching up on sleep, getting our next cargo aboard, and wading through the heavier-than-usual stack of paperwork. During that time, Chen tried twice to sneak off the planet. Both times, the transports were forced to return after an hour's worth of trying failed to get them a flapblack wrap.

By the time we buttoned up the rumors about her were just beginning to be heard, and as we headed for deep space I found myself wondering if she would be able to find passage on a transport even after her internal exile was over.

To my lack of surprise, I discovered I didn't really much care.

★ ★ ★ ★ ★

"Hi," Rhonda's voice came from the dayroom door. "Got a minute?"

I looked up in mild surprise, deciding to pass on the obvious retort that when TransShipMint got done with me I would have all the time in the world. "Sure," I said instead, waving her toward one of the other chairs at the table. "You come here often?"

"Hardly ever," she said, sidling over to the indicated chair and sitting down. Her left hand, I noticed, had stayed out of sight behind her the whole way, as if she was hiding something behind her back. "But I wanted to talk, and this seemed a good time to do it."

"Sure," I nodded. "What about?"

She nodded down at the reader on the table in front of me. "Working out how to pay off the TransShipMint Corporation?"

"Trying to work it out," I said, sighing. "Really just going through the motions. There's just no way I can raise that kind of money that fast."

"There was one," she reminded me. "I hear Chen offered to unbury your other account if you'd get Peter to let her off the hook with the flapblacks." She cocked her head slightly. "I wanted you to know I was very impressed that you turned her down. So was Jimmy, by the way."

I snorted. "Thanks, but impressing the two of you was pretty far down on my reasons list. We needed to scare her, and scare her good, or we'd have had her and the whole Chen-Mellis family hanging over our heads for the rest of what would have probably been depressingly brief lives. This way . . . well, at least we all have a chance of living through it."

"Assuming self-preservation outweighs her sense of vengeance," Rhonda pointed out soberly. "*And* assuming she doesn't figure out what's actually happening."

"I don't think there's any chance of her doing that," I said. "She doesn't even know about the InReds, let alone how they interact with younger flapblacks."

Rhonda shivered. "I guess it just feels too much like a magician's trick," she said. "Peter creates the illusion that a whole galaxy worth of the flapblacks are deliberately and actively snubbing her; when really all it is is a single Ancient InRed who's been persuaded to hang around her whenever she leaves the planet. It just seems so fragile, somehow."

"Only because you know how the trick's being performed," I pointed out. "And because you know that it would only work on a world like Parex where there's a single spaceport and no more than one ship leaving at any given time." I shrugged. "Frankly, if there's any magic in this it's that Peter was able to persuade one of the InReds to cooperate this way in the first place."

"Yes," Rhonda murmured. "It's rather sad, really, having to spend its last few weeks of life sitting on Chen instead of getting to listen to the *Freedom's Peace*'s music."

I smiled. "Oh, I don't know. You didn't see what they did to Chen during her last day in prison. Where were you, by the way?"

"I was working out a deal with Suzenne," Rhonda said, frowning. "What did they do to her?"

"Nothing much," I said, frowning at her in turn. This was the first I'd heard of any deal. "They just played one of the InRed's favorite melodies over and over again on her cell's speaker system. Knowing how *my* mind does things, I figure that tune will be spinning around her mind for at least the next month. What deal?"

"Oh, that's nasty," Rhonda said. "Brilliantly nasty.

Gives the Ancient something to listen to, and probably helps him identify her, too. Your idea?"

"Peter's," I said. "What deal?"

"Oh, it wasn't anything much," she said casually. "You remember how much Suzenne liked my beadwork? Well, I sold her my entire stock. Beads, hoops, pattern lists, fasteners, needles, thread, looms, finished items — the works."

"Congratulations," I said, feeling obscurely disappointed. After all of that buildup, I had expected more of a payoff. "She'll be a big hit at their next formal concert."

"I think so," Rhonda agreed. "She was already talking about getting one of the fabricators retasked to making a fresh supply of beads."

"Sounds great," I said, frowning. Rhonda, I suddenly noticed, still had a twinkle in her eye and seemed to be fighting hard to keep from grinning. "So OK, let's have it."

"Have what?" she asked, clearly determined to drag it out a little more.

"The big punch line," I said. "What did she do, offer you a 50 percent commission or something?"

"No, of course not," she said. "How in the worlds would I collect on something like that, anyway? No, I insisted on cash."

Her hand finally came around from behind her back, and I saw now that she was holding a small wooden box like the kind Bilko kept his poker chips in. "And that's exactly how she paid," she concluded. "With cash."

I frowned down at the box. It was one of Bilko's poker containers, all right. Clearly, there was something significant here I was missing. "OK," I said. "Cash. So?"

Rhonda rolled her eyes. "Cash, Jake. The only kind of cash they use on the *Freedom's Peace* . . . ?"

And with a sudden jolt I had it. *Cash.*

Reaching over, I unlatched the lid and flipped it up. And there they were, neatly stacked in the velvet padding: a triple row of shiny golden coins. United Jovian Habitat dollars, one hundred thirty years old each. A currency that hadn't been minted since the Habitats were reabsorbed by Earth over a century ago.

I looked up again at Rhonda. "How many do you have?" I asked, my voice quavering slightly.

"Enough," she said quietly. "I checked a couple of numismatic files on Parex, and it looks like they'll pull in somewhere between a hundred fifty and three hundred thousand neumarks." Reaching across the table, she pushed the box a few centimeters toward me. "They're yours."

There are times in every man's life when pride demands he argue. Far past the end of my financial rope, I knew this wasn't one of them. "Thank you," I said.

"You're welcome," she said. "For all our faults, we're a pretty good crew. It would be a shame to break a team like this up."

I smiled wryly. "Even Jimmy and his youthful impertinences?"

"Listen, buddy, those youthful impertinences stood up with you against a member of the Chen-Mellis family," she reminded me tartly. "And whether he's willing to admit it or not, I think your moral stand back on the *Freedom's Peace* impressed him a lot."

"I suppose," I said noncommittally. Still, I had to admit in turn that Jimmy's willingness to accept my judgment had impressed me, as well.

Not that I was willing to admit it out loud, of course. Not yet, anyway. "Still, it's sort of a pain. The problem with moral leadership is that you have to keep being moral for it to do any good. I liked it better when I could get what I wanted by yelling at him."

"Yeah, right," she said, patting my hand in a distinctly sarcastic fashion. "Don't worry, though — I'm sure you'll be able to handle it."

She smiled slyly. "I, on the other hand, being a lowly engineer, have no need of leadership of any sort, moral or otherwise." She tapped a fingernail against the box of coins. "And I'll tell you right now I intend to take utterly shameless advantage of you over this."

"Ah," I said, scooting my chair over to the cooler. "So, what, you want me to serve you a drink?"

"That's a start," she purred. "And then we're going to sit here together, all nice and cozy, and I'm going to tell you all about the wonderful new engines you're going to buy for me."

Additional copyright information